Exiled From Paris

Exiled From Paris

Growing Up French in the 1960s

Eric H. du Plessis

2010

Dedication

To my Mother,
And to the Memory of my Father

Preface

How appraise a memoir without taking into account the memoirist? This puts to shame the critical notion that an author doesn't count, doesn't exist, that only the text matters. I put aside such balderdash and will start with a few words about the author, Eric du Plessis, who is surely alive and well.

We met roughly two decades ago as both relatively new professors at Radford University in Virginia. I was struck immediately by the vivacity of the man, the limitless energy, verve and intelligence, and his ability to converse on just about any subject at all. He knows politics, he knows medicine, he knows both French and English literature, he knows the martial arts, he knows history and philosophy. And he carries on as a single father with two still young children.

Beyond mere conversation, Eric is a supremely intriguing man. He is a black belt in Aikijitsu, has served for many years as a martial arts instructor, can fly small aircraft, plays a mean guitar, teaches French and film courses and all the rest of it. He is tall, debonair (as the French usually are) and handsome. He has spent most of his professional life publishing academic and scholarly articles, as well as writing on Nietzsche and translating into English two hitherto obscure novels by Balzac. Obviously, I am impressed by both the man and his work.

Often in the past I have urged him to try his hand at fiction or creative non-fiction, encouraging him to write *as he speaks*. The long awaited upshot is this autobiographical novel which I had the opportunity to read long before its publication. I watched the work bloom from chapter to chapter, made suggestions, but mostly tried to keep up his confidence. He claims the book was the most difficult piece of writing he has ever undertaken, that it seemed unnatural to his background as a scholar and translator. The result was a feast for me because, however well I know Eric, his past had always remained a mystery. He never spoke of it, and I didn't ask.

The book itself is a delight to read. This is English prose at its finest. One even thinks of Conrad, but du Plessis' work is not as ponderous. If I dared to compare, I would rank him with Dickens – the vivid immediacy of almost cinematic scenes, the cliffhangers, the salient detail of character cameos, the suspense. This book is not a strict, chronological biography; the author chooses what one is tempted to call "archetypal" moments of the past, bringing them to life and letting them serve as extended Proustian privileged moments. Forget the trifling day-to-day dross. In this way the book reads like a novel, and it certainly utilizes fictional techniques, like those mentioned previously in this paragraph.

One finds just about everything a reader could want in Eric du Plessis' memories of youth and adolescence – a revealing social document, adventure, cultural history, splendid descriptions, remembrance to the finest details, characters who seem larger than life (again, more cinematic than flesh and blood, yet flesh and blood they remain), humor, high jinks, action, heartbreak, love, coming of age, and, yes, a hero! It is astonishing that the author can remember the details of a bedroom he luxuriated in momentarily decades ago, to the point that he can make that room come alive in the present moment. Beyond plot, characterization, dialogue, the work is an explosion of creativity and memory, in the Wordsworthian sense, when the poet, lying on that sofa, revives the dancing daffodils. And juicier yet, this book stands, in the end, aside from its genre as bildungsroman, as a magnificent love story. *Amor Vincet Omnia.*

Every writer knows how difficult it is to create a love scene charged with convincing sexuality. And yet it happens several times in this work, from the mysterious Michelle, the older woman who in effect novitiates the adolescent hero into sex, to the younger Emily who serves as Everygirl, and the almost transcendent, spiritual yet earthy Jennifer at the end who transforms the hero's life altogether, who seduces him without guile, who offers, at last, true love. And the author responds exactly as we would want him to: he succumbs utterly. And thus the final chapter remains ambiguous, tantalizing, charged with potential, as if calling for a sequel. For it is in the final chapter that the concept of exile, which permeates the work as a whole, comes to fruition. The varied previous exiles seem, in retrospect, test runs. And here one thinks of the great lovers of the past, Petrarch and Laura, Dante and Beatrice, even Romeo and Juliet, those willing to either die or sacrifice everything for love that surpasses the merely erotic. The book ends, thus, with a kind of vision, and vision it will remain until and if the author chooses to present us with another installment.

A final word on some of the astounding characters one meets throughout this book. Du Plessis' portraits of his mother and father are crafted with almost sacred devotion, though both parents remain real people in real time. We meet some unctuous, slimy characters as well, such as Alain, the roommate at the Y, the aristocratic, sleazy pedophile Edward whom the hero trumps, and the horrendous Father Mayeux, perhaps the most evil antagonist in the book. But the characters I like most are the women, from the author's sister Isabelle to his selected love interests. He describes women wondrously, down to the finest details of a bead of perspiration on the ridge between nose and upper lip. Again, the magic of memory come alive.

Eric du Plessis' memoir is therefore an immediate account not of events rooted in the deep past; it is almost their creation here and now, in the present. One can almost *smell* the perfumed flesh of, say, Emily, as one reads; one can, as reader, fall in love with her vicariously; one can imagine that she has remained Emily, exactly as she was, to this day.

In his autobiography, where fictionalized digressions occasionally intrude upon the facts, Eric du Plessis presents characters and situations that we cannot, nor would we want to, easily forget. They live on in our minds, as they live on in his. The transfer is complete. They step, flutter, strut and leap out of the pages as do characters in movies and the world's most sumptuous masterpieces.

Louis Gallo

ACKNOWLEDGEMENTS

I am indebted to Louis Gallo, the talented short story writer and poet, who encouraged me early on to escape the strictures of scholarship for the challenges of creative writing. My thanks also go to Susan Kwilecki and Philip Sweet who contributed their keen critical eye. All three read an earlier version of the manuscript and offered invaluable comments and suggestions. This book and its author have both been enriched by the gift of their enduring friendship.

Places, names and chronology have been changed to protect the anonymity of individuals still living today. Although the foregoing pages are based on actual circumstances and real characters, the author has occasionally altered the course of events and created composite protagonists who embody the characteristics of distinct individuals. And at times, as if to settle accounts with a still equivocal past, he has crossed the line between recollection and myth. Because of such liberties, this memoir should be considered an autobiographical novel.

One

THE SHIP'S BOW surges for a moment over the waves and plunges back into the sea. In freezing darkness the small ferry rises and falls as it plows the English Channel, a wondrous sight to a sixteen-year-old running away from boarding school. I stand on the top deck, partly shielded from the rain, shivering in the drizzle of this November night, and yet exhilarated as the coast of France recedes behind me. For this night's crossing, the ship is nearly empty, which makes me feel better because I dread the thought of attracting attention to myself. I slowly take in the full measure of the last twenty-four hours, reveling in a mixture of excitement and apprehension. I ran away from home once before, at the age of twelve, a four-hour escapade all the more futile since no one even noticed I was gone. This time is different. I have forged my mother's signature, evaded the scrutiny of the school's disciplinarians and stolen money to be here tonight on my way to England, the land of the Beatles and, according to my cousin, of enticingly promiscuous girls.

From the deserted observation deck, I wish I could already see the English coast, only twenty-five miles away. I am sad about my mom, though—how she will worry when the school calls tomorrow. But I've no such misgivings concerning my dad. He's larger than life, almost mythical to me, a genuine World War II hero in a land of collaborators. Still, his powers might extend further than I know, maybe all the way to the British Isles.... But my excitement overrides both guilt and fear. I will call my mother from London. The ferry is now far enough from the shore that I have lost any point of reference to situate myself in the surrounding darkness. The boat rides the surf more rhythmically, and its pitching merges in unison with the shapeless waves crashing along the sideboards. In this weather it will take two hours to reach Dover. I recede further into the shelter of the observation deck, my eyes riveted on unseen shorelines yet to emerge from the night. I sink into an armchair and let my memory drift back a few days....

This morning I walked out of St. Joseph Academy, a rigorous Catholic boarding school with a reputation for discipline, carrying a 24-hour pass to attend the fictitious funeral of my grandfather. The school is located in an arid and forlorn part of central France, away from tourist attractions or any other place of interest, in a small town called La Souterraine. In French the word means "underground," or "subterranean," referring to the neolithic river that runs deep under the town, supplying the largest aquifer in the region. The meaning of "subterranean" particularly befits the place. Surrounded by gray walls twenty feet high, the somber mass of the two-hundred-year-old building looms over the town from the only hill in this barren plain. I did not end up in this Dickensian caricature of a boarding school by accident. After exhausting the patience of a previous educational institution, I had spent the spring semester at home, a complete nuisance to my family.

Sending sons to boarding school had long been a respectable tradition in the more affluent circles of European society. French, German and British parents often disburdened themselves of their troublesome teenagers by exiling them to a remote and regimented existence. It was thought profitable in fostering esprit de corps and proper breeding in otherwise pampered and privileged kids. There was some merit to the argument, and most of us were probably the better for it, even if in those days no one breathed a word about the abuse we suffered within these cloistered walls of respectability. Both my parents worked, and since I had already distinguished myself by being thrown out of four private schools, they agreed that I should be made to share the sort of ordered life suitable for acquiring self-discipline and respect for others. By today's pedagogical standards, it seems cold-hearted to submit a ten-year-old boy in desperate need of attention to a lifestyle of rules and uniforms, but it is also true that I had become quite unmanageable.

Between the ages of ten and fifteen, I had been educated at Holy Spirit Preparatory, located near the frigid town of Amiens in Northern France. I still remember the initial interview between my parents and Monsignor Fallois, the headmaster. My family was determined to find a reputable establishment that would lock me in for at least a couple of years. I recall my mother asking the bald, middle-aged priest what sort of misdeed would warrant expulsion from the school, thus setting the standard by which I was expected to behave. The headmaster had a rather kind and benevolent way about him; he turned to my mom and said: "Madam, let us understand one another, at Holy Spirit, we do not expel students. Your son will simply be made to comply with our rules of conduct and discipline." And then he just looked at me, his benign smile a chilling contrast with the steel in his eyes.

Five years in that place did not break my spirit, though it took the rebellious edge out of my attitude. Yet the fifteen-year-old adolescent I had become started to chafe in this stultifying and unimaginative environment. I could have stayed another two years until I went to college, but I managed to convince my parents that the time had come for me to return to public school, and reclaim my place as a full member of the family. We lived in Saint-Germain, a privileged suburb of Paris with a historical castle and a lush national forest. In June of 1965, I returned a changed young man. Or so it seemed. If the sensible argument I had patiently woven for my parents finally convinced them, their decision to let me come home would prove disastrous indeed.

In the fall I was admitted to Saint-Erembert's, a Catholic establishment largely by name. The curriculum was the same as a public school, except for two hours of catechism each week. It was fairly expensive, and the tuition represented yet another imposition on the family budget. My parents had selected it because it was within walking distance of our house. It also had an enviable academic reputation, and if only by affiliation and name, Saint-Erembert's remained within that respectable tradition of French parochial education. I reveled in my new independence, and free from the constraints of boarding school, I celebrated my new life by refusing to do anything remotely connected to academics. I started to come home late, hanging out in local cafés and becoming quite proficient at pinball machines. On the surface, there wasn't much in my behavior that differed from that of my schoolmates. Scruffiness and nonconformity were almost a badge of recognition, but somehow my rebellion against all forms of authority and the headlong pursuit of academic mediocrity persisted with unusual intensity. The news of my spiraling grades reached my parents soon enough. In France, the school system relies not only on nine-week report cards, but also on a tradition that strikes fear in all students between the ages of seven and eighteen. Each month, they are ranked in every academic subject by means of competitive exams known as "compositions." The results of those tests are announced publicly, as the French believe that an educational philosophy based on public praise and humiliation is a proven motivator to excellence. Parents dread the rankings that consecrate their sons and daughters as first, second or third in math, or twenty-fifth and thirty-third in history and geography.

In the small community where we lived, such a system inflicted lasting social stigma, and our academic performance became the main subject of conversations at the end of each month. A mother would beam with pride informing her pediatrician that little Béatrice was first in social science for the third time in a row, while another would be more discreet about her son Alain, still dead last in language arts. Rankings alone proved more important than grades, and our parents were drawn with us into this obsessive ritual.

I had spared my family any notion of suspense by being ranked each month at the bottom of my class. I thought it a mark of distinction, a sort of quiet rebellion setting me apart from my peers. The only down side was a sharp reduction in invitations to birthday parties, since I was now pegged as a "bad influence" on my hardworking, rank-obsessed classmates. Actually, I relished in the rather comfortable existence as class dunce. A few teachers had reached the conclusion that I was learning-disabled and no longer expected any homework from me. I coasted along from September to Christmas, devouring the complete works of Arthur Conan Doyle in French. By February my overall GPA had reached rock bottom. I considered it a healthy expression of protest against society, but my parents were not amused. My flippant attitude started to infect family life as well, and the situation at home became increasingly difficult.

My father was a brilliant architect who left at 6:30 every morning to build skyscrapers in Paris, and he detested the role of disciplinarian. Both my older sisters found me insufferable. Mom did her best. Beautiful and exceedingly bright, she owned an art gallery specializing in seventeenth-century Dutch masters. I loved her, but she proved no match for the gangly teenager who was once her cuddly little boy. My family now bitterly regretted its decision to take me out of boarding school. I affected a slovenly demeanor and dressed in army surplus clothes, making it a point to appear unwashed, unshaven and unkempt. Before Easter my parents were informed that I would not be promoted to the next grade. In fact, I had done so well at doing nothing that the only prospect left for me looked like some sort of technical training. In a country like France, where, in spite of the revolution, social classes remain sharply segregated, this constituted a serious slap in the face. My parents were not snobs, but they expected me to remain within the social framework of a family that consisted of physicians and architects. My grandparents had been the first ever to actually work for a living, since generations of du Plessis before them had always lived on private incomes.

In this affluent suburb of Paris, social appearances were particularly important. At school, a few parents began to use me as a scarecrow to their children: "Look at Eric, the worst student in the class. This is what happens when you're disrespectful and refuse to do your homework. I feel sorry for his poor mother.... What a blow for such an upright and distinguished family...." I remember two of my classmates, the Blainville brothers. Pale-faced and overweight, the twins were the pride of their upper middle-class parents. They wore suits and black ties each day, standing at the top of the class in every subject but physical education, and didn't look as if they were having any fun in or out of school. One of them, attracted perhaps by a reputation that seemed perversely enticing, actually befriended me for a while. Our conversations during recess must have opened vistas into forbidden worlds, but it all came to an end when his parents insisted that he no longer have any contact with me, decreeing that I would probably end up as "a bus driver, or something ...."

Six years later, sitting in one of the ornate amphitheaters of the University of Paris medical school, I heard a startled voice calling my name. I turned around and beheld, a few rows behind me, the Blainville brothers, prim and proper in their little white coats, a look of disbelief in their eyes.

"du Plessis? What the hell are you doing here?" One of them finally asked, visibly perplexed.

"Well, just like you guys, getting ready for physiology. And how have you been all these years?" I answered casually.

"But, but how...? What...I mean, how did you...?" The expression in both their faces was a mixture of incredulity and despair. Eric, the class dunce, the scarecrow brandished long ago by their parents, was now one of their peers. From the look of their complexion and the color of their ties, they still were not having any fun. But at least they had worked hard all these years, and done it by the book. They had conformed and endured every privation imposed upon them. Now they reaped the fruit of their labor, sitting today in this prestigious medical school. So how could I in all fairness be here with them? I was an anomaly. Surely this was a gag, some sort of mistake. I let them wallow in their distress, never bothering to explain how hard I had worked to get here, rising to the top of my class and graduating with honors. I savored the irony of the moment, evading their pleas for information and never talking to them again. I would have given a lot to be a fly on the wall the next time the Blainville brothers met with their parents: "Guess who sat two rows in front of us the other day in physiology...? Eric du Plessis, that's who...! Well, thanks a lot mom and dad!"

After all those years, it still felt good to be an iconoclast.

While I did enjoy my role as the class dunce at Saint-Erembert's, I must also have felt a few pangs of humiliation, because I decided, just once, to surprise everyone by performing at the top of the class in at least one academic subject. For greater impact, I chose Latin. I had taken five years of fairly rigorous instruction in classics at Holy Spirit, but I had slacked off so much since then that I was hopelessly behind. I saw no way of catching up without tweaking the odds in my favor. We were studying *De Bello Gallico*, Julius Caesar's account of his conquest of Gaul around 57 B.C. Historically, it was quite interesting, but for the fact that we had to translate the Latin original into French, line by line, through long and numbing hours of uninspired instruction. Mr. Lanquenin was our teacher. Thin, gray-haired and forever sporting a tweed jacket and a purple bow tie, he seemed to revel in my academic ineptitude. I thought his class the perfect choice for my little scholastic coup. Each month we were given, well in advance, the next two hundred lines of translation on which we would ultimately be tested.

At a bookstore in Paris, I acquired a modern French translation of Caesar's work. With my photographic memory, I learned the entire passage by heart, regurgitating it line by line on exam day, in the course of a two-hour proctored ordeal. It usually took a week for teachers to grade the monthly exams, and then came another memorable French contribution to inept pedagogy: the in-class announcement of exam results. Teachers would call you by name, and you stood up as your grade, and sometimes excerpts from your work were read out loud to the rest of the class. To make this more suspenseful, the ritual invariably began with the worst performance, and the public excoriation would proceed, slowly working its way up to the top of the class. The first half an hour was devoted to the public humiliation of the less gifted, while the end of the period saw the celebration of the brighter students. Alternately subjected to praise and ridicule, we had all adapted to the process, with most of us laughing along with the teacher. There is no greater form of humiliation than a system which forces victims to participate in their own trial and execution, and yet no one, not even our parents, ever thought of questioning the intrinsic evil of this tradition.

The day came for the results to be announced. I was already savoring the scandalous fun that my sudden promotion in rank was going to create, the better to return to the comfort of established academic mediocrity. Buoyed by the stunning recognition of my true intellectual ability, I would then rise in the eyes of my classmates from mere incompetence to the much more envied role of enlightened rebel. As in the past, Mr. Lanquenin began by starting with the lowest grades:

"Mr. Lemercier, would you stand up, please? You have an F, as usual. I believe your academic incompetence truly borders on the supernatural....Mr. Desjardins, D-. I cannot resist sharing with the rest of the class your pathetic attempt at translating the third line of the text...Krylenkovitch: D. Your parents were not born in this country, and unfortunately you've inherited their inability to master the finer points of the French language....Legras: D, again. Your persistence in studying classics never ceases to amaze me, since your morphology seems more suited for manual labor."

After five or six hapless victims had stood up to face public derision, two things happened: a few heads began to turn to the back of the class, staring at me in disbelief since my name had not yet been called, and the door opened, allowing the principal to come in and steal his way into the class. This was done so discreetly that Mr. Lanquenin did not even acknowledge his entrance by making us all stand up to attention, as was customary each time an administrator walked in. He casually took a seat and blended in with the students who quickly turned their attention back to the teacher's relentless countdown. The principal's presence among us was a bit odd, though by no means exceptional. It was more the way he had come in and sat down so quietly that I found unusual. By now only three names remained, and my classmates openly gawked at me. This was getting uncomfortable. I had imagined I would end up in the top ten, but this close to academic perfection was embarrassing. My name finally came up and I stood.

"This is quite a surprise," the teacher intoned, "in first place, with what is undoubtedly the best translation I have ever read from a student, we find Eric du Plessis."

He paused to allow this intelligence to settle.

"The very same du Plessis we had been led to believe incapable of such a performance."

I was not enjoying the moment as much as I had anticipated.

"But then again," he continued sarcastically, "I am hard put to decide to whom I really should award this grade of A+."

His tone had suddenly taken on a sharper edge, and I noticed that the principal, who had been standing up for some time, drew nearer to him. There was something almost menacing in the way he casually leaned against the teacher's desk.

"Should I award it to Eric, or more appropriately to Professor Abel Lefranc of the Sorbonne, the author of what is arguably the finest translation of Caesar's *De Bello Gallico*?

And taking his cue from Mr. Lanquenin, the principal suddenly moved to the front of the class.

"Du Plessis," he began, his voice crackling with anger, "take your hands out of your pockets when a teacher addresses you! I read your Latin exam and I have satisfied myself that you are guilty of the most shameful example of academic dishonesty."

The students were still staring at me, but their faces had grown pale. Of course, this entire deception wasn't too bright. In my determination to succeed, I didn't bother to alter even a single word of the text I had memorized, thinking that no one could ever trace the source of my inspiration. Not so much disconcerted at being unmasked, I felt humiliated at being exposed so quickly. The principal took a few steps towards me.

"Get your personal effects out of your locker and follow me," he announced tersely. The words were well known: they always preceded someone's expulsion from the school. I walked out of the room without looking at anyone.

In the office, I waited on a chair while my parents were being notified. After the obligatory half an hour meeting between my mother and the principal, I was expelled from Saint-Erembert's. I was not too proud of myself, mostly because of my mother's embarrassment. We walked out of the school in silence and passed under the red brick archway. I turned around for one last glance. The basketball courts were deserted. From the second floor a younger student smiled and waved at me, his face pressed like a clown against the window-pane.

My being thrown out of school months before the end of the spring semester could not have come at a worst time for my parents. My mother's gallery required her undivided attention, and my father's architectural firm had just been retained to create the new headquarters of OPEC in Paris. I was left alone at home with the strictest instructions to work as hard as I could to pass the BEPC, the national scholastic exam that could still assure my promotion to the next grade somewhere else. Public schools in France are not allowed to grant diplomas on their own. Instead, they prepare students for national exams which impose upon all schools throughout the country a monotony of academic standards. Left to my own devices, I showed as much interest in school-related matters as when I was a student. I did the bare minimum to ward off my parents' scrutiny and retain control of my everyday life. I studied judo, spent hours devouring books in the library and discovered sex.

The object of my desires was Viviane de Pressigny. I had met her during my last year of boarding school. I was the only Protestant kid amid five hundred Catholic boys at Holy Spirit Preparatory, a hundred miles to the north of Paris. These were the early days of ecumenism, and it had been decided that I would also attend services every Sunday at the Reformed church. After making such a groundbreaking exception to their admission policy, the good fathers did not wish to be accused of proselytizing the lone Huguenot entrusted to their care. Since I could not be exempted from mass, as it would have created a deplorable precedent, my parents agreed that I would sing in the choir. This ensured my regular attendance, but avoided the appearance of trying to convert me. And so I sang mass twice a week for five years, in the old Latin ritual. The choirmaster's ability to extract competent renditions of polyphonic hymns out of forty recalcitrant teenagers was nothing short of miraculous. We even cut two records whose profits paid for the restoration of the chapel organ

Each Sunday at 10:30 a.m., I was accompanied by a chaperon down the steep hill to the Protestant church. Dwarfed by the massive presence of the cathedral, the small and unassuming building stood almost unnoticed as a token of Catholic magnanimity to its wayward brothers. This weekly outing allowed me to escape the confines of the boarding school and savor a bit of much-envied freedom. Often the chaperon would turn out to be a college student, and his lack of supervision enabled me to stock up on cigarettes which fetched quite a price among my classmates. One Sunday, during the social that followed the service, I made Viviane's acquaintance. She was a fair-haired fifteen-year-old, neither stunning nor unattractive, with the definite advantage of being generously endowed. It didn't say much about my maturity level, or the innocence of my intentions, but let's face it: as far as innocence or maturity were concerned, I didn't possess any, and each Sunday I looked forward to the sight of Viviane's ample breasts with great anticipation. We had become friends, but since our meetings were restricted to church functions, our relationship remained completely platonic. After I left the boarding school, we communicated sporadically, but in the month following my expulsion from Saint-Erembert's, I received an invitation to her sixteenth birthday party.

She lived north of Amiens, in a sumptuous eighteenth-century manor, surrounded by stables, tennis courts and three hundred acres of woods. She was an accomplished rider with several regional championships to her credit. The invitation meant that I would have to spend the night there. I did not know why my parents agreed so easily to let me go, since my attitude at home hardly lent itself to any favors. They remembered Viviane, whom they had briefly met at my confirmation service. She was an A student and perhaps they hoped she would have a positive influence on me. On her mother's side, she was related to the DeReich family, one of Germany's largest steel manufacturers. My parents' own ancestry obviated any suspicions of social climbing on our part, but Viviane's wealth and impeccable academic record did not hurt either. A couple of weeks later, I was allowed to leave for the weekend.

Viviane came to pick me up at the train station. She had blossomed in the intervening eight months and looked radiant. We chatted in the back seat while the chauffeur inexplicably treated us to an 80-mile-an-hour drive through narrow country roads. The estate was impressive. A two-story structure covered with ivy, with three separate wings huddled around a tiled courtyard and an Etruscan fountain in the middle. Her family was deferential and generous, and we enjoyed a pleasant afternoon in the company of twenty other teenagers. At five o'clock, the cars came up the driveway to pick up the guests, and I realized that I would be the only one left. Delighted at the prospect of spending the rest of the evening with Viviane's family, I was treated to a startling announcement: her parents were leaving for Paris within the hour, only to return the next day. They had prepared a guest room in the left wing, and a chauffeur would drive me back to the station in the morning. That left me, Viviane, her uninteresting seven-year-old sister and the staff as the only occupants of the manor that night. To this day, I still do not comprehend why her parents allowed me to stay the night without their presence. I thought myself a dangerous seducer, but her father probably had taken the full measure of this lanky teenager and pronounced him incapable of endangering his daughter's virtue.

I did entertain notions of being a budding Casanova, but in coldest fact I was totally inexperienced. I had kissed two girls in my lifetime. One had cornered me behind the rocks in the back of a Normandy beach when I was eleven, passionately sticking her tongue into my mouth while she took off the upper part of her bikini. I had thought the whole episode rather disgusting and added rudeness to injury by showing no interest in her anatomy. The other kiss was a better experience, but only lasted the time to say good-bye in a train station at the end of summer camp. I had surmised that Viviane was more experienced than I and resented the power differential it created between us. In my conversations with her the year before, I had remedied that deficiency by attributing to myself a romantic past I did not possess. My knowledge of lovemaking was entirely fictitious, and that of a woman's anatomy limited to the then-hairless centerfolds of girly magazines. Sure, I had grown up with two older sisters, the envy of my friends, but catching an occasional glimpse of them "*toutes nues*" did not count, since it was axiomatic that your exasperating sisters were utterly devoid of erotic attraction.

Later that evening, I found myself alone with Viviane. Her younger sister and the nanny had already bid us good night and retired to another wing. The room had a sloped ceiling with varnished beams and antique furniture. The tall windows were hidden behind thick curtains and the place was warm and inviting. Viviane owned one of those plasticky record players that teenagers loved in the mid-sixties: the one with two detachable speakers you could set apart on a thick rug, allowing you to lie down and discover the marvel of stereophonic sound. We listened over and over to the Beatles' "Eight Days a Week," and the fact that we didn't understand the words made the lyrics even more magical. We had exhausted conversational topics during the party and were now awkwardly looking at each other, knowing what we wanted, but not quite sure how to go about it. It must have been heartbreaking for a sixteen-year-old girl entertaining romantic notions to be paired with a selfish and immature boy with embarrassingly obvious intentions. Viviane's decision to lose her virginity must have taken quite a bit of determination back in 1966, when neither contraception nor abortion was available in France. She yearned for a very special moment, romantic and drawn-out, with dreamy looks in our eyes. I only wanted to get laid, and fast,—almost as a frantic rite of passage. In my mind, the satisfaction of my own desires was not even the main goal, and the incongruous idea of pleasuring her never crossed my mind. The only thing that mattered was afterwards, when the deed was done, and I could walk tall and proud, the equal of my older brother, whom I envied from afar. To get there, I would have done anything, told any lie and sworn any oath. Poor Viviane, hell has no lust like that of a horny teenager.

She dimmed the lights as we lay upon her bed, commencing a curious mixture of excitement and fumbling. Her breasts felt soft under my hands, but her kisses were oddly light and brief, like the pecking of a hen. She retreated under the covers, and insisted on removing her clothes while hiding behind the sheets. I don't know why, but I never got undressed. I just lowered my trousers to my knees, kicked off my shoes and jumped into bed with her. There was no tenderness or cuddling, only awkwardness made all the more uncomfortable that my pants had traveled down to my ankles, impeding the movements of my legs. But it was the dark triangle of tangled hair between her legs that captured all the attention of my eyes and hands. Never in my life had I touched a girl there. I let my fingers run through the thick mane of her hair, and the excitement I felt almost took my breath away. I did not dare anything else, for what lay below was both intoxicating and mysterious. I slid my body between her legs, as Viviane lay back with her hands above her head, taking quick and shallow breaths. I had no notion that she could actually enjoy any of this, and didn't have the slightest idea of what foreplay meant. And it was then that my lack of experience became obvious. Viviane had believed my lies when I boasted of a previous sexual conquest, and she had chosen me for this very reason as her initiator into sex. But the full measure of my inexperience was now revealed. Instinctively, I knew what to do next, but couldn't quite find my way home. The French language has a rather vulgar and yet pertinent expression to describe such a predicament, the verb "glander." Derived from the Latin *glans*, or "acorn," it means "to loiter about without purpose" and etymologically draws on the quandary of an inexperienced young man whose glans does not know which path to follow. Viviane was not exactly swooning with ecstasy, and my insistence at knocking on the wrong door must have finally awakened her suspicions. Suddenly regaining her senses, she closed her legs, maneuvered her body to the side and brought the entire proceeding to an abrupt end. Not a word was spoken between us. I felt humiliated as she sat on the edge of the bed looking embarrassed and angry. I scurried back to my room, nearly losing my way through a maze of corridors, and fell asleep on an unopened bed, staring at the ceiling and wearing all my clothes.

Starting in April, I was expected to work diligently at home, preparing the upcoming national exam. It was not a particularly difficult test. Tediously long, like a two-day version of the junior SATs, it was well within the reach of any high school sophomore willing to spend two hours of preparation each day. I did nothing, purposely immersing myself in books conspicuously absent from the official reading list, and hoped against hope that I would just wing the whole thing. My friend Jean-François, whom I had met at Holy Spirit Preparatory, had also left the boarding school to return to his family. Not particularly interested in academics, he was gifted for manual labor and had enrolled in a technical training program. In France you can't drive until you're eighteen, and so the real status symbol of a teenager is the treasured possession of a Moped. My friend owned a powerful Italian model that could accelerate all the way to 40 mph. I had to contend with a temperamental French Mobylette, an erratic second-hand bike prone to mechanical breakdowns. I compensated for the lack of horsepower by adding small amounts of ether to the fuel tank, a recipe passed on to me by the previous owner. It resulted in sudden, unpredictable bursts of acceleration, and the improvised mixture was probably responsible for destroying the engine in less than three months. J.F. and I would roam the neighborhood like two budding Hell's Angels, dreaming up all sorts of mischief and worrying our parents to death. And well they should have been: idle and bored in this affluent suburb, we both craved excitement.

I came up with a plan. My parents kept all sorts of fascinating books in their library: large picture books on the Himalayas and other exotic places on earth, alternating with complete sets of first editions of Molière and Voltaire, as well as medical and architectural textbooks. Up on the higher shelves lay the works of the best photographers in the world, including André de Dienes' luminous figure studies. The upper shelves had been a favorite of mine since I was thirteen. They sheltered large format editions of classic black and white photography, with nude models curiously devoid of pubic hair. Nestled within this eclectic collection was a large volume I had grown quite fond of: an encyclopedia of crime, criminals and con-artists, documenting some of the most ingenious and elaborate scams perpetrated during the last two hundred years. An entire chapter was dedicated to the art of breaking and entering, with particular attention to the use of skeleton keys, and the proper means of gaining illegal entry by defeating solid doors and impregnable locks.

It looked so simple on paper that J.F. and I decided to burglarize a house. All we wanted was to get inside the premises at night, and celebrate our success with a bottle of champagne. I began to reconnoiter the territory to identify the perfect target for our expedition.

Sprawling with opulent homes and manicured lawns, the neighbor-hood offered quite a few prospects. I found a large, two-story country house used only as a summer residence, and therefore uninhabited until June. It lay a little too close to the main street, but with its shut-tered windows and its lawn in disrepair, it hardly attracted atten-tion. We planned to strike the next week around 3 a.m. I carefully rehearsed the procedure described in the book on how to get past a securely bolted door. Since I did not have access to skeleton keys, I had decided on the more direct approach. The technique called for the gradual insertion of thin wedges of hard wood, preferably oak and ash, into the space between the door and its frame. With the help of a crowbar and a rubber mallet, the wood chips were driven into the progressively widening gap, building pressure and slowly disengaging the bolt from its receiving plate in the door frame. All that remained was to exert a slight amount of forward pressure on the door to gain access into the house. Nothing could be simpler. I cased the neigh-borhood late at night for unusual activity, police patrols or barking dogs, while J.F. used his father's extensive collection of power tools to cut and shape a complete set of hardwood wedges.

The big night finally came. I stayed up long after my entire fam-ily had gone to sleep. At two a.m., I slipped out of the house, silently pushing my Moped out of the garage and vanishing into the night. J.F. and I met up a couple of blocks away and I followed him, our equipment safely tucked in small saddlebags. We had hoped for dark clouds and rain, but it was a clear and beautiful night, as spring gently turned into summer. We continued until we got to about half a mile from our destination. Both of us stopped our engines and proceeded quietly on foot, pushing the Mopeds along, our hearts racing as we drew nearer to the driveway. To make sure we could not be recog-nized, I had insisted we wear masks, but all J.F. could find were black satin contraptions covering the eyes, the nose and the upper part of the mouth. We looked like a cross between an eighteenth-century costume ball and Zorro. I thought they made us sinister and danger-ous, though anyone coming upon us that night would have only been in danger of laughing to death.

And to cover all bases, just in case of complications, I also brought a gun. Not a real, functioning firearm, since in France the possession of a private handgun is something of a rarity. Two summers before, while playing cowboys and Indians with friends, I had convinced my mom that cap guns were ridiculously childish and that we all needed something a bit more convincing, though still completely harmless. The local sporting good store stocked my dream: a starter pistol, the sort of loud noisemaker used at races and athletic events. It was a small revolver made in Spain, and only capable of shooting blanks. But it could be fired in rapid succession like a real six-shooter, and the noise it generated was tremendous. To make sure it couldn't be converted into anything else, the barrel was obstructed by vertical steel posts welded in places, allowing only for gases to pass through. In the dark, however, these tell-tale signs could not be seen and the starter pistol looked as menacing as anything Edward G. Robinson had ever aimed at me from the screen. We slowly opened the gate and let ourselves in, leaving our Mopeds in the driveway and proceeding to the somber mass of the house. A flight of marble steps led to a massive double front door.

Trapped under the silk mask, my breath started to fog my glasses and made it difficult to find the tools. A recessed alcove shielded us from view, and we quickly set about our work. The technique I had memorized looked easy enough in the book, but proved much more challenging against a real door. I began to insert the oak wedges into the crack that J.F.'s crowbar was opening between the door and its frame, only to see them instantly spat out the moment he released the pressure. I broke out in a sweat. This was taking longer than anticipated. The only way for the woodblocks to stick was to hammer them in. I picked up the rubber mallet and began to drive the wedges inward. J.F. was getting worried that I made too much noise, but I reassured him and went on. Soon the process began to work. As the thin wedges made way for thicker ones, the door started to buckle under the pressure. In the glow of our flashlights, we could actually see the bolt slowly moving out of the frame. Another half an inch and we were in.

Then disaster struck. Quite a few details must have been omitted from the book, and I wondered afterwards if it were an accidental oversight or a deliberate attempt on the part of the publisher to protect himself from liability. The crowbar and the wedges had gradually applied a tremendous amount of pressure to the door, and as physics dictated, it eventually had to be dissipated in some fashion or another. The door, not as formidable as it looked, owed its massive appearance to layers of dark varnish over pine rather than real oak wood. Without warning, it split from top to bottom like timber in the iron grip of winter. The crack reverberated against every house in the neighborhood. We dropped our tools and hid deeper within the recessed alcove. To the left a dog began to bark, quickly followed by another. I froze with fear. Within seconds, a light came on and a window opened in the house directly beside us. A man appeared, peering out in our direction. We didn't dare breathe and stood against the door like statues.

Gradually, things began to calm down and I even stretched a bit when a sharp clang broke the silence. I had bumped into the crowbar and sent it tumbling down the marble steps. The dogs started barking again. That's when I heard the man's voice bellowing in the dark:

"I know there's someone out there. My wife is calling the police. Stay exactly where you are or I'll sick the dogs on you!"

Another light appeared in the house behind us, and a garage door opened across the street. We both stood there scared, uncertain of the next step. For all its detailed instructions, the Encyclopedia of Crime offered no advice when things went disastrously wrong. It was time to do something. Suddenly emerging from our stupor, we decided to run, flying off the front steps with the winged agility of terrified teenagers. We made it past the front gate and ran down the street to the salvation of our Mopeds. J.F. got there first, and his Italian pony instantly came to life. He revved the engine and took off, his headlight erratically slicing through the night.

I did not fare so well. I tried the engine, but it refused to start. One of the neighbors decided to take matters into his own hands and crossed the street, coming towards me...It was not the burly man in pajamas I worried about, but the threat of the dogs coming on his heels. Still trying to start the engine, I turned around and saw the meddling neighbor less than fifty feet away. Without thinking, I reached into my coat, drew the starter pistol and fired twice in his direction. The detonations were deafening, and the unexpected muzzle flash startled me. The man instantly dropped to the pavement. "Don't shoot! For the love of God, don't shoot!" he yelled out, writhing on the ground as if he'd been hit.

My engine suddenly sputtered back to life. I straddled the Moped, fired one more shot in the air and sped away, the cobblestones in the road sending shivers through the handlebars.

That night, after stealing my way back into the family house, I went to bed with the certainty of being arrested in the morning. The French inject a measure of romantic leniency in the ruthlessness of their criminal code: the police cannot enter a private residence and arrest criminals between ten o'clock at night and sunrise. No one came at dawn, but I spent the next three days anxiously scanning the local paper for the lurid description of our exploits. Our criminal behavior never made it into print. One of the trap doors of my fate had mercifully closed, sparing me the path to juvenile delinquency. I never saw J.F. again, and turning my back on a life of crime, I joined the Boy Scouts at the end of the month.

I am not quite sure why I came to that decision, but subconsciously I must have felt the need to distance myself from recent events by joining an organization known for discipline and a sense of civic duty. The Boy Scouts is essentially an Anglo-Saxon concept; and the idea of organized patriotism remains somewhat suspect in France. The culture doesn't lend itself to flag waving and merit badges, and in the collective memory of its people, the thoughts of brown shirts, insignias and singing around campfires are too reminiscent of Hitler youth and the rise of nationalism. Still, the uniform and paramilitary lifestyle must have appealed to the fascist fantasies assailing the mind of an angry fifteen-year-old boy. My parents seemed favorably impressed by my new interests and after a short period of instruction and initiation, I was bombarded with the rank of assistant pack leader. I had no prior experience and probably owed this semblance of authority to the fact that the local troop coordinator worked for my father, and that I was older than most members. My hair became shorter, though I was spared the customary crew cut. In June, we set out for a two-week training camp in Provence. My parents took advantage of this opportunity to visit southern Italy with my sisters, and I would return in time for a rigorous review before the dreaded exam at the end of summer.

My bucolic dreams were dashed soon after we arrived at the camp. I was to supervise a gaggle of twelve-year-olds and attend to tedious administrative duties. The location proved disappointing, our tents nestled in the pinewood hills of southern France, thirty miles from the Riviera. But I remained eager to do well and wanted to be accepted by the group. Perhaps as a test of good will, they put me in charge of latrine construction. Digging a deep hole in the root-clotted soil, I constructed a commode of some sort, building a proper shack to shelter the latrines from the elements. Despite the heat and the incessant buzz of mosquitoes and horseflies, I acquitted myself of the task in less than forty-eight hours. I thought it quite an accomplishment, until informed that my predecessor had completed the same project in a single afternoon. Our sleeping bags were cushioned with rotting moss and drinking water strictly rationed. Working on merit badges and studying the local fauna soon became tedious. I still had another twelve days to go and started regretting ever taking part in the entire expedition. The kids were nice, but I had little in common with them, and found it progressively harder to take an interest in whatever stirred their enthusiasm each day. A casual comment from a camp counselor did catch my attention: there was a Girl Scout camp less than two miles from our location. It had a small lake and a pontoon for water activities. The thought of girls in bikinis began to haunt me. In the sweltering heat, the latrines exhaled a stench that penetrated every recess of the camp, mingling with the smell of canned sardines and dirty socks. After a few days, I decided to mount an unauthorized expedition and pay a visit to the campfire girls.

At two in the morning, as my charges slept soundly in their tents, I put my training to good use and slipped out quietly with two flashlights and a compass. The moon was half-full and I found it easy to orient myself. I grew up in the Alps, and since childhood I have always found a forest at night a magical and privileged experience. With just a hint of apprehensiveness, it graces the night traveler with a reassuring sense of peace and tranquility. In the shadows, the surrounding woods teemed with industrious and invisible life, a quiet celebration of whispering calls, muffled sighs and imperceptible rustlings. Under the pale illumination, the darkened trees gave off intoxicating scents of resin and bark. I felt exhilarated as I walked on, with twigs and pine needles crackling under my feet. But I had underestimated the time it took to reach the camp, and didn't make it to the lake for another two hours. It was completely silent, and I could only make out the outline of large tents huddled fifty feet from the shore. There were no campfire girls, no midnight swim or naked bodies silhouetted against the lake, only the stillness of the night and specks of moonlight dancing on the water. After a few minutes, I retraced my steps. The deepening shadows and my exhaustion made it more difficult to find my bearings, and I got lost on the way back. I finally reached our camp at five in the morning, the hardened and knotted ground under my sleeping bag now beckoning like a soft mattress. I was abruptly stopped by the glare of several flashlights pointed straight at my face. The senior staff had noticed my absence and had patiently awaited my return. I thought they would be amused and understanding, but I was charged with dereliction of duty, endangerment of camp safety and violation of a half-dozen rules.

In the morning, without the benefit of a disciplinary hearing, I was made to pack my belongings and accompany the camp director in his jeep for a ride back to town. I thought my escapade rather harmless, but the scout council deemed it serious enough to expel me that very day. My parents had to be located before I could be sent home, which proved somewhat difficult. The camp leader finally found them in a hotel on the island of Ischia in the bay of Naples. I sensed once more my mother's embarrassment and my father's displeasure as I sat in a small room while the director gave an eloquent account of my nocturnal activities. In an attempt to salvage their vacation, my parents came up with a solution. Since no one would be home for the next two weeks, it was out of the question that I should be allowed to return there unsupervised, so they asked Jean-Claude for help.

Jean-Claude de Rochefort lived in Paris. A noted oral surgeon, he was a professor at the Dental School and a facetious man who could also be authoritarian when necessary. I worshipped him. He readily agreed to step into the fray and offered to keep me under his supervision until my parents' return. He was forty years old but looked ten years younger, and though he had risen to an enviable level of professional excellence in his specialty, he remained a perennial sixteen-year-old at heart. He followed my academic vicissitudes from a distance, taking me aside during family reunions for some much-needed advice. Wealthy and handsome, he was the embodiment of professional success and grace, and yet the younger set in the family always identified with him because of his two-seater Porsche and his irreverent swipes at the establishment. He remembered what it felt like to be an embattled teenager. For as long as I could recall, he had always taken care of my teeth. Despite a full schedule of surgeries and teaching responsibilities, he made room for my sisters and me, attending to our cavities long after his staff had gone home. His office was equipped with the latest technology from Germany: high-speed drills and the sort of automated dental chair that is the norm nowadays, but which in the 1960's was rather unique in private practice. I still remember him cleaning my teeth, regaling me with salacious anecdotes about his female students at the dental school, while doing imitations of Nazi interrogators from all those war movies mass-produced in the fifties.

"Ach so, you are ze one who vill not talk, ja? – But ve have vays, human vays to obtain informazion from you, mein guter Freund."

He was the only member of the establishment I respected. For my birthday, he would slip me five hundred Francs – no mean sum for a teenager back then – with a card that read "Pour le superflu... si nécessaire!" ["For things superfluous...yet so indispensable!"] His advice was summed up in words every rebellious teenager needed to hear: "buck the system and screw the bastards, but pass your exams with distinction: it is the key to your independence."

Jean-Claude had married my cousin Hélène, a stunning beauty fifteen years my elder who had first caught my eye when sunbathing in the nude at my great-uncle's estate. In my early teens, I took instant notice of her lithe and tanned body, finding it difficult to breathe each time she would go in or out of the pool. The prey of undefined stirrings and desires, I would let my eyes shamelessly caress her at a distance. My great-uncle's plantation in the French Alps included a sprawling eighteenth-century manor, with wide porches and a massive veranda that looked out over manicured gardens filled with exotic flowers. It was surrounded by a thousand acres of orchards and apple groves covering the nearby hills as far as the eye could see. From the front gate bordering the highway, a road half a mile long led to the main house. Spending summers there allowed my sisters and me to explore the maze of corridors and rooms that unfolded over three monumental floors, with balconies long enough for us to roller skate when it rained. The servants' quarters lay slightly to one side, with the children's rooms concentrated on the second floor, directly above the pool. Centenarian magnolias and towering oaks huddled around the manor like battlements to a castle. Vacations were spent playing and swimming in the afternoon, devouring French pastries the maid would lay out by the pool side. We also got initiated to curries and spicy African dishes created by Mani, the family cook from French Guinea. Six-and-a-half feet tall, massively built and so soft-spoken that his voice came out as a modulated whisper, he was the only black man anyone had ever seen in this Alpine enclave, twenty miles from the Swiss border.

Yet despite the enchantment of this playground, my cousin Hélène could at will interrupt my games each time she decided to sunbathe under my window. There she lay motionless for hours, beads of sweat glistening off her wondrous golden skin, her towel like a rose petal against the luxuriant grass of the lawn. I was still uninformed about matters relating to sex, and I experienced my first lust as a perplexing tide of emerging desires. I recall the day when I had accidentally overslept, and bolted out of bed to catch up with my sister at the pool. I met Hélène half-way down the backstairs. She walked up slowly, a towel in her hand and her sunglasses propped up in her hair. She had come straight from the lawn, not anticipating anyone on the way back to her room. I came to a stop, overwhelmed by the sudden proximity of her nakedness, impudently staring at the gentle sway of her perfect breasts. I had never seen anything so beautiful. Hélène allowed me to gaze much longer than I should have, and when we passed on the stairs, she smiled, ran her fingers through my hair and walked on up before disappearing at the top of the steps. When I finally reached the landing, flooded with the afternoon sun, I could still hear my heart pounding like drums in my ears.

A few years later, Hélène became Jean-Claude's wife, and she ceased to arouse my interest. But the good doctor still teased me for years about the incestuous desires I had once entertained for my nudist cousin.

Now, as he had done before, Jean-Claude stepped in to help with my turbulent upbringing. The plush comfort of his Paris apartment was a welcome relief from the strictures of a sleeping bag. He also took advantage of my presence to check my teeth, while entertaining me with stories from his past. In the late nineteen-fifties, he had served with the French army medical corps during the Algerian war. Stationed in North Africa, Captain de Rochefort was a reluctant participant in a political charade that had already claimed the lives of forty thousand people. France was fighting her last foreign war, trying to hold onto the oil-rich territory against a rising tide of murderous terrorists. Algeria had been an integral part of the French Empire for a hundred years, and over 400,000 soldiers would eventually ship out across the Mediterranean in a doomed effort to retain control of the largest desert on earth. Exiled to a Saharan outpost, Dr. de Rochefort provided expert care in oral surgery to a full detachment of the French Foreign Legion. These men had seen action all over the world, from the rice paddies of Cambodia to alligator-infested lagoons in French Guyana, and even within the army, the legionnaires were feared for their ruthless efficiency. At night, checking his bed sheets for scorpions, Jean-Claude would dream of his colleagues safely removed to a military clinic in Tahiti, another relic of the French colonial empire.

One morning, a sergeant was referred to his office for immediate treatment. The six-foot-five Special Forces instructor stood at attention next to the examining chair. He was bald and sported a gleaming metal plate screwed to the side of his skull, a souvenir from a Vietnamese mortar shell around Dong Khē.

"Doc," the legionnaire said, "I was sent in by the major. I don't really need to see you, but the men can't stand my breath anymore. So you got to do something."

And the sergeant sat in the chair. The infection he had nursed for months had spread through the gum and into the bone. Jean-Claude reached for a syringe to numb the swollen jaw, but the man grabbed his wrist and held it as tight as a vise.

"No needles, doc. I don't like needles.... I was interrogated by the North Koreans back in 1951, after the battle of Heartbreak Ridge. So you just go right ahead. Cut or drill, I don't really give a damn, but no needles. Got that?"

And to make sure the oral surgeon understood what was being explained to him, he drew a loaded .45 and jammed it into his ribs. Then he leaned back against the chair and opened wide.

"So what did you do?" I asked with trepidation.

"I proceeded very slowly," he replied. "I squirted a topical anesthetic over the infected tooth, removed the bit from the drill, substituted a brush and polished a healthy molar on the other side of his mouth for the next five minutes or so. He finally got up, lowered the hammer of his .45 to half-cock, saluted and left. I sat down in the chair, mostly because my legs were too weak for me to stand up. I reached for the Cognac I kept in the bottom drawer of the surgical cart and drank straight from the bottle."

I spent an exceptional week in Jean-Claude's company, almost forgetting the showdown with my parents at the end of the month. I hugged him when I left, grateful for his kindness and the seasoned strength I could sense behind his impish grin.

Two

I HADN'T HEARD FROM my parents during my stay with Jean-Claude, and their silence was both unusual and ominous. The family had returned from Italy, and though everyone appeared rested and tanned, the atmosphere around the house was tense. I pretended to hit the books in a feeble attempt to study for the national exam scheduled a week later in Paris. Cramming for the test became a temporary refuge, a reprieve from the storm I felt gathering. Even my sisters proved considerate, almost solicitous towards me, and in a close-knit family such as ours, deference indicated that something was amiss. My mother appeared more distant, as if restrained. No real discussion ever took place about the incident with the Boy scouts, and on a couple of occasions I had the distinct impression that conversations abruptly stopped as I entered the living room.

   I took the train to the testing center, and over the next two days sat in a proctored room from eight to twelve and one to five. I knew the moment I left that I had done poorly. The exam was knowledge-based, and it covered mathematics, foreign languages, history, geography, literature and natural sciences. To make matters worse, none of it was multiple-choice, since the French educational system puts its faith in essay-type questions. I spent the next two weeks mostly at home, eyeing the mailman in an atmosphere of uncertainty and dread. When results finally came in, my mother got to the mail first, opening the official envelope while I slept. It was a humiliating disaster: I had failed every subject. I knew what it meant even before my parents sat me down for a heart-to-heart talk. In their view, the decision to take me out of boarding school had been premature, and the only avenue left to me was a private school, away from family life. I raised no objections for I had surmised the outcome a few months earlier. What hurt the most, though, was the thought of going back to boarding school, something which at the age of sixteen I compared to civilized incarceration. But I resigned myself, sensing how frustrating this decision sat with my parents. There were few Catholic institutions willing to admit an academic liability, so my mother relied on the advice of St. Erembert's principal to find an appropriate boarding school – the same principal who had expelled me in the spring.

A tall and burly middle-aged man, he always seemed flushed, as if his naturally sanguine inclinations were constantly kept on a leash, with his thin ties strangling his bull neck in shirts too small for his build. He stammered in my mother's presence, and once loaned her a book from a Swiss naturopath which he believed could be helpful with my upbringing. It advocated the wrapping of turbulent teenagers in wet sheets for twenty minutes at a time, the better to soothe their rebellious nervous systems. Before she ever managed an art gallery on the left bank of Paris, my mother had attended the University of Paris Medical School, and still retained a keen interest in child psychiatry. She paid no heed to such nonsense and politely returned the volume without comment. I was left wondering how many hapless teenagers were forcibly made to suffer this treatment, screaming like wet mummies in the embrace of dripping sheets. Knowing the principal's disposition towards me and his fondness for unorthodox pedagogy, I thanked my mother profusely for standing between me and the sadistic aspirations of this lunatic.

The end of August came too soon. My parents decided to drive to the new school, trying to make the journey as pleasant as possible. As we left, I remember turning around in the back seat, watching the closed shutters of my room on the third floor slowly recede through the rear window.

Saint Joseph Academy was located about two hundred and fifty miles south of Paris. In a country like France, which is about the size of Texas, this represented quite a distance from home. There were no high-speed trains in the sixties, and even the interstate highway system was still in its infancy. The entire region is known as *La Creuse,* which literally means "hollow," or even "meaningless, without substance," and this ominous connotation resonated perfectly with the surrounding area. The place was dreary, the sort of rural enclave suffering the exodus of its younger population, who escaped in droves from the cattle farms to the alluring promises of industrial cities. The boarding school was a massive three-story edifice overlooking a town of a thousand people. The walls were twenty feet tall, and as my parents' car drove through the main gate, a veil of apprehension settled on my shoulders like a winter coat on a summer's day.

The staff greeted us with polite interest and perfunctory orientation sessions. In an effort to cut costs and foster a spirit of responsibility, the supervision of sophomores and juniors had been handed over to the senior class. Having lived in a boarding school for five years, I thought the arrangement quite disturbing. It allowed for unchecked hazing and little accountability since the seniors would not return at the end of the year. My feeling of unease became even more palpable when we met the students in charge: they appeared to have been selected for their muscular build. This wasn't good. We placed our belongings inside lockers in the basement of the gym, under the sneering supervision of a senior ravaged with acne. My parents had been told that the school maintained an active judo club, and they had bought for me a splendid new gi, the thick white uniform of judokas. Power, or the illusion thereof, plays a crucial role in the social interaction of teenage boys, especially in a confined environment. I put away my things, slowly unfolding the green belt I had proudly earned in the spring, making sure it would be seen, like an amulet warding off dangers yet to come.

My parents had planned to leave by late afternoon, and I dreaded the moment when the reality of it all would finally be inescapable. I put on a good show, brimming with confidence and abnegation for the sake of my own pride. I nearly lost it when they said goodbye. I would not see them again until All Saints' Day, if all went well, since the school's policy linked family visits to academic performance. I felt once again the tug of that invisible, yet intact umbilical cord between my mother and me. My dad put the best spin on the awkwardness of the moment. He stood out among the other fathers, looking like Clint Eastwood in a three-piece suit, handsome and quietly formidable, with that subtle aura of physical confidence women sense and men notice. Beyond the veneer of polished society, and long after their days in the schoolyard, boys remember the look in the eye of that one kid who could not be intimidated, that stare saying he was prepared to give you a hundred per cent, and you knew he meant it, and you backed off. My father was a quiet man. But from childhood he had kept that look in his eye, and putting it to the test with British commandos in World War II, he still carried it today into hushed executive boardrooms where it served him well.

He eyed the gray building with an expression we all knew—the critical gaze of the architect upon a poorly constructed edifice. But on that day, there was something else as well. Though he never went to church, my dad had been raised a Protestant and harbored a deep-seated mistrust of Catholic priests. It bothered him to strand me here. Before leaving, he made it a point to introduce himself to the dean of discipline, and bade farewell to the athletic young priest with a bruising handshake. I looked away when my parents' car finally started down the main alley and went past the front gate. Years later, my mother confessed that she cried on my father's shoulder for ten minutes as the small country houses of La Souterraine receded behind them.

Time slowed down. I had dreaded my return to boarding school as a recidivist his journey back to prison. But things were different here, as if the hardship I had experienced at Holy Spirit Preparatory were transformed into sheer boredom. I kept to myself, and beyond the perfunctory alliances one makes to survive in exile, I did not think I would find a friend. Yet three weeks into the semester, a late arrival caught my attention. His name was Christophe, a pale fifteen-year-old with an angelic face and freckles. The son of a diplomat, he had just arrived from abroad and taken his place at St. Joseph's almost unnoticed by the other kids. He sat alone in the courtyard during recess and in the back row in study hall. We became friends. Self-effaced and prone to melancholy, Christophe had an extraordinary, almost magical past. For the last seven years he had lived in New York City.

And suddenly this barren place became illuminated. Isolated as I was, Christophe's presence offered a way to escape dreariness and boredom. He began to share with me details of his life in America, opening up unknown vistas to my imagination. Exiled to St. Joseph's, I felt as if we were both locked away in the Chateau d'If, dreaming of Monte-Cristo, with Christophe's memory as a treasure trove of exotic anecdotes. His father had been the French consul in New York. Unexpectedly recalled to the Quai d'Orsay, the French Department of State, he had had no choice but to find a boarding school where his son could remain until Christmas. Christophe's exile was my gain, my salvation. Both of us felt out of place, and we ended up spending all our free time together. So much time, in fact, that the seniors thought we were queer for each other. I only knew the United States through the distorting lenses of television shows and picture books, for in those days traveling across the Atlantic was a privileged experience. I sat transfixed as Christophe related matter-of-factly his everyday life in America, sounding as fantastical to me as if he had lived on another planet.

He caused quite a stir in English class. Our teacher was Mr. Maxwell, a mean-spirited and sardonic Briton who wore dark shades on the gloomiest days of winter. We were doing a conversation drill when he happened upon Christophe. To his delight, the blond-haired late comer was completely fluent, in fact a graduate from one of New York City's junior high schools. We all sat in our desks completely amazed as the two carried on a lively exchange. It was magical, as if my friend had just stepped down from a movie screen, endowed with the linguistic abilities of Alec Guinness. He was excused from English class, writing book reports for the teacher who assiduously checked on him throughout the week. Though certainly drawn by linguistic affinity, Mr. Maxwell did not seem entirely indifferent to Christophe's green eyes and bewitching smile.

We made it a point to stay away from other students, and I sensed that our refusal to participate in their structured power play threatened the very fabric of the system. We were not paying our dues, and dissidents are distracting anomalies to any social structure based on privilege and intimidation. One of the seniors finally came over to challenge me. When I would not heed his demand to stand up, he viciously kicked me. I got to my feet. We were roughly the same height, but he had at least twenty pounds on me. He looked me in the eye and came close enough to spit in my face – the usual prologue to a fight. I did not budge, putting my hands in my pockets as if I were unconcerned with imminent harm. And it worked. All of a sudden the tension eased, the threat dissolved and the instigator backed off. I turned around and walked away.

I hadn't moved twenty feet before the attack came. It probably was just a taunt, a mocking gesture from a crestfallen bully in need of regaining his standing with the crowd. From behind, two hands wrapped themselves around my neck. The rear choke routine was a training drill at our judo club: without even thinking, I got hold of his arm, moved back against him and went into Ippon – the over-the-shoulder throw so popular with action movies. It had come out of pure reflex and the student sailed over my head, slamming into the wet mud with a wrenching thud. It knocked the wind out of him, and he lay there for a moment, visibly shaken. He rose slowly to his feet and hissed, "You don't scare me at all, du Plessis, not even a bit!" before ambling off into the main building. Christophe and I walked out of the courtyard. I was astounded at the speed with which these events had taken place. My technique was not ordinarily that proficient, and the near perfect execution of the throw owed as much to luck as it did to training. But no one needed to know, and as news of the fight rippled through the school, my reputation as a dangerous silent type was established. The seniors never bothered us again, and the fag jokes ceased that very day.

To Christophe, my childhood misdeeds and the colorful members of my family represented an endless source of wonder. To me such information was trivial when compared with his recollections of New York. And thus we became quite fond of each other, sharing the mail we received from home and talking about girls for hours. But the echoes from Christophe's former life stirred the darker recesses of my imagination. Since my arrival at St. Joseph's, I had occasionally entertained the idea of running away, but it had remained just a coping mechanism, a soothing fantasy to help me forget about this place. But feeding on my friend's exotic recollections, the notion gradually took on a more solid shape and moved into the realm of possibilities. Going to the United States was out of the question. I needed a passport, a lot of money, and I was simply too young to travel alone across the Atlantic unnoticed. If escaping from St. Joseph's had become more than a dream, I still needed a reasonable plan of action and a more realistic destination. As we drew nearer to All Saints' Day, the solution slipped into my brain: the place had to be remote and exotic enough for a taste of adventure, and yet not so far as to prevent a hasty retreat, if necessary. It all naturally pointed to London.

In the 1960's, England, that arch nemesis of the French, exerted a magnetic attraction on teenagers everywhere. While France and other European nations were busy resisting the tide of social change, holding the younger generation to the starched principles of centuries past, England had become a powerhouse of ideas. My father had often alluded to the reward of a trip to Berlin, Vienna or Rome, and though I thought these places interesting from a historical point of view, they elicited little enthusiasm in me. My dad was appalled to learn that London was now the "in" place. England had been the enemy of France for a thousand years, until two world wars forced them into an awkward alliance against a common peril. They were so uncomfortable as first-time allies in 1914, that the most flattering terms they could find to describe their newfound partnership were "Cordial Understanding." With its wretched weather and detestable food, *Perfidious Albion* and its condescending inhabitants were insufferable to my parents' generation.

But then it happened: an artistic revolution accomplished in ten years what centuries of strained diplomacy had failed to do. French teenagers broke ranks with their elders and reconciled with England, thanks to Rock and Roll and James Bond. A powerful tide of new music and exciting films were taking over our transistor radios and movie screens. In junior high, most of us signed up for English as a foreign language, rather than German or Spanish, because it was the language of John Lennon, Mick Jagger and 007. There was another powerful attraction as well: British girls. With their pale Anglo-Saxon looks, flaxen hair and bad teeth, they often said "yes" to horny Parisian teenagers. While young French women seldom consented to sex before college, English girls were more willing, and many of us left for summers in Brighton Beach, convincing our parents it would improve our English, and losing our virginity in the process. The early availability of contraception in England had made it the flagship of the sexual revolution.

What did I hope to accomplish by running away to London? I thought it a brilliant and decisive coup to attract my parents' attention. It would be the most powerful statement I could make about my exile in boarding school. Christophe attempted to dissuade me, arguing instead for a serious discussion with my parents during the upcoming break, though deep inside he probably knew I had already made up my mind. But I went home for All Saints' Day, and visited with my parents for the first time since they had dropped me off at St. Joseph's. Over two months had passed, but the excitement I felt upon my return to Paris was mixed. I had missed everyone a great deal but felt as if this trip were a rehearsal for the escape plan that was forming in my head. Rather than complaining about the school, I convinced my family that things were actually rather positive. My grades had considerably improved and I hadn't caught the attention of the disciplinarians even once. For my plan to work, it was essential that my parents think me well content. So I played the part of the reformed delinquent, and only my mother sensed that something wasn't entirely right, for I shrank from her attempts at meaningful conversation and averted my eyes each time her loving gaze would rest upon me.

There were two essential documents I needed to secure: my savings account passbook and a travel permit. Back in the 1960's, European borders were rather forbidding. Cars and trains were stopped for inspection, luggage was searched and identification required. These formalities presented me with a problem: it was illegal for someone under the age of seventeen to travel outside of France without a guardian. The only way around this requirement was a form, valid for three years, entitling the bearer to travel alone. My mother was in possession of such a document, and I knew where to find it. Two summers before, I had attended a training camp for the national junior swimming team in Switzerland, where I had a lot of fun, but did not make the cut. I waited until everyone was out of the house to go through my mother's antique writing desk, where she kept important papers. I loved that piece of furniture, an ornate Louis XVI secretary, with a lacquered rotating panel protecting rows of small drawers. Made of solid cherry and precious wood, it possessed secret compartments once reserved for classified documents and incriminating love letters. Today, it gleamed with the veneer of history, while the lingering scent of my mother's perfume stood guard over the two-hundred-year-old antique. Fortune must have smiled upon me, for I retrieved the travel permit in less than two minutes. The passbook was hidden in my room. I needed it to withdraw the balance of my savings account before I left, and was shocked to discover that it only held three hundred francs. That was a serious problem.

I left home with mixed emotions. The atmosphere was light and relaxed, since I was expected back in six weeks for Christmas break. I had no idea when I would actually return and took a good look at my room, suddenly feeling apprehensive at the thought of leaving. I even hugged my mother the way I used to, long enough to elicit a few taunts from my sisters.

The thrill of the preparations soon eclipsed the sadness of the trip back to St. Joseph's. Christophe listened and gave advice as I struggled with details and unexpected difficulties. Most of all, my financial situation was alarming. Even if I put together the allowance my father had given me, all my birthday money and the balance of my savings, I still couldn't come up with more than eight hundred francs. It was clear that I didn't have enough funds to travel to England and survive. I had a solution in mind, but it was not something I felt particularly proud of. In the end, I deemed it a necessary evil in the greater scheme of things. Moral relativism is easier when you're sixteen.

I had traveled alone before, but I was excited at the idea of crossing the English Channel on my own and actually leaving the continent for the first time. The main difficulty was getting out of St. Joseph

Academy. I had known for some time that I couldn't just scale the wall and leave. The town was small, everyone knew each other and trains and buses linking it to the civilized world were few. I had to leave by the main gate in broad daylight and without dissimulation. It meant that I needed a valid reason for my absence and an official pass from the father superior himself. Along with the authorization to travel alone outside of France, I had acquired something else from my mother's desk: three sheets of her stationary – immaculate Italian vellum, with a watermark of the family crest in the center. Using my sister's Olivetti typewriter, I composed a short letter requesting special permission to attend a memorial service for my grandfather, the noted cardiologist and a member of the French Academy of Medicine, who had recently passed away. I forged my mother's signature, then gave the letter with ten francs to a young waitress at a local cafe, with instructions to mail it a week later. Everything now depended on her. There was always the risk that she would keep the money and throw away the letter, but it was the only practical stratagem I could devise.

Ten days after the break, as we sat in study hall, I was called out of class at the headmaster's request. I walked the darkened halls and ascended the wide wooden staircase with intense apprehension. For all I knew, the young seminarian accompanying me could be an escort to my own trial and execution. But the old priest was uncharacteristically warm with his welcome, even rising from behind his desk as I entered the forbidding study.

"Du Plessis," he said in a kind tone, "I want you to know that all of us here at St. Joseph's share in the loss of your grandfather. I fear you will have to alter your regular schedule this week, for I have just received a note from your mother requesting your presence at a memorial mass in Paris. I know how inconvenient it must be to leave so quickly after your return, but you are a junior now, so consider it a sacrifice expected of one. Here is your leave of absence. You will catch the 8:15 for Paris in the morning. Please convey my personal sympathies to your mother. That will be all."

I felt exhilarated as I walked slowly back to study hall. It had worked! The school had not called home to verify the request, or even to confirm the time of my arrival. What yesterday had only been theoretical mischief had now taken root in the present. There was no turning back. My grandfather, the irascible physician and scholar, a knight-commander in the Order of Malta and a vocal anti-Semite, was probably turning over in his grave. I had never met him. He died two years before I was born.

The next morning I awoke two hours before reveille. I had spent the evening talking non-stop with Christophe. He did not take the whole thing seriously, believing instead that it was just a passing phase, something I had to prove – and something dumb to boot – since he felt certain I would get caught and wind up back at St. Joseph's within three days at most. Perhaps he secretly hoped it would not work, so that I would indeed return. I sensed his sadness and resentment at my leaving him here. But Christophe, my fellow exile in this place, had no interest in running away with me. There had never been a shred of rebellion in him, and, besides, you don't run away to London when you've lived for seven years in New York City.

It was cold when we said good-bye. At the last moment he handed me an envelope. Inside was all the money he had, and his wristwatch. He had tears in his eyes and we shook hands in silence, as if I were a soldier leaving for the front. But before I could say the words I had carefully composed, Christophe turned away and ran, disappearing into the gray dampness of the courtyard. It was the last time I would ever see him.

La Souterraine's train depot bore a striking resemblance to Neustadt, the fictitious train station in The Great Escape, a movie every teenager had seen when released in France the year before. I thought the analogy appropriate, since I did not feel entirely safe standing there waiting for the 8:15 to arrive. I worried that at any moment now a car would pull up alongside the tracks, and a couple of priests in black cassocks would rush the platform shouting, "Stop that young man, stop him...!" Not quite as dramatic as the SS tracking down Steve McQueen from the nearby stalag, but I was just as worried. I had to show the school's permission slip – my modern day "Ausweis" – to the stationmaster before I could even purchase a ticket. I carried a small suitcase, since I could not take any more clothes without arousing suspicions. I had only packed for an overnight trip and shivered in a dark two-piece suit, thin enough for a summer funeral.

But no one came running to haul me back into St. Joseph's, and the Paris express pulled into the station on time. Only later, ensconced in a comfortable seat with my forehead cooling against the frosted window, did I finally relax a bit. Once again, I reviewed in my head the schedule I had meticulously arranged over the past two weeks. At the most, I had three days to carry out my plan and get out of the country, before the school would call my parents when I didn't return from the "funeral."

Paris looked almost different when I got out of the Gare de Lyon train station. My being there illegally, as it were, lent the city an exciting feel of novelty. There was the slight possibility that I might run into an acquaintance of my parents, but hidden among ten million people it was unlikely. My first stop was my father's architectural firm, which was closed for the weekend. I ate lunch and stocked up on Gauloises cigarettes, not knowing if they were available in England. The night train to Calais did not leave until midnight, so I hung around in record stores until six. It was nearly dark when I arrived at my father's office, located on the sixth floor of a stately and opulent building. It stood directly above "Aron Fils de Tunis," the finest Tunisian restaurant in Paris, and as you ascended the immense stairwell lined with thick red carpet, delicious aromas and fragrant scents would entrance your senses. To make sure no one would accidentally be locked out, a secret key was concealed behind the eighteenth-century portrait which decorated the landing on the sixth floor. I sighed with relief upon finding it in its usual place and let myself in. The vast office was dark and silent. I felt my way down the corridor to my father's suite. Through the panoramic bay windows, the Eiffel tower rose majestically, its searchlight scanning the rooftops like a lighthouse in an ocean of flickering neon. A huge drafting table stood in the shadows like a prehistoric bird. There, my father's ideas were transmuted into bold edifices and skyscrapers.

I stood in the darkened office like a thief in the night. The only reason for my being there to steal the money I needed to run away. I was not proud of myself and felt restless, my dad's presence lingering behind the massive desk. I found the secretarial offices and turned on the lights. In the third drawer of one of the desks was a box containing petty cash. I had seen it when I worked there last summer, making copies on a German duplicator that had gotten me high on trichloroethylene for two weeks. The strongbox was still in the same place, and it was not locked. I opened it and stared in disbelief at a wad of banknotes in the coin drawer. Held together with a pin, crisp five hundred francs bills silently lay in the tray. I had anticipated a handful of ten and twenties, but not such a large bundle of cash. It was the beginning of the month, and the accountant must have placed in there all the petty cash needed until Christmas. What should I do? Each of these bills represented a week's lodging in a decent English hotel, but my father's dedication, his hard work and honesty tugged at my heart. For a minute I vacillated, uncertain of the next step, and then, quickly, I removed two bills from the bundle, putting the rest into the box and shoving it back in the drawer. I turned out the lights and scurried out of the office, my conscience somewhat eased by what I thought was commendable restraint.

For years, the memory of stealing from my father would haunt me. But decades later, during a memorable family reunion in Paris, all the children took turns confessing to my parents the misdeeds of our youth still unknown to them. And I revealed the episode from that night, finally unburdening my guilty conscience. My father looked at me with a smile and said:

"I will ease your conscience even more. The accountant never brought the theft to my attention for a simple reason. We discovered years later, after he had left the firm, that he regularly pilfered the strongbox, writing fictitious receipts and keeping for himself over half the petty cash. You could probably have taken the whole thing and no one would have been the wiser!"

As Mother Teresa once said about making the right choices: "In the end, it is between you and God. It was never between you and *them* anyway."

It was ten o'clock at night when I arrived at the Gare du Nord, the Paris station with trains bound for northern France, Belgium and England. It was cold and nearly deserted, an immense canopy of wrought iron and frosted glass hung over the tracks like the inverted hull of an ancient ship. The heat from gleaming and motionless trains condensed in the air and rose in silent volutes, ascending waterfalls to the top of the hangars. Not quite the airfield at the end of Casablanca, but the vaporous atmosphere and the smell of ozone gave the place an almost theatrical feel. I still had time to turn around, but I had made up my mind weeks ago, lying awake at night in the dormitory of St. Joseph's. Though I think of myself as a level-headed person, the most important decisions in my life have been made almost casually. I find momentous choices comparatively easy, because they are logical extensions of personal preferences and affinities built layer upon layer over the years. The real difficulty lies in harmonizing the choices I have already made with the particular circumstances in which I find myself. As always, the devil is in the details.

I purchased a ticket, only to see a third of my meager budget instantly vanish. My information was either inaccurate or completely out of date, and my wallet suddenly felt considerably smaller. The train left at midnight for Calais, on the French coast. From there, passengers transferred to a ferry and crossed the English Channel to Dover. Then the train ride resumed and continued to Victoria Station in London. I walked the length of the station in search of the platform, found the reserved car and climbed aboard, with thoughts of Caesar crossing the Rubicon. The only exception to France's chronic disregard for punctuality is its trains. They are so precisely on time that you can set your watch by them. Once we were underway, I couldn't see much of anything through the surrounding darkness, only slivers of light as the train sped through suburbs and rail yards. I felt excited, and stretched my legs on the plush comfort of the opposite seat. I lit a cigarette and relaxed, feeling the tenseness and anxiety of this entire day gradually ebbing away. My immediate concern was the border, but we would not be in Calais for another three hours. In the warm shelter of the seat and alone in this compartment, I clutched my suitcase and surrendered to the torpor gradually invading me. I fell asleep as the train reached the countryside, slicing through the night on the frigid plains of Brie.

A gentle nudge awoke me, and it took a moment to recognize where I was. The conductor punched my ticket and reminded me that we would arrive in Calais in twenty minutes. It was about three-thirty in the morning when I got off the train. The station was much colder than Paris. Twenty sleepy passengers and I were ushered through endless hallways and steep staircases to the ferry. The night air and the smell of kelp greeted us as we reached the embarking area. From what I could make out through the dimly illuminated dock, the port of Calais looked as ungainly and sinister as any industrial harbor. I had expected a police checkpoint, or at least custom agents, but no one paid attention to us as we walked up the gangway and into the ship. So far, it seemed that all my apprehension was for nothing. There were cabins for first-class passengers on the forward deck, but all of us were directed to the upper structures of the boat. Everyone huddled in the small cafeteria for coffee and a bite to eat. Tethered to the glistening dock with its engines growling, the ferry swayed as the tide rushed in. I was not hungry. Raised in the mountains, I've always found it difficult to relax on a ship, its perpetual movement sending signals of unsound foundation. The smell of diesel fuel and hydraulic fluid permeated the entire place. I left the shelter of the lounge and walked up to the observation deck. Within twenty minutes we had cast off and slowly eased out of the harbor.

And it is done. Shaking off the cold and the memories, I take a few steps onto the ferry's deck, watching the piers fade into dark as we head out to the open sea. I'm shivering, hemmed in on all sides by brackish waters and the fleeting shapes of rusted ships. But standing up there against the night, I feel exhilarated and free, with a smile that the blistering rain cannot dim.

Three

FOUR-THIRTY IN THE morning, not quite daylight yet. The rain stopped an hour ago and now the edge of twilight begins to shed its violet hues and turns to dirty gray. I am tired but not sleepy, standing with my hands on the railing of the upper deck, taking it all in. In my mind all things English will look different, so even the waves appear oddly shaped. And suddenly, to the starboard, it happens: a faint outline emerges from the dissipating darkness, revealing the coast of England. As we draw closer, the indistinct shoreline turns into cliffs and estuaries. Dover probably looks the same as Calais, but it does not matter to me. I only saw a glimpse of the French harbor on a rainy night, so its English counterpart takes on the mythical appearance of a citadel rising out of the morning fog. The ferry comes to rest alongside the peer and we dock, longshoremen bustling and yelling around us. Everything does look different, from advertising signs on the gangway to the faces of workers oblivious to passengers stepping out of the ferry. I don't think I've ever been so fascinated by the simple routine of everyday life.

I feel a touch of apprehension as we proceed towards the exit. British policemen await us at the end of the corridor. But there is none of the brusque behavior of the French police. It is five o'clock, and even though they're short-handed and tired, the port officials are remarkably courteous and professional. They look rather pale and thin, without much emotion in their face. When my turn comes, the custom officer seems to study my identification a little longer than the other passengers. He asks me something I do not understand.

My confusion and nervousness must be quite obvious. He asks again, more slowly this time and with a clear enunciation, but without any more success. I am embarrassed that my English is more deficient than I feared: I can't even comprehend a simple request. He pauses for a moment, as if to gather his thoughts, and then says, "Votre autorisation de quitter le territoire, s'il vous plait?"

His French is heavily accented but quite understandable. I smile with gratitude and produce the form allowing a minor to leave France without a guardian. That is all. I find myself walking on, following everyone else to the train station directly behind customs. I am in England, I truly, really am! Even the drab station house looks inviting. It is colder than I thought, and I clutch my suitcase against the wind, regretting too late that I didn't bring a coat. I purchase a ticket and within an hour I am seated comfortably on a train speeding towards London.

My knowledge of what England should look like is limited to postcards and James Bond movies, so what I see unfolding through the train window does not correspond to any of it. What is true of Rome and Paris also applies to London: the first sights likely to greet tourists on their way to the great capitals of Europe are often disappointing. Highways and railroad tracks invariably cut through the poorest neighborhoods before reaching the illuminated heart of the city. We meander through shanty towns and lugubrious industrial parks that rival the suburbs of Paris in ugliness and despair. But soon the train penetrates deeper into the orbit of London, revealing an architecture I have never seen before: narrow townhouses huddled together, each with bright-colored doors, and tiny backyards meticulously preened within brick walls. The lights come on inside the train as we roll through tunnels delivering us into the center of London. We arrive at Victoria Station, and I can't wait to make it past the turnstiles and cavernous halls, finally emerging into daylight and getting my first look at the city.

I am not disappointed. London is a wondrous sight, even if you were raised in Paris. I walk for hours through Piccadilly and Trafalgar Square, past Mayfair and Buckingham Palace, finally stopping, enraptured and exhausted, in dire need of breakfast. I find a neighborhood diner and discover how the British can serve a fabulous cup of tea in the most ordinary places. I enjoy my first day in London as if in a daze, realizing toward the end of the afternoon that I must find a place to stay. There are plenty of rooms available—November is not exactly the height of the tourist season—but hotels in the vicinity of Westminster and St. James Park are opulent palaces charging for a single night what I budgeted for an entire week. I settle for a more modest establishment, a family hotel whose white crenellated walkway looks like icing on a wedding cake. I fall asleep in the early evening, on an old four-poster bed, and do not awake for another twelve hours.

The next morning I continue to explore the city, but my initial enthusiasm is tampered by a sobering fact. Even in the most modest of lodgings, I only have enough funds to last a week, and that's if I survive only on sandwiches and water. I need to remember that I am not here on vacation. And there is something else as well, something tugging at my heart that I have tried to ignore for the last twenty-four hours: I must get in touch with my parents. I have no regrets at all being at last a free man in London. A month ago, this place was but a stitch in the fabric of my imagination, a mental refuge in exile. Now it has come into being, the fruit of calculated efforts and mischief, with consequences likely to unfold in some dramatic fashion. I'm thoroughly enjoying the freedom and suspense of it all. In French, "running away from home" is translated by the word "fugue," the same word describing some of Bach's finest compositions, as well as a psychiatric condition. I find it sweet that the French language has given adolescents in trouble both an affiliation with musical creativity and extenuation for traumatic amnesia. I picture the look on the headmaster's face back at Saint Joseph's when he discovers my treachery. His consternation at the collapse of a carefully constructed educational charade, and the ensuing publicity befalling his establishment. Most of all, I wish I could see the smile on Christophe's face when he receives a postcard from his uncle "Peter," a panoramic view of Piccadilly Circus I mailed yesterday. The events I have set in motion will now take on a life of their own. And this is my time, my own stand against a conformity I cannot abide. The act itself is hardly original, but I believe it will bring about a decisive change. I may be a rebel without a cause, but not without a heart. I will not make my mother suffer, nor drive my father to despair, and I will call today. Somehow, I don't know why, but it will turn out all right in the end. I do not mean this in a careless and irresponsible way, but all my life I have never doubted that the ultimate denouement of this play, and the unraveling of its decisive parts, would come about as they were foreordained long ago. Not that my own existence is deserving of privileged considerations, for I do not think of myself as anyone of consequence, but I have always known that pivotal events will only come to pass at their appointed time. In the limited dimension of this world, such a conviction may not relieve me of choices which seem quite real, but I still feel like a starry-eyed kid, a dazzled passenger on someone else's journey.

I must contact my parents and a part of me dreads it. I'm also worried about my father's initial reaction. What if he traces the call and comes over here? It is a risk I have to take. I decide to leave the family hotel where I spent my first night and search for cheaper accommodations. At a tourist information center near Hyde Park Corner I find a French-speaking employee who suggests a couple of possibilities within walking distance. The least expensive option is a youth hostel on Tufton Street, behind the Victoria Tower Gardens. Its appearance is much more modest than my previous lodgings. It is a gray three-story structure squeezed between a post office and a discount furniture store. Behind the reception desk sits a rotund middle-aged man who seems oblivious of my presence. Patiently, using simple words and a lot of gestures, I explain that I'm in need of a room. The manager scrutinizes me the way an entomologist examines a specimen. He is a first-generation Englishman, a former sailor originally from Sri Lanka, clearly annoyed at my inability to express myself more intelligibly. There is nothing like the intolerance of recent converts to newcomers in the faith. I'm grudgingly shown the rooms upstairs, discovering that the bowels of the hostel are even less glamorous than its storefront. Here you don't even book a room, you pay for some sort of alcove housing four boarders at a time. I haven't seen bunk beds since I was eight, and the exiguous quarters remind me of summer camp. The place is dreary, with paper-thin blankets and tired sheets. The only commodity provided in abundance is the heat, and the entire floor swelters around glowing radiators you dare not touch. No one is allowed to remain in the bedrooms between nine a.m. and three in the afternoon, though the reason for this policy is never made clear. There is a small dining area on the first floor, but no cooking is allowed on the premises. Only breakfast items may be kept in the refrigerator or in assigned food lockers. So much for my escape into a new world of glamour and adventure. I pay three nights in advance, leave my suitcase on the upper bed and walk out of the hostel.

The evening chill grips me as I search for a telephone booth. Armed with a pocketful of change, I manage to get through to the operator. She is sweet and exceedingly patient with my English as she routes the call to Paris. The phone rings for what seems to be an eternity and my mother picks it up.

"Hi, mom, it's me."

There's a pause at the other end. Students are not allowed to call from the boarding school. My mother is glad to hear from me, but her voice is hedged with apprehension. She wants to know if I'm all right, and is unaware that I have left. The school hasn't called yet to enquire about my absence. This is going to be harder than I thought.

"I'm O.K., mom, but I'm not in school."

The news takes its toll on her. Where am I? Am I staying with Jean-François or with someone else in Paris? She readies herself for the worst. Is there a girl involved?

"No, mom, it's nothing like that. I'm in England, calling from London."

I feel the shock and anxiety my mother is experiencing all at once. Her voice struggles to remain calm, but it breaks nonetheless, sending shards of guilt into my heart. She asks a dozen questions and I offer no explanations, only silence punctuated by my breathing into the phone, letting her know that I am here, that I am alive...I would so much want to confide, to talk, to explain, and yet I know this is not the time. She puts me on hold and I hear her in the distance, telling the rest of the family assembled around the dinner table. She comes back on and asks if I want to talk to my father. I decline. The conversation resumes with an odd mixture of pointed questions and trivialities. She's afraid to say something that might make me hang up and break this tenuous thread still linking me to her. Like all teenagers, I have at least once fantasized having my parents in the palm of my hand, begging for mercy. Well, here it is, and all I feel is the embarrassment of reducing her to a supplicating mother anguished about her child. And all the time, I sense my father's presence, looming at the other end, his silence more formidable than anything he might say. I'm going to lose it. I hang up and remain standing alone in the frigid phone booth, my breath steaming up the small window. I've never felt this far from home.

Hours later that night, I fall asleep in a overheated room that feels like a cramped cabin on a cargo ship, with the smell from three other men permeating the air, insinuating itself into my dreams.

The next day I meet the boarder who sleeps in the lower bunk. He's from Belgium, barely twenty-one, with eyes that seem to elude any direct contact. He doesn't tell me what he's doing in London, nor does he share any personal information. Something like distrust, and possibly danger, emanates from him. At first I had hoped for conversation in French and maybe a few survival tips from this fellow expatriate, but there will be no friendship between us. I go downstairs to the breakfast area, only to realize that I didn't buy anything to eat the night before. There is a coffee machine in the lobby, and for a shilling it regurgitates something that passes for a cup of tea. I sit down and try the morning papers, but cannot understand the headlines. The rooms will be off limit at 9:00 am, so I decide to go back upstairs and take my chances with the shower in the corridor. And this is when I see her. She's seated twenty feet away finishing her breakfast. I'm not good at guessing someone's age but she looks like a full-grown woman, definitely not a girl. Perhaps it is because of the half-darkness in the room, but everything about her appears in tones of black and white. She's attractive but poised, with something about her that discourages familiarity. I don't know why I keep standing there between the newspaper rack and the door. She must have been looking at me for some time, with the sort of indulgent expression women keep for lost puppies.

"Comment t'appelles-tu?"

The question comes with the measured diction of provincial upper-class. But she uses the "tu" form of informal French, either to create an instantaneous distance between us, or perhaps to make me feel more comfortable. I am out of my depth here, and left guessing which is which. She slides a dish of pastries across the table, while her eyes beckon me to the other chair. She does not shake my hand but nods imperceptibly and introduces herself. Her name is Michelle. I throw away all caution and pride and latch onto her breakfast invitation as if she were throwing me a life-jacket. I don't know why but I decide to tell her the exact circumstances of my being here in London. Besides, I think she can see right through me. She has an elegant, almost classical face, with something else that draws me in. I've often equated a woman's beauty with the degree of symmetry in her features. Though unremarkable by other standards, Michelle's almond-shaped eyes and full lips are perfectly symmetrical.

By the time we leave the room, I still know next to nothing about her. She's a high school teacher in London, trying to find an affordable apartment. Her room is on the third floor, which is strictly reserved for women – no male visitors allowed. She is twenty-six. Twenty-six! It's both scary and fascinating. I don't know how I muster the courage, but before she disappears into the elevator I offer to return her kindness and invite her to dinner that night. She cocks her head and looks at me quizzically. I'm sixteen years old. There is the same maternal look in her eyes as my mother's girlfriends used to have—if they had only known the salacious fantasies some of them elicited in my brain. I remember Mireille, the thirty-year-old liberated anthropologist who came for tea on Thursday afternoons, smelling of incense and wearing thin African robes with nothing underneath. She must have known her powers on a fourteen-year-old boy, because she always greeted me with a kiss that landed on the corner of my mouth, just enough to make me dream.

Michelle stands in the elevator with a frown that hesitates between bemused interest and reprimand. But she nods her assent and whispers "je t'attendrai ici à huit heures," just as the door slides shut. I'm in love.

The weather is cold and gray. I spend most of the day trying to familiarize myself with the subway system. Michelle said she would wait for me at eight. I am back at the hostel at 7:30. I wish I were better dressed, but I only have two days' worth of clean clothes. She arrives ten minutes late, long enough for me to start worrying, and suggests we walk to a nearby Chinese restaurant for dinner. London and Paris are both magical places at night. Their neon and streetlights shine and glitter each in their own particular way. London appears suffused and discreet as it reveals itself more slowly, though the billboards in Piccadilly stand as a garish exception to British restraint. The trees in Grosvenor Gardens are bare, stiffly silhouetted against the night sky. It all feels a bit odd: I've run away forty-eight hours ago, and here I am walking to a dinner date as if everything were perfectly normal. The seriousness of all that has taken place in the last two days yields to the simple reality of a sixteen-year-old's instant infatuation, un-hindered by time, place or circumstances.

The restaurant is small, warm and intimate, with tiny tables and candle light flickering inside rice paper cubes. Michelle is a good listener, and not very talkative by nature. I get the feeling she will not reveal herself as readily as I do. We talk about my situation and my family, but her interest appears motivated only by a desire to protect. She gives me advice on the best way to reconcile with my parents and quickly resume the school year once I am back in Paris. But I've no intention to return to France. I imagine myself staying here in London, working as a stage hand at the Royal Albert Hall, with a view to a career in the theater or the movies. Michelle is kind enough not to laugh openly at the naiveté of my plans, but she remains guarded in matters concerning herself. All I learn is that she's been here for six months, waiting for her visa to be upgraded, so she can work full-time for the London public school system. Of her family and private circumstances I know nothing. I do wish she would quit looking at me as if I were a child, and instead consider me a valid romantic prospect. But she is twenty-six, experienced and sophisticated, and I am a teenager whose conversation and interests she must find tedious.

Michelle is the first real woman I went out with, if you can call our dinner an actual date. She draws me out of my reverie with a laugh, gently rearranging a lock of my hair:

"You need to go back to school," she says protectively. "How would you survive in London? You've never worked a day in your life. You're a good-looking kid, though. You remind me of those angelic teenagers Leonardo kept around his studio. Of course, his interest in them was not always a matter of aesthetics."

My classical education is so deficient that I smile without understanding the allusion. I would want nothing more than to go back to her room and make love to her, but all I get from across the table is a maternal gaze into which my desire dare not intrude. It's not yet ten o'clock when we leave the restaurant, and Michelle asks if I'd be interested in a late-night movie. I would love to, and we're off to a theater in Eccleston Place. The night air feels invigorating as we walk along the Thames. I draw closer to her and take her hand. She smiles and leaves it in mine.

The movie theater is an old art house, and tonight's fare is not exactly what I would choose for my own entertainment. For the next hour and a half we sit in a totally darkened room watching Ingmar Bergman's *Persona*. It's black and white, in Swedish with English subtitles, and much too bleak to a teenager in need of affection. Our age difference is showing: Michelle sits there transfixed by a movie she's already seen, and I only have eyes for her. We are seated so close that our knees and shoulders constantly touch, with her mouth taunting me each time she turns her head to whisper translations of the subtitles. The surrounding darkness deepens her communion with the film, but it only fosters my hunger for her toffee-scented breath. A half an hour passes, and as she leans once more towards me, with her lips brushing against my ear, I turn my head and kiss her. She hesitates for a brief moment and then kisses me back, though her heart is not in it. When she redirects her attention to the screen, I just rest my head on her shoulder, closing my eyes and enjoying the tickling of her fragrant hair upon my face.

We talk on the way back, but Michelle knows I have to call my parents, and that I'm doing everything possible to procrastinate. She thanks me for dinner in the lobby, saying good night with a kiss on the cheek. I try not to appear disappointed and swagger out the door, satisfied that I did kiss her for real a few hours before. Notches on your belt, like illusions of the mind, are pathetically important to teenagers.

I choose the same phone booth as the night before, bracing myself once more as the phone rings at the other end. My sister answers. She's dying to ask me a hundred questions, but the phone quickly changes hands and my mother takes over. She sounds both relieved and angry, asks what my plans are while trying to rein in her mounting exasperation. I decide to play tough and reiterate my conditions: her promise that I will never have to return to St. Joseph's, or any other boarding school, for my willingness to come home. But to my surprise, she refuses. There will be no conditions whatsoever, and I'm in enough trouble as it is without dictating terms to anyone. I will go back to La Souterraine and stay there until Christmas. At that time, and only if my grades and conduct warrant it, will they consider transferring me to a public school in Paris. My mom is doing all the talking, but I know that my dad is sitting next to her, holding the other receiver and listening in. In the 60's, the old black rotary phones came with an additional ear piece tucked in the back. Unknown to me, my father is running the show. Though he detests the role of disciplinarian and always defers the day-to-day running of the household to my mother, he has made a major exception on this occasion, taking charge personally. I'm unaware that for once my mother is just a mouthpiece relaying his decisions. This was hard on her. Years later, she would recall how worried she was.

"I didn't think you could possibly live alone in London," she confessed. "Since you were not legally allowed to work, I feared you might turn to larceny and crime to survive, or be the prey of all those pederasts lurking around the City."

Her numerous vacations in London before the war had not left her with the best impression of Englishmen. "We can't lean on him too hard," she told my father, "or he'll leave and we may never again know his whereabouts." These were real concerns, but my dad held fast and refused to give in an inch. Though he didn't particularly like the British, he respected them. Two years as a paratrooper in Her Majesty's airborne commandos in World War II had left him with an appreciation for English civility and their keen sense of fair play.

I press the point further and threaten never to call again, but my dad anticipated such a move. I'm shocked to hear my mother reply that it would be a most unfortunate decision, but that I have to live with my choices and their consequences. I don't know what to answer. My strategy isn't working and my own mother no longer seems to care about me. I'm outraged and scared. I hang up on her and storm out of the phone booth, slamming the red paneled door in anger.

I decide to call my mother's bluff and let three days pass without giving her any news. But if this silent treatment is depriving her of much-needed sleep, it is also taking a toll on me. The original excitement and appeal of London is gone as my escapade enters into its second week. The days grow short and colder, with the pale illumination of the city fading into gray as early as five o'clock. My financial situation is critical. I'm now skipping breakfast, surviving mostly on fish and chips, and with just enough money for three nights at the hostel, I can already visualize being left out in the street. Michelle commiserates as best she can, and though she's not financially able to help, she still buys me dinner every night and does my laundry. I begin to spend quite a bit of time reading in public libraries and in the London subway. Dug deep beneath the city, its stations offer warm and propitious shelter from the cold, just as they did in World War II, protecting stoic Londoners from German bombs.

I talk briefly with the Belgian who sleeps under my bunk. His name is Alain. He remains carefully vague as to the reasons for his presence in London, and still evades most of my questions. I find his eyes and physical appearance disturbing. There's something not quite right about him. I should have the decency of going beyond the surface, but I cannot. It is most unfair that we should distrust those ill-favored in appearance, but readily grant the best of intentions to grace and physical attractiveness. I bemoan the high cost of living in London, but Alain brags that this is of little concern to him, casually opening his wallet and flashing its contents. Though I only catch a side view, I'm shocked by the thick wad of banknotes within. It's an impressive, if not reckless boast, leaving me more curious as to why he remains in this dilapidated hostel, when he could easily afford more elegant lodgings.

The oppressiveness of the room makes it difficult to sleep, and I find myself wide awake at three in the morning. The two Norwegians left yesterday, and for a while the place is home only to me and the Belgian, snoring on the lower bunk, still in need of a shower. He sounds completely asleep, with the deep and rhythmical breathing of dream states. The last thing Alain does before lying down to sleep is to suspend his precious leather jacket from a peg, so that it hangs precisely at face level on his bunk, allowing him to keep an eye on it. Each night, he also goes through the same ritual before he retires: he places his gold chain, watch and wallet in the inside pockets, tucked away in a bomber jacket that makes him look bigger than his actual size. Two days ago, I only toyed with the idea of robbing him, but desperation now convinces me to go ahead and do it. It's just a matter of finding an opportune time, and this one looks as good as any. I don't care about his watch or the gold chain. What I have in mind is the money he displayed so ostentatiously before me. There isn't a sound in the room besides his breathing and mine. I will have to operate silently, and getting caught in the act would probably turn very nasty. I lie down on my stomach and let my right arm hang gently over the side and down towards his bunk. My hand finds its way through the folds of his jacket, descending along the lining and locating the inside pocket. Darkness and the necessity to move very slowly make this more challenging than I had expected.

At last my fingertips find the wallet and begin to pull it up slowly. It's heavy and the edges get caught in the fabric. The heat of the room and the concentration required bring beads of sweat into my eyes. All I can do is stop and rub my face into the pillow to get rid of the stinging sensation, while my hand precariously hangs inches away from the Belgian's face. At last I'm able to free the wallet and slowly lift it up to my bunk. I pry it open, removing the thick bundle of money and stashing it in my underwear. Then I lie down once more on my stomach and proceed to do it all over again in reverse, all the while fearing the sudden grip of Alain's fingers capturing my wrist, wrenching me off my bunk and sending me crashing onto the floor. But the Belgian does not awake, and I remain there, lying perfectly still on my back, listening to my heart returning to its even and slow rhythm. I would love to get out of bed and visit the bathroom, just to find out the extent of my wealth. But I remain there, drifting in and out of sleep, until daybreak.

Alain is up before I am. He gets dressed, puts on his jacket and vanishes. I wait a few minutes and then cautiously walk down the corridor to the bathroom, getting in and locking the door behind me. I switch on the light, retrieve the money and quickly sift through the bundle of bills. I can't help but let out a string of profanities as I count the loot. It's real money, but it is made up exclusively of one-dollar bills. Alain could boast by flashing the edge of an open wallet, all you really saw was the side view of a thick bundle of bills. I am furious to be taken in by such a cheap trick. Like children saving their allowance, the Belgian keeps his money in small bills. So he is broke after all, which explains the reason for his choosing this run-down hostel. I should put it all back, but doing so would be just as risky as taking it. I don't feel very proud stealing from someone as hard-up as I am, but I remain stuck with the wages of my dishonesty. Later on that morning, I stop by a branch of the Midland Bank and convert all of Alain's fifty-eight dollar bills into British pounds.

As the end of my second week in London draws near, I find myself with little to do. Sad to say, my precarious circumstances have considerably mollified my rebellious stance and that night, listening for once to Michelle's advice, I call my parents. My mother is relieved to hear that I am well, but to my surprise she no longer sounds as worried as she once did. There is no answer to my last ultimatum and we talk instead about fairly trivial matters, as if this situation has now taken on an air of normalcy. I casually mention the possibility I might have to do some modeling for a British fashion catalogue – a complete fabrication on my part, but one that would have sent my mother into a frenzy just a week ago – but this, too, elicits no particular reaction from her. I'm disconcerted and the whole conversation leaves me with a bitter taste in my mouth. A year later, my mother would confess how much effort and acting skill this air of nonchalance and impassivity demanded of her.

I buy a take-out Chinese dinner for two and meet Michelle in the TV area of the hostel. I do not confide in her my disillusion and worry, since it would not be in keeping with the debonair and confident exterior I wish to project. We eat together, cuddling on a small sofa and for once totally alone, but my plans for some degree of intimacy are unceremoniously interrupted by Alain who storms into the room, disheveled and out of sorts. He's been robbed. Someone stole money from his wallet, a rather large sum he says, over a thousand dollars. Michelle and I sympathize with his distress. When did he first notice the theft? Could a professional pickpocket have relieved him of the money in a crowded street? Shouldn't he be reporting this to the police? Ensconced in the sofa and with Michelle's legs resting on my lap, I must not look the part of a suspect. My suggestion of calling the cops brings a twinge of irritation in his face.

"I'll kill the bastard if I ever find him," he shouts on his way out of the room. He also turns down my offer to share our Chinese dinner, never knowing he had paid for it.

It can be dreadfully cold in London in November, and the more so when you're hungry. As required by the hostel, I paid again for three nights' lodging in advance, and this morning I find myself once more on the verge of financial ruin. Evading the rigors of the weather, I discover a warm and fascinating shelter in the mini-casinos around Piccadilly Circus. Such establishments are completely new to me. There are casinos in France, but only the sort of luxurious palaces featured in Hollywood movies, and strictly off-limits to those under twenty-one. The smaller London casinos feature only slot machines and are far from glamorous, catering instead to working-class customers. They are uniformly vulgar and loud, with gaudy neon signs and skimpily-dressed hostesses. Cigarette smoke and human sweat permeate the rooms, but you can spend hours shielded from the cold while playing one-arm bandits and sipping cheap beer. I can only afford the penny arcade, so I sit with my coins, hypnotized by the rhythmic staccato of slot machines, numbers and symbols falling into ordered rows of flickering colors. I'm only drawn out of my fascination by the occasional chime of tokens tinkling into the metal trays. It's of course an exercise in futility, since the odds are ultimately in the house's favor. But the coins that I lose are not a total loss: they're the price I am willing to pay to keep out of the cold and bide my time, a sort of rental fee against inclement weather and boredom. I'm finally out of money and about to leave, when a hand casually stacks a pile of shillings on top of my machine. I look up and see a young man who turns around and smiles. I assume he has just chosen my machine as his next stop, but I am mistaken. He points to the coins and says:

"You seem to need them more than I do. I've been winning non-stop for the past two hours, so I figured I'd spread the wealth and help you out a bit!"

And thus I make Edward's acquaintance. He's thirty-one, a lecturer at the London School of Economics and an inveterate gambler. He has a nice way about him, something passionate that distinguishes him from the more reserved individuals I have met thus far. Edward also has the distinct advantage of speaking French well enough to carry on a conversation, a talent he first volunteers upon hearing my fractured English. We leave the casino and walk into a nearby pub just as the rain comes down like a cataract, washing Piccadilly clean of passers-by and pigeons. We talk for hours. He seems fascinated by what I've done within the past two weeks. His own life appears ordered and settled. The youngest son of a member of Parliament, he is trudging through his doctoral dissertation without much enthusiasm, spending his free time traveling, gambling and having fun. When we leave it is already dark and the streetlights are on, mirrored in puddles of rainwater. He has a car and offers to give me a lift, and I enjoy my first drive through the streets of London in the comfort and speed of a Triumph TR4. Edward drops me off and we agree to meet again the next day for lunch at the National Gallery, near Trafalgar Square. I can't wait to tell Michelle what an exciting afternoon I've had, but I'm shocked when she doesn't share my enthusiasm.

"You mean to tell me that you met this guy 'Edward' in one of the penny arcades around Piccadilly?" she asks precipitously.

"Yes, I did," I answer, "Why do you look so concerned?"

"Because, sweetie, you walked into the most notorious pick-up place for pedophiles in all London."

"Come on," I reply aggressively. "You're not suggesting that this guy is interested in me in that way? I would have sensed it instantly. Edward is a decent sort. There is absolutely nothing suspect about him."

The look on Michelle's face reflects her consternation at my naiveté.

"I have a bit more experience of this town, and of Englishmen, than you do," she answers sweetly, "mark my words, you're being set up. This guy isn't interested in your personality or life story, your looks are what he's after. Please listen to me just this once and stay away from him. Tell you what, don't show up tomorrow and I'll take you out to dinner to make up for it."

I like it when she's concerned about me. Her eyes are pools of grayish-blue where I could lose myself. She leans over and lightly kisses me on the lips. I'm about to give in, but against my better interest something in me wishes to rebel. It is almost as if she were jealous. I thank her for the advice, promise to be careful and ask her to meet me after dinner tomorrow night. She acquiesces with a reluctant sigh and retires early. My eyes follow her as she leaves the room and walks up the stairs. What I wouldn't give to accompany her.

The next day at noon I stand in front of the National Gallery. I love the massive steps, the extravagant fountain and the entrance way, because they remind me of the Church of the Madeleine in Paris. I've spent afternoons in that museum, marveling at the collection and escaping the freezing rain outside. Edward is punctual and seems delighted to see me. We drive to his favorite Italian restaurant in Portobello and enjoy a pleasant chat on the way. It's an expensive place with exquisite food and seamlessly efficient service. We have lunch on the second floor, in a booth overlooking the avenue. Edward tells me of his family and upbringing. A great conversationalist, he is also a good listener who is not above poking fun at his shortcomings. When we reach the dessert, he offers his help in securing legal employment for me. He knows of my romantic aspirations to work in the theater, and it so happens that his father sits on the board of the Royal Albert Hall. I'm thrilled at the offer. Edward goes on to suggest that a du Plessis should be lodged in more proper surroundings when visiting London. His flat in Kensington has three unoccupied guest rooms, providing complete independence and privacy. He generously offers that I move in whenever I please. This is a dream come true. I remain speechless, struggling for words to express my gratitude, when it happens.

What I thought to be an accidental brushing of his foot under the table gives way to a more pronounced and unequivocal overture. Edward's legs have encircled my left knee, while the spark behind his winsome smile turns into lust. This is so unexpected that for a moment I do not know how to react. Michelle's warnings return like cymbals in my ears, and the feeling that gradually comes over me contains more sadness than anger. I liked him and feel betrayed by his lack of honesty and the way he ensnared me. Edward reads the astonishment in my face. The sudden change of mood in the room is palpable, and under the table, his legs beat a hasty retreat.

"I am so sorry, Eric. I didn't mean to embarrass you like this in a public place."

But Edward doesn't get it. He misconstrues my stupefaction as bashfulness, an old-fashioned frown at such deplorable liberties. My pleasure in sharing his friendship was unguarded. Our age difference should have alerted me, but I was flattered by his interest in someone so much younger than he, never thinking it would encourage anything else. I don't understand why he couldn't be forthcoming about his intentions when we first met. The moment of surprise over, my inclination is to walk out of the room, but I'm shocked by the celerity with which my brain searches for ways to take advantage of this situation. I may be cold and hungry, but I didn't think myself capable of such unrehearsed deviousness.

"Don't worry, Edward, it's nothing at all," I remark casually, even managing a smile. "I'm just not used to the English way of expressing feelings so unreservedly. In France, one has to be more discreet, so please allow me to proceed at my own pace."

And I raise my glass to accept his offer to move in with him. Edward is instantly reassured. He picks up the conversation where we left off and proceeds to discuss our schedule for the next week. I have retreated inside my shell, nodding here and there and smiling to encourage him. He must be wealthy, and there's got to be a way I can benefit from his infatuation without endangering myself. I tell him I'd love to come and live with him, but – and here I lower my voice, trying to look convincingly embarrassed – there is a delicate matter I need to attend to.

"Is there some other guy you're not telling me about?"

"No, it's nothing like that," I reply, "but I had financial difficulties and ran up quite a bill at the hostel. I owe five days' rent to the manager."

"But," he retorts, "that man is a brute who never extends credit to anyone."

Edward is better informed than I thought, and must have known other boarders from the hostel. I'm searching for an appropriate reply, when he preempts my efforts.

"But then again, the old limey must have made an exception for you."

I choose to ignore the allusion.

"So how much do you owe?"

I quickly compute the exact amount in my head, thinking he probably also knows the room rates, and whisper, as if genuinely shamefaced,

"A little over forty-five pounds."

He laughs at the triviality of this sum, making me regret I didn't come up with a higher figure. I leave the restaurant with his arm casually around me. I can't stand his company much longer, but even as we sit talking in his car Edward still doesn't give me the money. Instead, he calls my bluff.

"There's nothing for you back there in that hostel, or in France for that matter. Why don't you just move in with me tonight? I could come by and pick you up at nine. We'll settle everything right there. What do you say?"

I don't know whether Edward really teaches economics, but he's quite adept at creating opportunities and getting an early return on his investments. I agree. There is little else I can do. He beams with anticipation and speeds away, disappearing in the afternoon traffic. What have I done? I walk absent-mindedly into the subway station in need of a place to sit. And to think my mother's worst fear is to imagine her innocent boy, preyed upon by pedophiles roaming around Piccadilly.

I return to the hostel and wait for Michelle to get back from her teaching job. I'm both excited and nervous at the prospect of putting my plan into action, and relieving Edward of a sizable amount of cash. The moment she comes through the door and sees me, Michelle knows something is going on. We sit in the dining room and I tell her all about my lunch, and the way Edward came on to me. She smiles half-heartedly, reassured to see me unharmed. And then I proudly reveal my plan for the evening, and the little stratagem I intend to use as a way to get back at him. Michelle is aghast at the thought.

"You must be out of your mind," she says forcefully. "Have you any idea how dangerous this could be? That high-class predator of yours is more treacherous than you think. He may appear charming and harmless, but I know his kind. He'll turn nasty if he's crossed. Besides, if he truly is the son of an MP, he may be shadowed by private security – the sort you really don't want to meet. What makes you think he'll come alone tonight? That plan of yours may backfire, and I don't want you to end up with your head bashed in on some back street in Soho. Go ahead and laugh, but that judo of yours won't make any difference."

She appears genuinely worried, and her alarm takes some of the wind out my sails. But what can I do now? I don't even know how to get in touch with the guy.

"Just don't be here when he shows up and he'll get the message," she implores.

She takes me in her arms with an urgency I wish she'd manifest in other circumstances and holds me close against her, but my resolve does not waver.

"I appreciate your concern, but I can't do what you're asking," I reply. "I would look like a coward."

But it isn't just that. Deep inside me, from the recesses of childhood memories, a ground swell of anger and outrage has been surging all afternoon. My plan for tonight is a harmless prank compared to what I'd really like to do. But I don't feel like explaining and slowly release myself from her arms. Something must have changed in me, because her eyes no longer shine with maternal solicitude. Maybe for a moment there, I aged a couple of years.

"I'll be fine." I say, trying to reassure her. "If you wish, I'll call you on the house phone around ten to let you know how things went."

I give her a hug and disappear into the lobby and up the stairs to the second floor. Once in my room, I quickly gather all my clothes and personal effects and pack my suitcase, laying it flat on my bunk. Then I sit by the corridor window, light up a Gauloise and wait, peering out onto the street below.

Shortly after nine, a taxicab pulls along the curb and stops. At first I pay no attention to it, but after a few minutes the rear window rolls down, revealing a face looking out to the entrance. It's Edward. From where I'm sitting, he can't see me. I'm surprised he did not drive his own car and chose to take a cab instead. It's also odd that he doesn't come inside and ask for me at the reception desk. It all feels a bit more sinister than I anticipated. Whatever the reason, Edward remains in the cab. From his remarks during lunch, I gather he's been here before, and may not wish for the manager to see him or for his car to be recognized. I feel no emotion as I study him from the second floor window, only the rush of adrenaline that precedes a satisfying prank. I go downstairs and walk out to the cab, catching Edward's smile framed in the window. He does not come out but leaves the door open on the opposite side, inviting me to get in.

"Is everything ready? Are you all packed?" he asks rather nervously.

"Yes, it's all set," I reply. "All I need is to pay my bill and I'm free to go."

"I'll be glad to help you do that," Edward answers, "just as soon as you bring your suitcase in the taxi."

He's not as naïve as I thought, and this added precaution confirms that he is no stranger to this sort of transaction. I leave the cab and return to the hostel. Once inside, I pause for a moment to assess the situation. I'm not about to let him have my own suitcase, of course, but I must find a solution and quickly. I run back upstairs. No one is in the room. I pace the floor for a minute, when out of the corner of my eye the solution suddenly presents itself: the top of Alain's suitcase is peeking out from under his bunk. It is not locked. I feverishly stuff in his boots and every piece of clothing I can find lying around the room, hoping he does not come barging in unannounced. I stop to catch my breath and comb my hair in the mirror, before going downstairs and calmly walking to the cab. Edward helps put the suitcase into the back seat, visibly satisfied by its reassuring weight. Only then does he give me the money. I exit the cab once more, assuring him I will return momentarily. Back inside the lobby, I look in my hand to see what I've got. It's more than I thought: three bright-red twenty-pound notes neatly folded in half – a small fortune. The reception desk is deserted. I rush through the dining room and continue toward the rear of the small kitchen in search of an emergency exit, but can't find one. This is getting ridiculous. I run back upstairs to the second floor looking for the fire escape, without any more success. A wave of panic slowly passes over me. I pick up my suitcase and, breaking all the rules, continue on up to the third floor into the area reserved for women. A male boarder's presence in these quarters is synonymous with immediate expulsion. There are two doors left ajar to my right. No one is in the first, but as I open the second, I come face to face with Michelle.

"Eric! What on earth are you doing here?"

"I have the guy's money, and he's waiting for me out there in the street. I'm just trying to get out of here. Where the hell is the back door?"

"The back door?" she replies with a look of desperation. "There isn't any! Only last month the fire marshal threatened to close the place down if the manager didn't take care of the problem."

No wonder Edward went along so readily with my brilliant plan. He knew the hostel did not have any other exit than the front door, so he could simply get a hold of my suitcase as collateral and wait for me to reappear. I can't believe how stupid I have been not to prepare my getaway more carefully. Michelle lets me in, then closes the door and watches me pace the floor like a rat in a cage.

"I think the best thing to do right now is to call the cops," she says. "You're a minor. He'll run the moment he sees a policeman entering the lobby."

I know she means well, but I'm not about to follow her suggestion. Long ago I promised myself I would not let other people do the thinking for me, and would face alone the consequences of my actions. Michelle's room looks out onto the rear of the building. There is a window in her tiny bathroom; I try to open it but it resists. The sash finally comes loose and bursts open, sending specks of broken paint onto the floor.

"What are you doing" Michelle asks, truly worried. "We're on the third floor. You're going to kill yourself."

I look outside the window. The back of the building is dark and damp, plunging straight down to a small courtyard below. My fingers rub over the asperities of the stone as I feel for a handhold. I locate the drainpipe carrying rainwater from the roof. It is sturdy and obligingly follows the back of the building all the way to ground level. Michelle is convinced I'm going to break my neck and does her best to dissuade me, but she doesn't know this is hardly a problem. And it's not recklessness on my part: eight years of mountain climbing in the Alps with my dad – not always at my own choosing—have made me familiar with vertical drops and challenging rock faces. The descending pipe and multiple footholds afforded by protruding bricks make this an easy task, even in the dark. I entrust my suitcase to her keeping, climb over the railing and disappear from view. It's wonderful to look like Errol Flynn to the untrained eyes of a frightened and beautiful woman. The descent is effortless, and within a minute I find myself on street level. There is a small alleyway leading up to an iron gate, secured with rusty chains and padlock – a firetrap indeed. I climb the gate, and as I pass over the top, one of the pointed spears lodges itself in my outer pocket and tears it off my coat. Landing safely on the other side, I run into the first street and hail a passing cab.

By now Edward must be fuming. I wonder whether he's finally decided to come inside the hostel and look for me. I must know, so I ask the driver to turn into Tufton Street and pass slowly in front of the entrance, while I hide in the back of the cab. The Austin FX4s are the pride of London, the best taxis I've ever seen. They come with such a cavernous backseat that you can dive into them with a suitcase in hand, and have enough room left to stretch your legs. I see the cab still idling in front of the hostel. Edward has opened the door and ventured outside, staring at the entrance and stomping his foot on the pavement in a fit of impotent rage. We pass unnoticed just a few feet from him. It's a rewarding sight. I rest my head against the plush comfort of the seat and close my eyes, a smile of satisfaction on my face.

Four

THE DEVERE CAVENDISH in Regent's Park is the sort of luxurious hotel I often admired and envied on my frigid London walks. Defended by uniformed footmen and forbidding porters, it enjoys an unblemished reputation for opulence and taste. Michelle had already introduced me to its palatial restaurant. Once a month, she would defraud the establishment by enjoying a sumptuous continental breakfast free of charge. Though she never gave me the exact details, she had acquired a guest key and never bothered to return it. Breakfast at the Cavendish is an elaborate affair, and an experience much prized by the London upper-class. The only identification required is a room key which ushers you into a luminous patio of wild orchids and crystalline fountains. The honor system – that hallmark of civility and character in Anglo-Saxon society – was unheeded by Michelle's more Gallic pragmatism, except for the relative parsimony with which she used the precious key. Each time, she entrusted her fate to the inefficacious memory of the head waiter, hoping the rightful occupant of the room would not also decide to enjoy the hotel's legendary breakfast.

Even in the off-season, a room at the Cavendish costs a minimum of forty pounds a night, which for me is pure folly. But I have my fill of narrow bunk beds and rank bathrooms, and tonight is cause for celebration and a bit of fun. I give the cabby the hotel name and enjoy a seamless ride through the tranquil avenues of Saint James gardens. The illuminated lobby is a startling contrast to the reception desk of my hostel. I book a room on the seventh floor, and, escorted by a porter in livery, discover a lovely suite overlooking the park. The place has the definite feel of affluence and discretion that defines true luxury. I call the hostel and Michelle answers the house phone on the second ring. She is relieved to know that I'm all right and chuckles upon learning of my new address. I have no fresh clothes or personal effects with me and ask if she could bring my suitcase over. I'm aching to find out what happened after my flight from the hostel and eager to show off my present lodgings. Despite the lateness of the hour, she gracefully accepts and will join me around eleven o'clock. I'm thrilled, but the night's activities have taken a toll on my appearance. Looking at my reflection in the gilded mirror of the bathroom, I am surprised the night staff even let me in. I shed all my clothes and ignore the shower to enjoy my first real bath in quite some time. The size of the tub is in keeping with the lavish appointments of the room. It is the sort of deep enameled contraption I used to enjoy at my uncle's estate. Standing on four cast-iron paws and fed by a roaring flow of steaming water, it is large enough to accommodate two bodies at a time.

I emerge from the tub twenty minutes later, soothed and rested, and wrap myself into a plush bathrobe. The embrace of the warm cotton is wonderfully soft. I open the French windows and step out onto a small balcony, leaning against the cold railing. The city lights twinkle through the bare branches of the park, as rumors of a distant world gently ebb against the impregnable walls of the Devere Cavendish. I'm called back into the room by the doorbell. Michelle has brought my suitcase and a late dinner from the deli. This is the first time we're afforded any sort of privacy in a bedroom, and I really don't know how to act. She takes a long look at me and smiles at my newfound prosperity, before dropping into an inviting armchair. There will always be an aura of detachment and reserve in the way she carries herself, something undefined like discreet gracefulness. Attractive without ostentation, she reminds me of Gene Tierney in "Night and the City." And though she dresses as if to escape notice and conceal her figure, my teenager's eyes are drawn to her curvaceous hips the moment she sheds her coat and scarf. Michelle admires the room, but she's also dying to tell me what happened after my escape. She gets up, kicks off her shoes and stretches out on the bed, a quiet odalisque in a long white sweater. Being naked in a bathrobe adds a definite touch of intimacy to our reunion, but her enthusiasm stems more from the news she brings than from being alone with me. Once again, I try to make the best of the situation. We settle upon the bed and she tells me of the night's events, as I sink my teeth into a warm garlic sub.

"The moment I saw you land safely in the courtyard, I closed the window and cleaned the debris from the bathroom floor," she begins. "No one else saw you exit the building, so I made my way downstairs, chuckling at your audacity, and decided to wait by the house phone in the lobby. I had not been sitting for five minutes when the front door opened and a young man hesitantly walked in. Elegantly dressed and passably ruffled, he went to the empty reception desk, turned around, and, upon seeing me, enquired as to whether I knew of your whereabouts."

I prop myself on an elbow and cut her off, unable to wait.

"Was it Edward? Did he give you his name?"

"Actually, he didn't," she continues with a conspiratorial air, "but from your description, I felt certain it was him. I answered in the negative and he ventured deeper into the lobby, reluctant to attract attention and carrying the suitcase you had brought into the taxi. The dining and TV areas were deserted, and he appeared unwilling to proceed to the second floor. He was just fidgeting there by the coffee machine, when the Belgian guy and the manager came walking down the stairs, engaged in a heated exchange."

I love the way she describes the entire episode, and how her teeth sparkle through the impishness of her smile.

"Alain had apparently gone to the manager's apartment to report the theft of his suitcase and most of his belongings," Michelle goes on more slowly, teasing my impatience.

"He was livid from the loss of his personal effects which, coming only days after the theft of his money, had driven him to exasperation and rage. As you may imagine, the manager's sole concern was the legal ramifications of these events, and the negative publicity they might have on prospective boarders. By the time they reached the landing, they were yelling at each other. 'What kind of a place are you running here?' Alain asked, shaking with anger. 'There's no security. Most of the time, you're not even at the front desk answering inquiries and screening guests. Anyone can walk in and out of this place and rob us blind. This is an outrage. I demand compensation for the two losses I suffered because of your carelessness and incompetence!'

The manager stared with sullen anger and drew close enough to spit in Alain's face.

'Sir, you will please take note of the sign above the reception desk,' he replied, hissing between his teeth. 'It states quite clearly that the management isn't responsible for any loss or theft occurring on the premises.'

Michelle pauses and can't resist a sip from my drink.

"Despite the fierceness of the exchange, the linguist in me couldn't help but savor this collision of heavily accented English," she adds with a knowing smile. "It was as if the culture shock between Asia and the West had come down to the two of them. The Belgian was beside himself, screaming and gesticulating inches away from the manager, while the latter retreated into an oriental shell of glowering restraint. The whole thing was about to degenerate into physical violence, when both men became aware of Edward's presence, discreetly making his way out of the lobby. The manager leaped with unexpected agility and placed himself between the young man and the door."

"I told you never to set foot in this place again!" he said in a menacing tone.

Edward's golden complexion turned to gray.

"I can explain," he replied. "This is a simple misunderstanding and I was just seeing myself out."

Alain bounced in turn to the manager's side. He had just noticed the suitcase in Edward's hand.

"And I suppose you're also going to explain what you're doing with my luggage?" he asked, his eyes flashing.

Though wedged between the Belgian's indignation and the manager's wrath, Edward remained heroically collected. All he desperately wanted was to get out of this place unharmed.

'Forgive me, Sir, but this cannot possibly be yours. It belongs to a friend of mine, and I was just bringing it back here as a courtesy.'

'Oh, really? What kind of a fool do you take me for?' Alain snarled back, rolling his shoulders like an animal ready to pounce. He stepped forward, and over the manager's objections, wrenched the suitcase from Edward's grip, before laying it out on the floor and opening it.

'These are my Belgian army boots!' he howled, 'See, my name is stenciled on the inside. You son of a bitch!'

"Edward had grown horribly pale," Michelle adds with a dramatic pause. "He stammered a few words in his defense, but it was too late. Alain sprang to his feet and viciously punched him in the stomach. The Englishman dropped to his knees like a calf on a slaughterhouse floor. He could hardly breathe. The manager and two other boarders drawn in by the altercation quickly restrained Alain and led him away to the kitchen."

Michelle interrupts her narration with a sad smile.

"I felt sorry for the guy. He had no clue. He slowly got up and leaned against the wall, trying to catch his breath. The manager returned from the kitchen and walked up to him, right in his face. Poor Edward seemed more worried about the look in his eyes than the abuse he had just suffered. They didn't exchange a word, but Edward made a hasty exit. I looked out the window into the darkened street. The cab was still waiting with the engine running, wisps of smoke blanketing the asphalt. Edward stumbled against the curb and threw up on the sidewalk before diving into the safety of the car and disappearing in the night. I don't think he'll ever come again within two city blocks of the hostel."

It is odd. Though at first I rejoiced in the cruel irony of Edward's downfall, reaping greater humiliation than what I had personally brought upon him, I am not savoring the tale of his undoing. Michelle, too, notices the change.

"What is it, sweetie? Are you feeling all right? Is it the food? You're white as a sheet."

"I'm fine," I reply. "I'm just not very hungry right now. Would you please excuse me for a moment?"

I go to the half-open window and step out onto the balcony. The chill of the night is invigorating, but I can't shake the uneasiness that has come over me. Michelle quietly wraps her arms around my shoulders, brushing her lips against the back of my neck. The warmth of her breath is a soothing remedy.

"I know something is troubling you. Though you've made light of Edward's advances, I also sensed something sad and dark hovering about you all afternoon. Did he hurt you in any way? Did anything happen that you're not telling me?"

At first I attempt to deny there might be anything beyond the rather amusing events of the day. I take the greatest care for my voice not to betray my state of mind, and stoically continue to stare straight ahead into the distance. But Michelle stands too close to be taken in by this pretense. I try to stave off the storm welling up in me, but it's useless. When I finally turn around, she is not surprised by the tears on my face.

"I'm so embarrassed," I finally tell her. "I wanted to impress you with the luxury of this room, and all I can muster is this mortifying outburst."

Michelle leads me back into the warm refuge of the room. She walks to a king-size bed that speaks of decadence and lust, rearranges the thick pillows into an alcove, and invites me to join her within the plush comfort of this improvised shelter. This is unexpected. My fantasy of being alone in bed with her has finally come true, and yet, at this moment, I'm not particularly interested. I know she wants me to talk and unburden myself of whatever it is that oppresses me, but I don't know what to say, or where to begin. The awkwardness of conflicting emotions for once leaves me at a loss for words. But Michelle is wonderfully patient, as she looks upon me with genuine concern. I feel safe. Her eyes reflect not a hint of judgment and I cautiously begin to open up.

"Whatever transpired these past few days has caused certain memories to return and speak loudly, as if they intended to be heard. Your intuition serves you well: I was molested as a child, and I've never told a soul."

Against the more or less conscious devices that have sealed the deeper recesses of my memory, the words now emerge, breaking through and taking form. I can't believe I'm actually aiding them to come forth, least of all in this place I had chosen for quite a different purpose. These are the words I never spoke to family or friends, the shame guarded by impenetrable labyrinths, images lying deep like recumbent effigies. Soon they're going to rise and infuse life into events I never wished to remember. I am now the only obstacle between silence and truth, and I feel as if a sewer were coming out of me.

I was eleven-years-old and a student at Holy Spirit Preparatory. Located in the barren plains of northern France, the boarding school enjoyed a well-deserved reputation for academic rigor, with a particular attention to character-building discipline. It was there my parents had sent me when it became obvious that raising me at home was no longer a tenable option. For reasons I've never completely grasped, I had become the epitome of the unmanageable brat. No doubt my father's chronic absence from home, because of constant professional obligations, played a part. As did his reluctance to assume the role of disciplinarian during weekends and vacations, the only time he could exert any real influence on me.

I had entered the boarding school at the age of ten. This was not a particularly rash decision on my parents' part, as a sizable portion of upper-middle class youth was subjected to the same fate. A challenging academic program, and the addition of a regimented lifestyle, was thought best to foster skills of adaptation, responsibility and discipline. I embraced boarding school with enthusiasm. For a cantankerous kid raised mostly by a mother and two sisters, an initiation to life in the close proximity of five hundred other boys seemed truly exciting. Of course, there was a downside to this new lifestyle. Beside the fun of summer camps or Cub Scout activities, strict regimentation was largely unknown to most of us. At Holy Spirit, the living arrangements were Spartan. A regulation-size locker was the extent of our privacy, its exiguity purposely limiting the amount of each student's possessions and wardrobe. We could only fit four days of fresh clothes and three pairs of shoes into it, but it didn't really matter since we all wore uniforms: a long grayish smock that went past the knees, with a row of red buttons on the right. The good fathers insisted on this dress-code to bring a measure of monastic equity to the student body. Lest anyone be tempted to equate individual worth with personal wealth, they made sure that the least fortunate among us looked just as drab as the richest. But they had not reckoned with the resourcefulness of vanity. Our shoes became the only way to identify the more prosperous among us, and students trudged through the courtyard mud in extravagant oxfords. We were assigned an individual sink for our morning ablutions, and royally granted a single shower every Saturday afternoon. Unsurprisingly, the locker rooms reeked of armpits and dirty feet, a situation made worse by the fact that deodorants were frowned upon by male teenagers in the early 60's. The dorms were huge and resembled the sleeping accommodations of a field hospital. They consisted of three interconnecting rooms, each as vast as a hangar, with one hundred and sixty-five gleaming beds arranged in perfectly aligned rows. Narrow and uncomfortable straw mattresses were fitted to the iron frames. Above us hung industrial-grade mercury-vapor lamps, whose stabbing glare made it impossible to remain in bed once they had been turned on. Our daily life followed immutable regulations, with discipline rigidly enforced. And yet we had a prodigious amount of fun, as if this stringent code only served to rally the collected resiliency of five hundred boys.

   We awoke each day at 6:15 to the glare of overhead lights and a resounding *"Benedicamus Domino"* shouted in Latin over our sleepy heads by Father Desmarets, the energetic dean of discipline. Following his injunction to bless God for our rest, we all dropped to our knees in the aisles and mumbled a sleepy rendition of the Lord's Prayer. We then shuffled off to our lockers, got dressed without the benefit of privacy, and filed out like pigs in a chute into the pre-dawn darkness for twenty minutes of calisthenics. Following time-honored rules that seemed oblivious to basic nutrition, we were herded back into study halls, shivering cocoons of cold sweat and red cheeks, longing for breakfast which only came at 8:00 am. In time, we all adapted, finding that the bonds of friendship outweighed the impositions of communal existence. From a pragmatic point of view, even Rousseau might have approved of our docility, but then again the grand pioneer of natural pedagogy had abandoned his five illegitimate children to a public orphanage.

Discipline was accepted as a necessary evil. By contemporary American standards, it qualified as child abuse. Corporal punishment was meted out at regular intervals by both faculty and staff. In its milder form it consisted of slaps in the face, or twenty blows from an oak ruler upon the tips of outstretched fingers. We all learned fairly rapidly a basic fact of human physiology: fingertips contain an inordinate amount of sensitive nerve endings – all exquisitely responsive to pain.

At Holy Spirit the rules were obvious, and breaking them resulted in a well-known schedule of reprimands and punishment. At least the system was democratic and free of capricious interpretation. The idea of introducing five hundred kids to the basic tenets of civility was no different from the modern precepts of a social contract. Noble sentiments to be sure, but the classic flaw of French pedagogy – failure to appreciate the emotional dimension of children—resulted in an educational system built on fear and humiliation.

If an infraction occurred in a classroom, the teacher would ask you to stand and come up to the front of the class. There was a yellow line on the floor, indicating how near you were to stand. Teachers' desks in France are not as democratically arranged as in the U.S. They're erected on a sort of tiered podium, allowing the faculty to watch over the entire class from a vantage point four feet above the floor. Once a student had aligned the tip of his shoes with that fateful yellow tape, he usually heard the standard injunction: "Stand up straight and put your hands behind your back." If you wore glasses, you were first instructed to remove them. This procedure left you standing with your face precisely leveled with the top of the desk, and conveniently positioned within reach of the teacher's hands. You were then asked to repeat out loud whatever it was you had been sharing in a hushed voice back in your seat. And as you stood there, exposed and apprehensive, you felt the collective dread of your classmates pulsating behind your back. Some teachers were kinder than others, only using the suspense of the situation as a way to maintain discipline, but others were not so inclined. I remember my history teacher, Mr. de Barennes, an impoverished aristocrat afflicted with a case of childhood polio that had left him with a fearsome limp. I always hoped he would slap me hard enough the first time, so that I'd remain out of reach of a backhand and not feel the impact of his signet ring. His family's coat of arms, once held high on chivalric battlefields, was now reduced to smacking the faces of recalcitrant teenagers.

We took it all in stride and at least didn't have to endure the caning still administered in British boarding schools. Most of the students chose to comply with the rules and led a peaceful and or-dered existence. Others, iconoclasts and rebels, made it a point to test the limits of the system and distinguished themselves as inveter-ate troublemakers. I enjoyed a special status apart from the other kids – I was the only Protestant amid five hundred Catholic boys. This ecumenical exception bestowed upon me a measure of singularity, a formidable asset when you are but a cipher in the social edifice of a boarding school. Chapel was compulsory, and I dutifully attended as a choirboy, singing mass in Latin twice a week. My peers saw me as a dissident of sorts, led astray by the errors of my ancestors. More or less accepted as a fellow Christian, I was afforded an inkling of what it must feel like to be a Jew in a sea of Gentiles.

Evening study hall was traditionally the time when we availed ourselves of the sacrament of penance. The cold anonymity of the chapel's confessionals was thought to be a deterrent to the students' interest in their spiritual lives, and so we were encouraged to sign up and meet our teachers in their private quarters after hours. This was a welcome diversion from the boredom of study hall, a room so quiet you could hear a pin drop. Outside of class, discipline was enforced by graduate students, selected mostly for their muscular build. That year, our assigned tormentor was Mr. Lee, who capitalized on his enig-matic Chinese looks and rumored expertise in martial arts to rein in the roomful of eleven-year-olds entrusted to his care. I can still pic-ture him behind his desk, towering over us on that elevated platform, inscrutable behind his tinted glasses. For two hours, Mr. Lee would sit and carefully attend to his fingernails, a ritual that earned him the nickname of "Lee Mah Ong," a spurious Chinese homonym of "lime à ongles," meaning "nail file" in French. We thought we were the cleverest kids in the entire school.

Being the token Protestant within this Catholic fold, I was exempt from the rule requiring students to go to confession. I enjoyed a sort of dubious notoriety as a spiritual bad boy, a speck of Luther's shadow amongst consecrated souls. The vast majority of diocesan priests at Holy Spirit were decent men who loved teaching and lived out their ministry with sincere abnegation. Their shortcomings were no worse than the human frailties affecting all mortals, but these were magnified by the expectations placed upon them in this Catholic enclave of French society. Father Charroux, the overweight professor of Classics, stoically faced ridicule in a culture intolerant of obesity. But his size belied the swiftness with which he could suddenly move across a classroom and pounce on an offender. Down the hall, Father Leborgne remained a mystery to all. The gaunt math teacher had piercing eyes and a yellow complexion that spoke of mysticism and mortification. Yet he despised corporal punishment, and would always offer us a form of alternative retribution. We could avoid physical pain by learning thirty lines of iambic heptameters in forty minutes, and reciting them without fault to the entire class. I owe much of my photographic memory to his kind and creative pedagogy.

And then there was Father Mayeux.

I didn't know much about him, because he taught older boys, but he was not hard to notice in a crowd. Six feet tall and red-headed, he looked fit enough to come out of the French Foreign Legion. Thick-lipped, square-jawed and with a regulation haircut, he walked the halls in the evening, lugging gallons of mineral water – his prescribed regimen against the kidney stones that afflicted him. He never said much, sported an amiable smile and blended seamlessly with the half-darkness of the corridors. Rumors circulated that he was once a promising boxer, but abandoned the sport upon entering seminary. I will never know what designated me as the focal point of his darker instincts.

Though I wasn't required to go to confession, I would still escape the boredom of evening study by filling out the request slips that went out to the faculty. Most of my teachers welcomed the visits as a distraction from the ordeal of contrived penitence. We talked about history, religion and world events, and the priests were astute enough not to confuse my propensity to fit in with a genuine interest in Catholicism. In my five years at Holy Spirit, not one ever tried to convert me.

Since I always initiated the meetings, I was surprised to be called out one evening for a visit I had not requested. Using his prerogative as a resident priest on the faculty, Father Mayeux had summoned me to his apartment. At Holy Spirit, teachers lived on the third floor. At some point in the past, a decision was made to allow priests to hear evening confessions in their studies. It was a welcome improvement over the creaky confessionals in the chapel. But somewhere along the way, the idea was also lost that the inhospitality of the confessional was designed for a purpose. Emptying one's heart of reprehensible acts is a deeply personal experience, and it places the penitent in a particularly vulnerable position. The drab environment of the confessional provided a public setting the least conducive to creature comforts or inappropriate advances. The wire mesh over the small window separating priests and parishioners, and the lack of lighting within, offered shamefaced sinners the protection of anonymity.

Father Mayeux's private apartment was quite a departure from such a place. Comfortable and warm, it featured thick carpeting, a plush sofa and a door sound-proofed with heavy velvet drapes hanging on the back. An imposing desk, stacks of books and a lingering scent of Amsterdamer pipe tobacco lent the place a quaint touch of quiet scholarship. I sat down at the priest's invitation, rather intimidated, with my eyes still scanning the details of the richly appointed room. The reason for his calling me tonight was his concern for my education. Though technically not one of my teachers, he had followed my academic progress at a distance. Of course, he had heard of my being the lone Protestant in the school, but he had also noticed my performance at swim meets, especially when our team had won the regional freestyle 4x50 meters relay. I didn't know of any faculty member interested in swimming competition, but he assured me that he was an assiduous supporter.

"You're very modest, Eric, and that's a wonderful trait of your character," he said in an admiring tone. "But it would have been hard not to notice your team's dedication and accomplishments last week."

I beamed with satisfaction. I thought of myself as a braggart and fairly mediocre swimmer, but this was the first time anyone had ever complimented me. The best I ever managed from the coach were exasperated looks and grunts of discontent. Father Mayeux rose from behind his desk and came to sit beside me on the sofa.

"Since you're not Catholic, I will dispense with the decorum and formal setting of confession. I want to talk to you not as a priest, or even a teacher, but as a friend. You're an interesting boy, obviously gifted and above the average intellect of other students. In me, you will find a friend and an ally you can trust."

I nodded in appreciation and he drew closer. Instead of the usual school uniform, I was still wearing the gym shorts and sweater required for physical education, our last class of the day. He stopped talking and placed his hands around my thigh. I froze. The only physical contact I'd ever experienced from the faculty had been corporal punishment. Something in the back of my head still trusted that his examination of my leg proceeded from his interest in athletics. But he asked me to stand and came closer still. I could feel his breath on my face. His fingers swiftly moved from my leg to my belt, and within seconds his hand was inside my shorts. I stood there so startled that I forgot to breathe. The room began to reel and I remember taking hold of an armchair to keep from falling. Father Mayeux was oblivious to my distress and kept panting as if he had run a mile. Both his hands were now stroking me in an attempt to elicit some reaction from my terrified flesh. And then I noticed what was happening to him. While I stood there clenching my fists and closing my eyes, he had opened his cassock and exposed himself. I had never seen a man's erection in my life and I stumbled back against the sofa. But he just grinned at my stupefaction and forced my hands upon him.

A feeling of repulsion closed in around my throat, and I feared I was going to lose my dinner on the carpet. I stared out of the open window to escape the oppressiveness of the room, as if help would come from the night itself. But even the lights of the basketball courts had been turned off. There was only darkness outside, and darkness within.

Father Mayeux must have finally noticed my anguish, because he backed off and reluctantly turned around to adjust his cassock. I didn't know it then, but I narrowly escaped the imminent insult of his lust. The assault on my senses was making me ill, and in the end my innocence saved me from a more repugnant violation. He opened the door and peeked into the hallway.

"You're a smart kid," he said. "Smart enough to remember that anything happening here remains strictly private, as confidential as if I had heard your confession. And besides," he added, "you wouldn't want your buddies to know what passed here just now, would you?"

The secrecy over what had taken place was sealed by invoking confidentiality and insinuating guilt in my conscience. I walked down the half-lit corridor and took the stairs to the first floor. Only then did I notice the tears on my face. I couldn't return to study hall like this and veered to the left, seeking refuge in the gymnasium. The darkened hall was empty. I closed the door behind me, went past the pommel horse and parallel bars into the fencing room. I remember standing there in the shadows, shaking like a leaf. I tried to make sense of what had taken place, but could find no explanation. My naiveté was such that I had no knowledge of the relative seriousness of this event. Were other kids subjected to this? And what was "this" all about anyway? I felt disoriented and afraid, but could not understand why. And yet innocence invariably knows when it has been infringed upon. At the level of a child's intuition, I knew something wrong had happened, and that Father Mayeux's actions were inappropriate. But I did not know what to do. The most puzzling part was that I felt guilty, and yet could not relate this to any of my own actions. Why did I feel ashamed if I had done nothing wrong?

I sat on the hardwood floor. The lights of the parking lot came faintly in through the high window panes, casting an eerie glow about the room. Somehow I felt safe there, protected by rows of fencing masks and shimmering swords hanging from the walls. When I returned to study hall, I had made up my mind never to come near Father Mayeux again, or talk about this to anyone.

Children have a remarkable ability to bury the things that trouble them the most, but in my case I only partially succeeded. For the next few days, I kept an eye out for the tall figure of the priest, worried he might materialize around the corner of every corridor, or at the end of the darkest hallway. In fact, I was protected from further contact because he wasn't one of my teachers, and the classrooms and living quarters of the older boys he supervised were segregated from mine. Life in boarding school is by definition a cloistered experience, and it doesn't require too much imagination to feel trapped and powerless. Time gradually removed that sense of imminent threat and I started to breathe easier and worry less. Evening study hall remained the only part of the day when my mind wandered. From the back row where I sat, I kept looking at the other students, wondering if any of them had shared a similar fate. After three weeks, my fears abated and I felt reasonably free of anxiety, but I was unaware of the depth and relentlessness of Father Mayeux's obsession.

The dorm where we slept was a large hall where efficiency and the need for supervision obviated any attempts at comfort or style. Our white enameled beds were arranged in eleven rows of fifteen units, which allowed the staff to monitor one hundred and sixty-five boys every night. After evening prayers we all lay there in silence, instructed to fall asleep with our hands visibly on top of the covers. The lights were turned off at 9:00 p.m., plunging us all in sudden darkness. I usually went to sleep fairly quickly, my dreams disturbed only by the occasional sound of someone talking in his sleep, or the watery echo of a boy relieving himself in the huge chamber pot left in each corner. The staff would make one inspection before ten o'clock, stealthily passing through the rows of beds with a flashlight, just to check on us. And if we had not already figured out what went on under the sheets, the relentless scrutiny of our keepers provided us with a few ideas. I had not yet entertained such notions, and it would be another year before I became interested in the crumpled *Playboy* magazines older boys rented out for fifty cents a night.

It was around three in the morning that I was drawn out of my sleep by a gentle but persistent tug at my pajama sleeve. I awoke. And there, in the half-darkness, rising by the side of my bed, I recognized Father Mayeux's face. The shock of discovering his presence in this place was so great that I couldn't make a sound. It was almost surreal. The priest had crawled under the rows of beds to reach me at the center of the room. And there he was, sitting on the floor, his head oddly silhouetted against the white sheets, a finger on his lips urging me to keep silent.

"How are you, Eric? I couldn't sleep because I kept thinking about you."

The look on my face must have reflected the most complete stupefaction, but he went on whispering in my ear.

"The first time we met, we really didn't have the opportunity to get to know each other. I'm going back to my apartment, and I want you to leave the dorm and join me. Sleeping together will allow us to get better acquainted."

I couldn't believe the extremities to which he had stooped in getting to me that night. In a room filled with boys, he could easily have gotten caught; and his complete disregard for scandal was a telling measure of his lust.

The unreality of his being there by the bedside, and the silent presence of all my friends gave me strength and a forthrightness I would otherwise have lacked.

"Leave now," I said, "get out of here this instant, or I'll scream!"

And I shrank away from him, gathering my legs as if I were going to kick him in the head. He disappeared as stealthily as he had come. I was left squatting against the cold metal of the bed board, with my heart pounding in my chest. I stayed awake until dawn, peering at the shadows, startled by every noise, fearing he might reappear at any moment, leaping upon my couch and carrying me away in the night.

The audacity of his visit stripped me of the fragile sense of safety I had managed to build during the preceding three weeks. I became so twitchy and irascible that my friends remarked on it. I felt as if there were no reprieve from him, and even wondered whether his next appearance had simply become inexorable. I didn't think there was anyone I could turn to for help. A child tends to feel the pain and hardship of a single crisis as if it were the state of his entire world, and so I settled for a life of constant dread. But the precariousness of my position must have caught the eye of Providence. That week in language arts, we were studying *Letters From My Windmill*, a collection of short stories from Alphonse Daudet, a delightful writer and keen observer of human folly. I had been assigned a book report on "Reverend Gaucher's Elixir," in which a resourceful monk saves his monastery from impeding bankruptcy by producing a prodigiously popular brandy. In time, the priest-turned-master distiller is so immersed in his duties that he becomes an alcoholic. He must then balance the financial survival of his religious order with the salvation of his soul.

It was a sunny afternoon and I requested permission to leave study hall and go to the library in search of additional information on Daudet. The book report was coming along well and I was so completely absorbed as to become oblivious of my surroundings. The hallway narrowed to a windowless corridor before it reached the library, and it was there that I came face to face with Father Mayeux. We were alone, and his materializing so unexpectedly brought me back to the shock of our previous encounter.

"Eric! What a delightful surprise!" he bellowed. "As a matter of fact, I was thinking about you this morning. The new basketball supplies have arrived and I was on my way to the gym. Come along and give me a hand."

And there he stood, blocking the corridor, towering over me, with his hands on my shoulders. I'm not quite sure how it came about, but rising all at once from my reading in study hall, the words of the distraught monk in Daudet's story sprang intact to my lips, and I heard my own voice say:

"Aren't you the least bit concerned about what is going on here? Well, I am, and to tell you the truth, Father, you're preparing for yourself an eternity of pitchfork and flames in the depths of Hell."

The words had such an effect upon him that he let go of me and shrank to the wall as if stunned by an exorcism. His jaw dropped, and he stared at me with utter dismay. The disproportion between my youth and this warning coming out with unexpected ease completely disarmed him. He turned around and vanished into the hallway.

Father Mayeux never again tried to contact me. In the next three years that I stayed at Holy Spirit, I don't believe he ever came within two hundred feet of me.

The warm comfort of the bedspread brings me back to the reality of the hotel room. Michelle is looking upon me with sweet tenderness. I am grateful for her listening so patiently. Strange how small details remain so vividly preserved under the still waters of the past. Strange also how present events can elude the guardians of buried pains, snatch these memories and drag them out into the light. Evil seems to have a way of materializing unexpectedly around the corridors of time, winking at us for a moment, only to disappear for another twenty years.

"How do you feel?" She asks as she draws closer and rearranges the pillows behind my head.

"I'm not really sure," I answer with genuine puzzlement. "Something like sadness and anger...Because of him, it has taken me years to enjoy even the brush of a hand on my body. I still avoid being caressed, as if the thrill of a girl's touch upon my skin is irreparably sanctioned as a threat. I can't even abide a back rub, and out of personal preference, my doctors have always been women. Father Mayeux's actions are burned deeper into me than I suspected. I despise him most of all for what he's altered in my sensibility."

Michelle looks at me with pained solicitude, but she also takes care not to interrupt the faltering course of this confession.

"For years I fantasized about returning to the school and doing him harm," I go on, "but today I'd be satisfied if he could just measure the enormity of what he's done. I would like him to walk into class one morning, sit down at his desk and suddenly realize he is facing a room filled with all his victims. Every single boy he violated standing silently behind the desks, lining the walls and obstructing the door –

each face a defiled memory, each stare an indictment. I wish he could see us all in a single glance and be shamed to the marrow of his sins."

Michelle reaches out and takes me in her arms. The soft cocoon she created upon this magnificent bed becomes a refuge. Our faces touch—I taste her tears mingling with mine while she cradles my head between her hands and kisses me. I'm taken over, subjugated and captured by the rapturous agility of her lips. This is a woman's kiss like I've never known, and its intensity relegates my teenage fantasies to insipid abstractions. In pure disbelief, I watch Michelle removing her sweater and taking my face into the warm fragrance of her breasts. Nothing matters any more, not the past, not the pain; there is only the moment at hand as the room blurs and disappears. The sensuality she awakens in me commands such intimacy that I'm scarcely a witness to this celebration of my senses.

"I can't have sex with you, Eric. You're too young," she whispers, her voice at once firm and sweet, "but in my own way, I will love you tonight."

And she makes me recline against the pillows, opening the top of my bathrobe and letting her fingers brush against my skin. The touch of her hand is electrifying, making me giggle when she remarks that I don't have any hair on my chest. And then, slowly, languorously, her lips and her tongue begin to send shivers into me. She works her way down and doesn't stop when she reaches my navel. I let my head sink back against the velvet touch of the bed. Distant murmurs of the city come in through the half-open windows and I close my eyes, abandoning myself to Michelle's loving dexterity. I never dreamed a woman's hands and mouth could wrench such pleasure from my flesh. And I succumb to the wondrous intoxication of this night, falling asleep with the caress of her breath on my shoulder.

A kiss on the corner of my eye draws me out of my sleep. Michelle is standing by the bedside, a sweet smile on her face.

"I've got to leave, sweetie. It's one-thirty in the morning and I can't be late for work. Go back to sleep and rest. I'll call you around eleven. No, don't get up for me, I'll get a cab from the reception desk."

I'm still in a daze, emerging from soft and warm plenitude. She leans over and I marvel once more at the perfect symmetry of her mouth. Then she turns off the lights on her way out, quietly closing the door behind her.

I lay there in the half-darkness of this sumptuous room, completely at peace. And it occurs to me that Michelle has not just satisfied my longing for her, she has reached into a wounded past whose gates are slowly closing up again. Speaking the words I dreaded has given form to memories I denied for so long. But because of this, the most pernicious of these relics will no longer dwell in silence and poison me from within. At last they can fade away, like shards of darkness dissipating in the light. More than satiating my hunger, Michelle has assuaged the fear in my flesh. Her kindness has emptied me of shame.

Five

THE RIGORS OF AN early winter plunging London into darkness and ice have taken the edge off my seditious disposition, and the thought of going home has now insinuated itself into my mind. I do not wish to return to France vanquished and begging for forgiveness, not after all I have gone through. Yet I feel that my career in London has reached a crisis and find little purpose in prolonging this demonstration any further. Something tells me that I should quit while ahead, and from a less noble but pragmatic perspective I also realize that staying here will soon become impractical. However loath I am to admit it, I miss my family, and, yes, the luxury of having the means to eat for the next forty-eight hours.

I call Paris from my hotel room, since there is no point in hiding any more. As a last expression of pride and independence, I resist the temptation of a collect call, bowing instead to the exorbitant rates the Cavendish charges its affluent guests. My mom answers and I can feel instantly how relieved she is to hear me. I'm unable to disguise my own excitement. Something has changed in the tone and manner of our conversation. I find myself unguardedly confiding in her, resuming the closeness we have always cherished. We are on the same wavelength, both appeased and reconciled. My mother and I are too much alike not to get irritated with each other once in a while, but the steadfastness of our affection has never allowed the sun to set on our anger. Now that the dreaded preliminaries are over, we discuss the circumstances of my return.

My father anticipated this change of heart, but he has attached a few stipulations of his own. As a sort of peace offering, an enticement as it were, he agrees that I will not return to St. Joseph's. I expected a drawn-out battle on this issue, but my dad is a capable strategist. By single-handedly removing this hurdle, he puts me in the position of having to agree with my own conditions. But there are other contingencies as well. This will not turn into a hero's welcome, and my sisters are on notice not to treat me as the prodigal son—no fattened calf for my return. Instead, my father has arranged for me to meet with the directors of admissions of three private schools in Paris. He leaves me with the task of convincing them why they should admit, in late November, someone with a catastrophic academic record, when hundreds of qualified applicants are begging for a slot in next year's classes. I'm confounded by the way he has engineered all this. Since when does my father know anything about local colleges? And how on earth did he manage to expedite interviews with prestigious institutions known to take a couple of months just to answer requests for catalogues? I always thought my father uninterested in my education and unfamiliar with the academic labyrinth of Paris. That has always been my mother's province, and this sudden change leaves me wondering just how far his connections extend. But I'm not at the end of my surprises. Only later, when I have returned to Paris, will I discover the full measure of his powers.

Still, I am grateful for his generosity and for not making me crawl under the yoke of humiliating terms. But I also recognize his subtle and effective combat tactics. He gives me an opportunity to redeem myself by putting me in charge. Of course if things don't work out, I will only have myself to blame. I didn't expect this. My willingness to come home, and his agreeing to what two weeks ago was an insurmountable obstacle, have come and gone without discussion or resentment. I find the resolution of this conflict rather anticlimactic and am left a bit frustrated, as if I hadn't really won anything, which is precisely my father's intention.

I thought the actual details of my return had yet to be discussed, but my mother spells them out as if already agreed upon.

"Your father and I would like you back in Paris tonight. To speed things up, you could take the Air France flight out of Heathrow this evening."

I'm thrilled. I've never flown before and this is a delightful surprise.

"That sounds great," I reply. "Are you wiring me the money for the ticket?"

"No, I'm not," my mother answers. "Your father doesn't think it's a practical idea."

I bristle at the thought. Is it that he doesn't trust me and thinks I might abscond with the money? In 1965, a one-way ticket from London to Paris without prior booking cost as much as two hundred and fifty pounds. My dad probably calculated that I could survive another six weeks on that amount. And though my feelings are hurt by such a suggestion, I must admit the idea briefly crossed my mind.

"So, how do we proceed?" I ask her.

"Do you remember Langston?" she answers. "Well, he's agreed to help."

Langston is one of England's most successful fashion photographers. After the war, he started a model agency and did so well that it spread to France, the United States and Hong Kong. His pictures are everywhere, from *Vogue* and *Marie-Claire* to billboards along the interstate. I think he dated my mother before she met my dad. My sisters used to joke that he was still in love with her, and he spared no expense treating my parents like royalty when they were in England. Of course I know of his photographic talent from a different perspective, as Langston's work occasionally graces the cover of *Playboy* magazine.

"He and his wife will expect you at their house tonight in Hyde Park. He has offered to drive you personally to the airport and help you check in. You will get the ticket from him. It is a short flight and your father will come to pick you up at the other end. What do you think?"

"I think it's great," I reply, though I can't help thinking that all this is happening too much like clockwork. Coming to England was quite an ordeal, requiring careful planning and time, but my return is being engineered in a matter of hours. Of course I came by boat and train, and the distance between London and Paris is easily bridged in an hour by plane. But suddenly, the grand scheme of my quest for independence is crumpled in time and significance to less than an afternoon drive in the country. The realization also dawns on me that my parents' plan must have been hatched some time in the last two weeks, waiting to be implemented when I'd indicate my willingness to come home. After masterminding my getaway in such a grand fashion, I hate to appear so predictable.

My mom gives me Langston's address and phone number with instructions to contact him within the hour.

"I won't come to the airport," she adds. "Your father insisted upon it. But I will be waiting for you at home."

Her voice is sweet but veiled with a hint of apprehension. She needn't worry about me or my frame of mind when we finally meet. I know I will unreservedly rush into her arms the moment I see her. A tremendous weight has been lifted off my shoulders, and though my hotel room is still a much appreciated luxury, it pales in comparison with the comfort of home, now within my reach. I dial the number my mother gave me and a maid answers. I'm still fairly inept speaking English on the phone, unable to use facial expressions or gestures to compensate for my lack of vocabulary, but I manage to leave a message for him to return my call at the Cavendish. Michelle already rang me up this morning and will join me here for lunch. I don't know how to break the news to her. I'm worried I will come off as an insecure adolescent caving in to his parents' directives.

The lobby of the hotel is a richly decorated hall filled with crystal chandeliers and condescending portraits of British arrogance in India. But there is an island of grace and charm emerging out of the musty splendor of the room. Her name is Emily, one of the clerks manning the registration desk. Eighteen years old and a freshman at Magdalene's College in Oxford, Emily is the manager's daughter. She earns extra money by working at the Cavendish on weekends. Back in the 60's, teenagers and college students in Western Europe had a hard time finding temporary jobs. The idea of trusting an adolescent with a real occupation was not a popular notion, but exceptions were made for the children of upper management.

Emily noticed me wandering through the lobby the night before and we had struck up a conversation. She seemed to think we were the same age and I certainly did nothing to dissuade her. Blue-eyed, about a foot shorter than I, she has an adorable turned-up nose and magnificent hair, a brown mane framing her face and reaching down to the middle of her back. I will learn later the reason for her choosing this hairstyle: it's partly to conceal her ears, which she thinks embarrassingly misshaped. She has a slight overbite that for some reason I find attractive, and the whiteness of her smile is a welcome contrast to the unappealing dentition of British girls. There is an immediate affinity between us and we spent an hour ensconced in cavernous leather seats, giggling and teasing each other like kids, my obvious attraction to her making up for the deficiencies in my vocabulary. As the saying goes in French, "le courant passe," meaning our mutual inclination felt as natural as instant conductivity. I didn't bother enlightening her as to the reason for my presence here, and she had that wonderful British discretion of not asking. I hoped she would think me independently wealthy, just passing through London in the off-season. It's funny how immediate compatibility reveals itself in a tactile and physical way: while laughing together, our hands touched and lingered more than once, though we barely knew each other. Regrettably, an older gentleman in livery had interrupted us, and with exquisite manners convinced Emily to return to her duties at the registration desk before her father noticed.

I'm pacing the main lobby, waiting for Michelle. The vitrified smoothness of the parquetry, gleaming with deep tones of cherry and oak, makes me feel as if I were gliding across the floor. A large atrium, bathed in natural light from the open ceiling, waits at the end of the hall, but before I can continue my exploration, a bellboy materializes beside me. I'm wanted on the telephone and follow him back into the main lobby. Emily's smile flies in my direction as I pass the desk. I sink into a red leather chair and take the call. It's Langston. Though he speaks French fluently, he makes it a point to address me in English. He doesn't sound at all like the jovial Briton I once met at my parents' house. His voice is rather stern and businesslike, immediately setting the tone for our conversation. He will pick me up from the Cavendish at four o'clock and we will pass by his house on our way to the airport. He intends to stay with me until the plane takes off. I don't regret my decision to come home, but I still chafe at being talked to as a teenager. In the end, self-esteem is a matter of perspective.

I have about four hours left of complete independence and I decide to inspect the hotel's famous collection of antique swords at the other end of the hall.

"Well, Your Excellency," someone intones behind me, "are you being lured back to a life of privilege and luxury?"

It's Michelle. She catches me completely off-guard, and the smile on her face draws me out of my melancholy. Somehow I don't need to explain much, as if she's already surmised that I am leaving. But she's famished and seems eager to set out in search of a nearby lunch. I am definitely slow on the uptake this afternoon, but her insistent stare finally gets through to me: Michelle doesn't wish to remain in the lobby under the scrutinizing gaze of the staff. Not if she is to continue defrauding the restaurant with impunity.

We're about to leave when Emily comes sauntering over to introduce herself. She can't resist the fun of intruding on Michelle and smiles at her, putting her arm around my shoulders. She looks quite attractive under the suffused glow of the chandeliers, beaming with all the carefree insolence of youth. Michelle acknowledges her presence with a stare in sharp contrast to the girl's becoming smile. Then she buttons her coat like a queen adjusting the clasp of a mantle, and looks at the meddler as if she were just furniture. Though Emily is no match for the poise and maturity of Michelle's quiet beauty, she seems to enjoy the way her unabashed youthfulness exasperates her rival. I've never been wedged like this between the impishness and the scorn of two women, but it's rather interesting. Michelle finally takes my hand, leading me out of the lobby so quickly that I barely catch a glimpse of Emily's triumphant smile.

Our lunch is bittersweet. We got to know each other in a restaurant and it seems it will become the setting for our goodbye. I cannot eat anything and my hand reaches across the table for Michelle's. I want to mention last night and what it meant to me, but she gently places her fingers over my mouth. She will not talk about it. Slowly she returns to the way she was when we first met, gradually distancing herself from me. I feel as if I'm not the one who is leaving. Rather it is she who seems to have stepped onto a boat moving out with the tide, stranding me on the shore. Even her expression has regained the sort of benign detachment with which she first greeted me, and there's nothing I can do about it. She chose a public place to say goodbye so as to discourage tears and heartbreak, and I am left frustrated by my inability to express my feelings, my gratitude or the emptiness inside me as she prepares to leave. I did not think it would occur in such a dispassionate manner and hoped we would return to my room after lunch, but it is not to be. Things are happening too fast; we're already outside on a crowded and windy sidewalk. I can't believe we will part like this. I want to hold onto her and prolong this moment, but to no avail. She takes me into her arms. Of course, she will write, of course, we will meet again, but I can't make out the words she speaks. All I see is her breath condensing in the air, settling as a soft mist over her eyes. The taste of her perfect mouth passes briefly over my lips and she's gone. By the time she reaches the other side of the street she is as far away as an ocean. Michelle disappears in the crowd and I am left on the street corner, jostled by strangers, my heart in pieces for the first time in my life.

Back at the Cavendish, I seek refuge in my room before checking out. The place has lost the appeal it once held. Everything about it, from the bed to the tub, reminds me of Michelle. I've never experienced heartache before and have no notion how long it lasts. I step out onto the balcony. This will be a place to remember. Oddly enough, as time passes, I discover a sort of bittersweet comfort within my distress, solace and sorrow banded together. I feel guilty that the pain I experienced so vividly less than an hour ago is already dissipating, unable to derail the anticipation of going home tonight. I look in the bathroom. I had thought of stealing the monogrammed robe and taking it back to Paris as a souvenir, but I relent. Like the memories it stirs, the robe must remain here—a privileged object in its own place and time. A picture of my own disarray, it lies discarded and rumpled upon the tile floor. I take in as many details of the room as I can, as if staring at them will score their outline deeper into my memory. I close the door. The room number is gracefully etched in blue over a white enameled oval.

Emily is still behind her desk. Usually she leaves at one, but today she's decided to earn a few more pounds and stay a bit longer. Her eyes smile even when she purses her lips in a futile attempt to look professional. She has prepared my bill and hands it over on a silver tray. I feel the old-fashioned engraving of the hotel's crest raised against the soft vellum of the document. With taxes and telephone charges, it comes to fifty-two pounds and six shillings for one night. I casually leave sixty pounds, the three crisp and resplendent notes I earned the night before. Emily thanks me and passes the tray to the bursar, never suspecting that I don't have a penny left in my pocket.

We say goodbye almost in a businesslike manner, hemmed in by other employees and separated by the imposing partition of the registration desk. She hopes I will return soon, and so do I, though it is unlikely that I ever will. Emily shakes my hand as she gives me the receipt, and we both allow this contact to last longer than it should. I like the freckles on her nose. A porter follows me to the lobby and places my suitcase upon a golden cart by the valet service. I decide to take a seat and wait for Langston. The vast armchair sighs discreetly as it absorbs my weight within its fragrant and cushioning skin. I look at the receipt in my hand. Emily has written something on it, a few lines I don't understand. But she has also included her address and telephone number. I turn around, craning my neck towards the registration desk, but she's already left.

A half hour later, a gentle pat on the shoulder draws me out of contemplating the fire that illuminates the lobby. It's Langston. He is not as tall as I remember, but again that was two years ago and I have grown a foot since. He's pleasant yet fatherly in comportment. With a snap of his fingers, my suitcase is brought out to an awaiting car, and within minutes we are slicing through the evening traffic towards his house in Hyde Park. He drives a Rolls-Royce Silver Shadow; adorned with precious wood and soft leather, the tranquil interior is impressive in its refinement and taste. Langston still insists on speaking English, I guess to maintain a sort of power differential between us, but his enunciation is generously clear and measured. As we pass the gate to his house and drive through a manicured Japanese garden and shallow ponds, I discover that his home is in keeping with the discerning affluence of his car. It looks like a sprawling French country house magically tucked away in the heart of London. And the distance alone between the main gate and the front steps is impressive enough, given the scarcity of real estate in this part of the city. Night is falling when the Silver Shadow pulls up alongside the entrance. I look around as I step out of the car: small footlights dot the grounds, lighting up a red brick path to an illuminated indoor pool. As shadows gradually engulf the garden, the iridescent glow of turquoise water streams through the gable windows, taming the chill of this November night.

The house is warm and inviting. Thick Persian rugs and subdued lights create a soft and intimate atmosphere. I realize I'm famished, not having eaten a thing since last night. Langston's wife appears in the foyer and introduces herself. Her name is Xansi, a former model of his. Born in Singapore but educated in England, her beauty radiates through the room like a succulent orchid on a mahogany floor. They must have entertained for lunch, because the remnants of a splendid buffet can be seen on two large dressers in the dining room. I swallow hard. Dinner won't probably be served aboard the night flight to Paris.

"Would you like something to drink, or perhaps even a bit to eat before you leave?" Langston asks knowingly.

My eyes betray my hunger. I make a commendable effort to decline, but can't resist when he places a plate in my hand, inviting me to help myself to whatever I wish. Years later, the amount of food I ingurgitated would become a family classic in the annals of ill-mannered gluttony. I sit with him in one of the smaller living rooms as he opens a bottle of Chablis.

"You know, Eric," he begins nonchalantly, "I started out with next to nothing and slowly worked my way up, determined to succeed. That meant sacrifices and tough choices. But as you can see, diligence and consistency of effort do pay off in this life."

The topic of the conversation and his conciliatory tone are unmistakable. It's the fatherly pep talk he probably promised my parents hc would give before I left.

"Do you realize that you have none of the social or financial handicaps I had to surmount?" he goes on. "You were born into privilege, with education guaranteed, countless opportunities, a retinue of distinguished ancestors and loving parents. Your mother alone is a most inspiring example. Her beauty, intelligence and devotion to your happiness are gifts you ought to treasure."

I detect in his voice a hint of envy and irritation, as if I were unappreciative of the sort of exclusive attention he once longed for. But I'm thankful for his generosity here tonight. I acquiesce and assure him I intend to make a fresh start upon my return to Paris, taking my responsibilities and my future seriously. He gets up and goes to his study to make a few business calls while his wife comes into the room and invites me to visit the greenhouse. Xansi is tall, about thirty-five, with a bewitching scent of sandalwood emanating from her hair. The glassed-in exotic garden is attached to the mansion by a covered walkway, and she spends the next hour introducing me to an astonishing variety of tropical flowers growing under artificial light, oblivious of the British weather outside.

The Chablis gives me a bit of a buzz, but I do try to pay attention to the tour, and this is more meritorious than it seems. Xansi only wears a diaphanous sarong and I find myself struggling to maintain eye contact, my gaze drawn to her amber breasts pressing through the vaporous cloth.

The time comes to say goodbye, and Langston leads me out to the courtyard, illuminated by lamp posts from the turn of the century. He opens the car door and jokingly insists that I sit in the back.

"This way," he adds, "you'll really get to Heathrow in style."

And as the Rolls-Royce effortlessly speeds along the causeway, I measure how my departure from London is far more distinguished than my arrival two and a half weeks ago. The back of the Silver

Shadow is spacious enough that I can stretch my legs without touching the front seat.

"There is a small refrigerator in the center console," Langston informs me. "Help yourself to whatever you wish. It'll take at least half an hour to reach the airport."

The thick leather seats smell of almond. Through the windows city lights gradually recede into dark, and soon London itself dissolves into an indistinct somber mass. Large overhead signs coax the car towards the airport, and I'm suddenly reminded that I have never flown before and that tonight is going to be quite an experience. I wish my mind could dwell on nobler sentiments, or that the thought of Michelle would ride along with me, but all I can think of is the thrill of my first flight.

We park and penetrate inside Heathrow airport. The imposing cathedral of glass and steel is a dazzling sight. Just before we stop by the Air France counter and check in, Langston pauses and discreetly gives me my ticket. I follow him through the crowd to the departure gate, where a white Caravelle is being readied on the tarmac, like a bird of prey slowly released from its tethers. This is it. My obliging escort cannot proceed beyond this point without a boarding pass. He smiles broadly and shakes my hand, making me promise to return and visit him again under more auspicious circumstances.

"I'll be going now," he says. "I promised your parents I would stay until the plane takes off, but I'm not going to insult your intelligence. I feel I can trust you at this point, can't I?"

I assure him that he can and thank him profusely for everything. Once he's left, I feel liberated. I walk around the departure area and decide to investigate the duty-free shop, overflowing with luxury goods like open chests on a treasure island. There's something about an international airport at night that is fraught with mystery and awe. People around me seem oblivious to the excitement this place generates, but I feel as if I were walking on air, powerful and worldly, like a secret agent on a mission to save the world. A sultry voice on the PA system announces the imminent boarding of our flight and mercifully repeats it in French. I surrender my ticket, transit through the sudden cold of the outside air and climb the steps onto the plane.

The interior is smaller than I imagined, though I will find out later that the business-class alcove I have been assigned is more comfortable than the narrow seats entrapping the rest of the passengers in coach. The French-built Caravelle is a medium-haul airliner linking London to Paris in less than an hour. I have a window seat, so my first take-off is a truly wondrous experience. Tiny blue and red runway lights keep flickering by with increasing speed. As the engines scream, my back is abruptly pressed against the seat with a delirious sense of infinite velocity. We lose contact with the ground and I'm ushered into three-dimensional space, with an unearthly sensation of a sudden void below me. The closest thing I can relate it to is the feeling you experience as a child, when a tall swing dives into its downward arc, sending that delicious tickling sensation in the seat of your pants. I've been in quite a few planes since then, and flown solo as a student pilot for a year, but I still marvel at the thrill of becoming airborne.

Once we reach cruising altitude, I unbuckle my seatbelt and press my forehead against the window, trying to make out details in the night below us. I think of Michelle but find it difficult to channel the thoughts wandering in my mind. I can't say that I really miss her, though I imagine it will be quite different once I have put several hundred miles between us. Why am I unable to summon some deeper and achingly romantic feelings in my heart? Emily's freckled smile keeps intruding, so that my thoughts of Michelle feel almost superficial, as if she were no longer important. I'm grateful for last night, but I also find that obligation and desire don't necessarily mix. I guess I'm somewhat resentful that we didn't actually make love. What a memory it would have been to lose my virginity in London at sixteen! To a teenager, the transformation between rebellious adolescence and manhood would have been complete. But I surmise that my youth and our age difference proved too great an obstacle to her sense of propriety. I let my mind drift along with that thought as the stewardess offers me my first pack of Gauloises in two weeks. I don't know it yet, but I will see Michelle once more, and when I discover why she didn't sleep with me that night, I will need a chair to sit on. Figuring out the way women think will be the challenge of a lifetime—an exercise in incorrigible frustration.

The cabin is now bathed in soft bluish light and I close my eyes, lulled by the gentle hum of the engines. The immediacy of my return to France is in sharp contrast to the longer and laborious journey of two and a half weeks ago. We're about to fly across the English Channel, and as the coast of England disappears behind me, my thoughts gradually converge towards my destination. Paris is only forty minutes away, with its spacious and glittering airport. And somewhere beyond the cold runways and within the tranquil lounge of a terminal, my father already waits. I imagine him looking at walls, ceilings and girders, approving of details known only to him, but critical of others. Orly airport, located fifteen miles to the north of Paris, was an admired showcase of French architectural design and engineering in the early sixties. My dad was one of the three principal architects who conceived and supervised the audacious undertaking. I remember how proud I was during school break, when he would take me along for an onsite inspection. When the airport was inaugurated, people marveled at the harmony of the structure, its magnificent layout and bold design. Honored and congratulated, my father did his usual disappearing act, fleeing official functions and returning alone later. His eyes never missed much, and away from the concert of admiration and praise, he only saw the flaws. And even up here, twenty thousand feet above the somber waves of the Channel, I can see the look in his eye just as if he were standing in the center aisle.

There is a black and white portrait of my father I particularly like. It was taken in 1942 when he was sixteen. Set in a thoughtful and freckled face, his eyes already speak of the determination and will befitting an adult twice his age. His gaze is neither harsh nor unfeeling, it just lacks the sweet hesitation and timidity of a teenager. To me my father means both the warm safety of family and the distant awe of myth.

Born in 1926 to privilege and wealth, Jean-Pierre du Plessis was the oldest son of a family whose ancestors once produced a duke and a prime minister in the service of France. His father was a stern and genial mathematician heading one of the largest shipyards in Europe.

The weight of expectations placed upon his shoulders robbed him of the carefree childhood he might otherwise have enjoyed. A flu epidemic and an outbreak of tuberculosis decimated the children of his generation. My grandmother lost two sons and a daughter to an infant mortality that struck both beggar and king with equal ferocity. I recall my father telling me how, once a month, he would have to accompany his mother to the cemetery. Inconsolable since the death of her first-born son, she had named my dad after the unfortunate little boy. And for years little Jean-Pierre was made to stand in front of a headstone bearing his name, listening to his mother grieving for his brother. At an early age, my father learned what it feels like to see someone walk over your grave.

My grandfather was determined to shield him from such overprotective attention, and every Christmas, Easter and summer vacation were spent skiing and climbing in the Alps. Public display of affection was dismissed as weak sentimentalism, and discussing one's inner feelings frowned upon as socially inappropriate. Soft-spoken and self-effaced before the towering presence of this patriarch, the quiet teenager accompanied him on his mountaineering expeditions, sleeping on vertical rock faces tethered by ropes and hooks four hundred feet above glaciers. My dad seldom expressed a word of dissent to his father, who in turn barely knew his son. And he grew powerful, not just in strength and resiliency, but impervious to pain and fear. I don't think I've ever met a man as immune to intimidation as my father.

As it was then the tradition in French schools, students stood at attention in two rows of perfect immobility before silently entering their classrooms. One morning, a physical education teacher noticed that Jean-Pierre du Plessis' body stood two inches out of the impeccable alignment of his classmates. A former drill sergeant, he was incensed by this breach of discipline and decided to teach the offender a lesson he would not soon forget. Without warning, he took a few running steps behind the students and kicked my father into line. The blow was severe enough to send him careening into the other students, slamming head first into the floor. The fifteen-year-old slowly picked himself up and walked back to the teacher, who insisted that he apologized for his deplorable lack of discipline. Instead of an apology, my father hit him so hard that his body traveled ten feet across the floor, crashing into a trophy case where he remained unconscious, wedged into broken glass and splintered wood. Without uttering a word, Jean-Pierre du Plessis calmly reclaimed his place among his petrified classmates.

My grandfather was summoned at once and found his son waiting between two gendarmes in the principal's outer office. Being expelled from the Lycée Condorcet in such a fashion was unheard of in the quiet circles of Parisian society. My dad braced himself for the worst, expecting to be sent to the strictest military academy. I remember questioning him on this particular incident as we negotiated a crevasse on a Swiss glacier.

"Did grandpa really throw the book at you?" I asked, awed by this uncharacteristic display of outrage.

"Actually, he didn't," he replied. "And that was the oddest thing of all. As the chauffeur drove us off, we sat in the back of the limousine and he looked me straight in the eye. 'I've already heard the headmaster's account of what happened this morning. Now, I would like to have yours, and quickly.'"

"What did you say?" I asked, remembering how intimidating my grandfather could be.

"I told him the truth," he answered. "And then, to my surprise, his face creased into an indulgent smile and he said: 'You did precisely what you should have done, and responded with honor and courage to a despicable violation. Officially, of course, I cannot approve. But you are my son, and I am not dissatisfied with your conduct.'"

Three days later, my father was quietly allowed to complete the academic year at the Lycée Louis-Le-Grand. He never spoke to others of the reason for his late admission, but no one as much as bumped into him for the rest of the term.

My grandparents' residence in a monumental Parisian mansion was a study in stylish extravagance. Spanning the entire fifth floor of the building, its bay windows looked out onto Boulevard Suchet and the Bois de Boulogne, an enchanting harbor of magnificent oaks and quiet lakes refreshing the west side of Paris. Decorated with Roman statues and Cambodian bas-relief, the apartment sprawled like a museum over eight bedroom suites and regal kitchens. The corridors were so long that my sisters and I used to roller-skate over their exquisite parquetry, sending the Portuguese maids running for cover.

My grandmother lived as did her ancestors, oblivious to any changes in French society. Her considerable wealth shielded her from such ridiculous notions as social justice or the emancipation of women. She indulged in every luxury but distrusted modern technology. While her immense kitchen had ovens capable of accommodating a hundred guests, it included only one minuscule refrigerator for milk, butter and cream. Everything else was bought fresh daily, with leftovers royally bestowed upon the staff who left each night with enough food to feed a family. Several owners of exotic grocery stores down on the boulevard probably owed their early retirement to twenty years of my grandmother's patronage. She gave unreservedly, yet there was no kindness in her eyes, as if each of her gifts were a test. I remember how, every year, she gave my father and his brother the same present for their birthday: a blank check, with only the scrawl of her imperious signature. Some gifts are venomous beyond their apparent generosity.

When World War II broke out, my grandfather was too old to participate and my dad too young to enlist. The Germans poured over the border and crushed the French army in the most humiliating defeat of its modern history. In time, even the street signs in Paris spoke German as the population bitterly settled in for four years of Nazi occupation. My grandfather resigned his directorship of France's largest shipyard, refusing to build destroyers for the Kriegsmarine. He rode out the war in contemptuous exile, his family nearly starving in an unheated mansion. Wartime restrictions turned everyday life into a numbing grind of deprivation and despair. By 1942 my dad was sixteen, a precocious honor student in the twelfth grade. He belittled his academic achievements, remarking that good grades didn't deserve any praise, since there was little else to do in occupied Paris.

At what point did he make up his mind to join the resistance? Even to this day, I never get a straight answer. The *maquis* was still in its infancy, and the mood of the French oscillated between collaboration and resigned passivity. The only clear response I obtained from my father was the sense of urgency that he felt, even as a teenager.

"Each day before sunset, the Waffen SS marched down the Champs-Elysées, singing and drowning everything in its path with the drumming of their boots," he recalled without animosity. "You knew their superb voices and synchronized arrogance were bent on eradicating everything decent. It became impossible to remain a bystander. You either facilitated the spread of this darkness, or you took a stand against it. There was no in-between. Just a choice. And the clarity was unmistakable."

A discreet network of the French resistance operated in Paris and offered passage to England for anyone willing to join. This was a dangerous undertaking. Travel was restricted, and communication with allied powers prohibited under penalty of death. My father contacted the underground, lied about his age and started attending meetings. Recruits were eventually taken to the coast of Brittany and ferried over the Channel with the help of local fishermen. Once in England they joined the British army, and those who qualified began special training as paratroopers. The likelihood of being caught in transit and summarily shot by the Gestapo was real, while the chances of surviving both the training and the missions were negligible. My dad was gifted in art, and he used his talent to falsify his identification and pretend he was eighteen. It worked. He only informed my grandfather once he had been selected.

"I thought he would disapprove of my plan and of the deception I had used," my father remembered, "but his reaction was unexpected, almost affectionate in its restraint. He rose from his desk and looked at me kindly, the way he used to when I was a child, and simply said, 'You needn't say anything more. I will tell your mother after you've left. I am pleased with this decision. You haven't shown yourself unworthy of your ancestors.' And then, as if recovering from this rare display of personal sentiments, he sat behind his Regency desk and brought our meeting to an end with a gruff, 'Don't forget to close the glass doors on your way out.'"

My father reached England in November 1942. Assigned to a Royal Air Force base in Northampton, he joined two hundred other volunteers. They came from occupied France, Belgium and Luxemburg, sharing a common eagerness to fight and a chronic inability to speak English. The training proved grueling, with British officers openly contemptuous of the continental recruits. Old animosities die hard, especially when they ride on centuries of mutual distrust, conquest and carnage. England had been France's enemy since William the Conqueror, and the two had warred for nearly a thousand years with all the tenacity of inexplicable hatred. Of course, if you were French and Catholic, it was rather obvious which side God favored in this rivalry. After all, if Joan of Arc's voices were divinely inspired, then Heaven itself had saved the faltering kingdom of France back in 1429. Though Joan had been relegated to ancient history for five hundred years, British Catholics were filled with consternation when Rome made her a saint in 1920.

But even if it had pleased Providence to take sides in the petty continental politics of the fifteenth century, revenge was now at hand. British officers were given the task of transforming anemic French students into killing machines. Her Majesty's Royal Commandos were not intent on carrying passengers, and the training turned as rigorous as it was deadly. For the next three months, they all went through boot camp and airborne school. By the time they boarded the planes for their first jump, their number had dwindled to ninety. Wartime restrictions did not allow for the luxury of a safety, the second parachute that saved your life in case the first one failed to open. The chutes were recycled after each use, inspected by matrons and widows who contributed to the war effort by folding and packing them. Before each jump, the entire commando silently prayed the ladies had not overindulged in the sherry that kept them warm in unheated hangars.

When danger did not come from bailing out of airplanes or manipulating plastic explosives, it sprang from the soldiers themselves. Now grizzled and mean, they longed for action and turned their training against one another, triggering brawls in barracks that claimed the lives of a dozen men. I'm still trying to imagine how my freckled-face sixteen year-old dad became an implacable soldier, able to kill without hesitation or remorse. Thirty years later, he summed up the transformation that took place in those young and kindhearted intellectuals.

"Each time we jumped, something would go wrong, either with the equipment or the men," he recalled.

"Our main concerns were the propellers, much too close to the outer door, and the proper opening of our parachutes. Hurtling towards earth at a hundred and fifty miles an hour, it was a relief to feel the leather harness suddenly gouging your body, yanking you upward as the chute opened above your head. A friend of mine from Luxemburg wasn't so fortunate. His equipment malfunctioned three days before graduation and he fell eight thousand feet to his death. We were using an abandoned airfield as a landing site, and from above you could clearly see the star-shaped impact of his body on the cratered runway. I guess we had all fantasized enough about such an accident that we couldn't resist looking at what was left of him. What stuck in my memory was the way his body lay splattered on the concrete. It had crumpled to a torso with the thighbones coming out of his shoulders."

As a child, I never learned about my father's participation in the war. He earned his wings and left airborne school to join the Royal Commandos in February of 1943, along with sixty-eight surviving volunteers. When I studied World War II in the eighth grade, some of my classmates' fathers were hailed as heroes of the French resistance, their exploits proudly recounted to enraptured teenagers dreaming of John Wayne in *The Longest Day*. When my turn came to relate my father's tales of bravery, I had nothing to say. Not that I didn't ask him, but the answers I got were invariably vague and boring. Something to do with transporting radio crystals across enemy lines. Not quite on a par with blowing up bridges, killing Nazis and saving the world.

The lack of inspiring stories in which my dad played a pivotal role consigned him to the ranks of collaborators. Surely, if I had nothing to say that was because he stood by passively during the occupation, or worse, openly approved of Nazi Germany. I compensated for this dearth of courage and bravery by immersing myself in history books. I remember one night in 1964 when I was home on Christmas break, reading about British Commandos in the last two years of the Third Reich. And there, amid the thrilling description of their deeds, I found a resistance fighter with the same name as my father's. The age matched as well, so I knocked on my parents' bedroom door. They were reading in bed. I sat next to my dad and showed him the passage in the book.

"Look," I said, "isn't it wild? This guy was only seventeen when he served with British paratroopers in Holland. His name is identical to yours: Jean-Pierre Léopold du Plessis."

My father lifted his gaze from his reading and looked at the page.

"How about that?" he remarked, not particularly interested. "That's an interesting coincidence. A lot of soldiers took on assumed names during the war."

I was about to return to my room, when my mother abruptly slammed the book she was reading upon the bed.

"That's more than I'm prepared to tolerate," she said. "Your son is now fourteen and old enough to know. There is a fine line between discretion and the refusal to acknowledge one's merit!"

"Old enough to know what?" I asked.

My mother's outburst was uncharacteristic. She looked at my father, searching his eyes for a reply. She was a fierce debater, and he knew better than to get into an argument with her. That night, he finally resigned himself and took refuge behind his newspaper.

"Go ahead if you wish," he sighed. "I guess it's inevitable. He may be old enough after all."

"Old enough to know what?" I kept asking, mystified by their exchange.

My mother turned to me.

"The young man in the book is not a coincidence," she said gently. "He's your father."

I was astonished. I got up and ran around their monumental bed, yelling with excitement.

"Told you," my dad muttered, "he isn't old enough."

"But, Dad," I implored, "why didn't you tell me? Why did you say you were just a courier, running errands for the resistance?"

He folded his newspaper and dropped it beside the bed. I sat near him, my natural admiration turning into hero worship. He gathered his thoughts for a moment.

"I chose not to for several reasons. First of all, what I did during the war was necessary, but also ruthless and graphic. This was twenty years ago and it belongs in the past now. None of this has anything to do with the person I am today."

"But why didn't you give me at least some general information?" I asked. "According to this book, your unit carried out incredible missions. Think of the stories I could have shared with my friends!"

"That's precisely why I decided not to reveal anything until you had the maturity to understand, and to keep such information to yourself," he replied. "Had you known any of this when you were ten, you would have only been interested in how many people we killed."

"Well, of course," I answered proudly. "And...how many Nazis did you kill?"

"You see," my father sighed to my mom, "I knew it would come to this."

She stood up and looked at the two of us with bemused affection.

"I'm going to get a box of family photographs from the forties. We'll all sit down to a late snack and sift through it. I am sure your father won't mind enlightening you on a couple of points...will you, dear?"

And she smiled at him, with eyes against which his powers, past and present, were completely useless.

That night I learned for the first time some of the things that sweet-faced adolescent had done during the war. I still treasure the black and white photograph taken a few months before he left for England in 1942, but I can no longer look at it without thinking of the fearsome deeds behind that gentle smile.

Immediately after jump school, my father was inducted in a special unit of the Royal Commandos, whose mission was to operate deep behind enemy lines in occupied Holland. The War Office had put together a particularly effective team of saboteurs and demolition experts. Dropped stealthily during the night, the small units incinerated ammunition and fuel depots, destroying power plants and hindering German troop deployments. An added refinement of the missions consisted in assassinating upper echelon SS officers whose whereabouts were revealed by the local resistance movement. Away from the battlefield, the Germans traveled in armed convoys protected by an elite detachment of bodyguards. The discreet operations quickly turned into open warfare, with the targeted officers taken out in gruesome and spectacular fashion. The cost to the British was high. Units originally planned for multiple missions seldom returned from their first assignments. My father must have been gifted for this task: he and a few others made it to Holland and back three times between 1943 and 1944. His fourth mission would prove his last.

It is the only war story I ever heard from him, and he recounted it in detached tones that night, as I sat transfixed on my parents' bed.

The commando was comprised of nine men. They wore no dog tags or identification. Once the mission was completed, they would be on their own behind enemy lines, working their way back to the coast where a boat waited at a secretly arranged location. That night, on a flight to the north of Antwerp, the seven new recruits sang at the top of their voices over the roar of the engines. They couldn't wait to be over the target, already high on army-issued amphetamines, unaware of the carnage awaiting them. My father and another man sat at the back of the plane. The only veterans of previous missions, they just stared at each other, resigned to enter a darkness all of their own within the greater night of this war. The flight began uneventfully, with danger materializing only as they neared the coast of Belgium. German artillery was quite adept at shooting down transports flying over from England. The twin engine Whitworth Albemarle climbed as high as it could without a pressurized cabin, tracer shells exploding in the night sky like monstrous flashbulbs and rocking the plane as if it were a fly caught in a fan. Close to the target, the men stood and hooked their static line to a cable hung inside the plane. The hatch would then open—a large manhole into the darkness below – and the freezing night stormed the cabin with the howl of a two-hundred miles an hour wind. When the green light came on, the men jumped, each cable pulling on a chute, opening it like a giant corolla floating in the dark.

That night my dad was the last to go, and he disappeared through the hatch as he had done many times before.

"I knew almost instantly something wasn't quite right," he recalled, with his usual flair for understatement. "For some reason my static line wouldn't release, and instead of diving after the others, I remained attached to the plane."

Unaware of the incident, the pilot turned around for the flight back to England. My father's body was dragged under the plane and repeatedly slammed against the fuselage until he passed out. The steel clasp from the line eventually broke away, flinging his unconscious body into the night. But Providence smiled once more upon him: his chute miraculously opened, and he reached the ground alive.

"When I came to, I was glad to be in one piece; but as I tried to comprehend what had happened, my problems became rather obvious. I was unconscious when the chute finally opened, and the tangled straps had tightened around me like a noose, snapping a collarbone and dislocating my shoulder. I landed in a swamp, eighty miles from the other guys. Still, it would have been all right if a local farmer hadn't told the Germans he saw a parachute in the night sky."

He stayed a day in the swamp, crouched behind frozen reeds in four feet of muddy brine.

"The SS came in the morning with dogs," my father added, "and I knew that if I remained submerged, I had a chance to escape detection."

"But you were wounded. Weren't the pain and the cold horrendous?" I asked.

"Not really," he replied. "I kept slipping in and out of consciousness. Most of all, I didn't want to die of something ridiculous like hypothermia, not after this ordeal. It's strange what things go through your mind when you're up to your neck in a cold swamp at night. Your life functions start shutting down. You're unable to stop defecating in your uniform, and you really don't care."

I tried to imagine him, shivering, starved and broken, soaking in cold mud and human waste within the greater infection of a swamp, and concluded that men from his generation were made of harder stuff. In late afternoon, he crawled out of the sludge and walked two miles to the first farm he could find. Noticing a bucket of fresh milk cooling on a window sill, he approached stealthily to taste his first meal in twenty-four hours.

"It's only after I got close enough that I realized my mistake," he said wryly. "It wasn't fresh milk, it was quicklime used for coating the outer wall. That's when I gave up. I was already half-delirious at that point, so I didn't really give a damn any more. If I was going to die, at least maybe I could get a drink before they shot me."

He collapsed against the door. But, woven long ago, the threads of his destiny and those of the man inside, converged in his favor. A farmer opened up and sheltered him, even arranging to have his fractured bones treated at the hospital as a construction accident. Two of his toes were frozen and had to be amputated, and he lost sensory nerves in part of his right shoulder. He later refused the pension the French government awarded him as a wounded veteran. My dad preferred to look at his injuries as an interesting challenge for an experienced rock climber. By the time he made it back across the border, the American First Army was liberating Normandy. Months later, he learned that this accident had probably saved his life. The other members of the team did reach their target, but none made it back alive to the boat. They all vanished without a trace, slipping like thousands of others into the shadows of forlorn graves.

Apart from this account, and the information I found in the history book, I gathered only a few anecdotes. I sensed my mother knew quite a bit more, but she deferred to my father's wish for silence. Years later, my dad and I became much closer, and when climbing together in the Alps, he occasionally let his guard down and revealed something from his past. But even that proved limited. He had closed the door on that part of his life and didn't wish to look back.

"Listen," he once said to put an end to my curiosity, "it was long ago, in a war now almost forgotten. I've had to kill people, and those memories are for me alone."

To a teenager with a fertile imagination, my dad's silence only added to the mystery. In the early sixties, my friends and I marveled at 007 on the movie screen, but I sensed that the real thing, without fanfare or glory, lived at home right next to me. The little I had learned was stupendous enough, and his modesty made the rest loom as the stuff of legends.

And this is my father. The man I'm about to confront after this plane lands, and to whom I must render an account. More than ever, his approaching presence takes on the dimensions of a myth. The Air France Caravelle is already beginning its descent towards Paris. I look out the window. Ten thousand feet below me a scintillating carpet of illuminated towns and cities unravel itself, denser and more luminous as the plane draws nearer its destination. Almost frantically, I try to focus on the details of this flight and commit them to memory, but I can't concentrate on anything. Though fascinated by my first landing, all I can think of is the meeting about to take place, the reckoning I have dreaded for weeks. Somewhere inside that airport my father awaits, as patient and immovable as deep waters

Mom at Five in Hanoi with her Manservant

Mom in College in 1944

Dad in 1942, before joining the R.A.F

Mom and Dad in 1964

Boarding School, 1964

University of Paris Medical School, 1970

Exiled to Virginia

My Sister Isabelle in 1966

My Sister Florence in 1965

My Great-Uncle and Great-Aunt in 1965

Six

It is half past eleven when I step off the plane and walk into the main terminal of Orly, its vast corridors eerily quiet and its lights dimmed for the last flight of the day. The airport is shutting down for the night, home to captive passengers in transit trying to sleep on rows of plastic seats. I'm apprehensive and yet animated by a lingering sense of rebellion. I have no intention of coming home with my tail between my legs, so I briefly stop on my way through customs, put on a pair of dark glasses and light up a Gauloise. And then, suitcase in hand, I resolutely proceed to the arrival area with a swagger. Families are waiting past the security point, running to greet arriving passengers, but I don't see my father. He may be late after all, and I'm both relieved and disappointed. I wait for ten minutes before walking to the darkened concourse, looking for the airline courtesy counter. I may have to make a call but lack even spare change for a pay phone.

The transition between the terminal and the main lobby is a steep bank of escalators delivering passengers to the ground floor on a gleaming cascade of articulated steel. I let the mechanical stairs carry me, standing tall and confident enough to take on the whole world. And this is when I see him. Waiting near the bottom of the escalator, my father stands like a statue in the nearly deserted hall, his arms folded and a look of irritation on his face. I guess the shades and the cigarette remind him too much of my attitude before I left. I bury the glasses in my pocket and quickly crush the Gauloise in an obliging ashtray.

The frown eases off and he smiles, a becoming smile. For a Frenchman, my dad is surprisingly undemonstrative when showing affection. In a Latin culture where fathers and sons kiss on the cheek, his accolades are always stiff and somewhat reticent. But tonight he greets me wholeheartedly, picking up my suitcase as if it were a twig and escorting me to the parking lot. The drive to Paris is fairly pleasant. I answer his questions on specific events in London, trying to adopt a tone halfway between enthusiasm and contrition. As the car eases through the traffic, he listens and nods, a hint of a smile passing over his lips. When we draw nearer to our house, he slows down and adopts a noticeably firmer voice.

"I want you to know how annoyed I have been these past few weeks," he begins, with a sidelong look in my direction.

"You gravely upset the life of this family, at a time when obligations in Paris and overseas demanded my undivided attention."

I shrink within the exiguity of the car seat. I had hoped he would save the fatherly talk until tomorrow, but the time has come.

"I think I understand why you ran away and what you've been trying to tell me, but I wish you had expressed your teenage discontent by involving only the two of us. You have no idea how little your mother slept for nearly three weeks. This is the last time I see her aggrieved by your shenanigans. Do I make myself clear?"

"Yes, quite clear," I reply. "I'm really sorry I hurt her feelings; it was never my intention."

He seems satisfied by the look of genuine contrition on my face.

"There's one more thing I want to say before we reach the house," he adds, turning towards me and gently poking me in the ribs.

"Petit con!" He lets out with a grin, as the last of his exasperation whistles through his teeth—"little asshole." My father rarely curses, but paradoxically this is his way to express forgiveness and to draw the curtain on the entire episode. I grin back at him, sealing in the half-darkness of the car a complicity that has endured ever since.

The gates to the house are open and we drive on through. My mother stands on the front steps. I fly out of the car and rush into her arms.

"You've grown taller," she remarks, fighting back tears and rear-ranging my hair the way she always does.

Though it is late, my sisters stayed up for me. I remember my father's wish that this would not turn into a welcome for the prodigal son. I enjoy a late snack, doing my best not to gloat or monopolize the conversation. It feels wonderful to be back. An hour later, I'm at last reunited with my room. In the center, laid out like a treasure chest on a pirate's island, is the large steamer trunk I had brought to boarding school in September. Someone at St. Joseph's expertly packed all my belongings and sent them home two weeks ago.

I feel reconciled, resting my head on the bed and letting the ca-ress of flannel sheets slowly lure me to sleep. But the door cracks and my sister Isabelle pokes her head inside.

"Are you OK, kiddo? Need anything?" she asks.

"I'm fine," I reply. "Thanks for staying up for me."

"You'll fill me in on all the details tomorrow," she whispers. "I promise I won't breathe a word to mom. Just tell me, did you get laid in London?"

Since we were five, my sister and I have never kept a secret from each other.

"Well, not exactly," I answer sheepishly.

"*Not exactly?*" she retorts. "Wow! You've got to tell me every-thing in the morning...what's her name?"

"Michelle," I mumble, finally succumbing to sleep.

I enjoy a couple of days of respite before my mother sits me down, outlining a schedule filled with appointments and deadlines. My father has arranged for interviews with three private lycées in Par-is. These establishments combine the last two years of an American high school with the first four semesters of college. Those graduating with a baccalauréat can then study law or medicine at eighteen, mak-ing it possible to qualify for the bar by the age of twenty-three. Medi-cal school takes longer, incorporating pre-med, basic sciences and clinical studies into a six-year curriculum. The schools my parents have decided upon are prestigious, each with exacting admission cri-teria, and their catalogues are completely silent on accepting students in the middle of a semester. My mother makes it a point to mention that these places are not just selective, they're also inordinately expensive. This is a financial burden my family could do without, since in France state universities are practically tuition-free. They charge a modest registration fee, in the vicinity of three hundred dollars a year, a sum thought outrageous enough to trigger student protests each fall. French students have never heard of a college education costing thirty-thousand dollars a year. But I can no longer apply to a state school, having burned my bridges with numerous evictions and an academic record suggestive of a learning disability.

I won't ask again how they succeeded in lining up these interviews. When I did, my mother looked out the window.

"Your father made a few calls," she evasively replied. "Phone numbers and people I had never heard of before. You would be well-advised not to query him on the matter."

Paris in late November is just as frigid as London, but I no longer need to hide from the rigors of winter. I was hoping for a card or a letter from Michelle, but so far I've received nothing. My first appointment is with a well-known college located near the Arc de Triomphe in the financial district. I wait in the antechamber of the admissions office, skimming through a brochure extolling the school's international reputation. The roster of former students reads like a compendium of European celebrities. When I'm finally ushered into a plush and somber office, my eyes strain to adjust to the half-darkness. Thick green drapes hang from two French windows reaching the ceiling. Only slivers from the afternoon sun are allowed into the room. Behind an antique desk a diminutive administrator sits, absorbed in a letter even as the door discreetly closes behind me. At least thirty seconds pass before he deigns to notice my presence. He never rises from his seat but peremptorily designates a chair for me to sit on. He is bald with rapacious eyes, and his expression communicates resigned exasperation.

I don't appreciate the subterfuge of letting me stand while he continues to read, but I promised my dad I would be polite and receptive to courtesy. The imposing décor of the room and his surly demeanor are probably intended to intimidate and set the tone for the interview, but it doesn't work. The director of admissions looks like Donald Pleasance doing one of his sniveling characters, and his efforts to project a formidable presence only accentuate his lack of stature. I remain attentive to the point of deference, but it is obvious neither of us expects to see the other again.

The evening dinner with my parents is rather tense. I'm grateful my father made that interview at all possible and I feel I'm letting him down. Yet both my parents do their best to remain supportive and hopeful, allowing me a generous amount of personal freedom during this process. They would no doubt prefer to choose the college themselves, and I wouldn't exactly be in a position to dissent.

My second interview a few days later brings about the same result. My aversion to authority and discipline obviously has a lot to do with it, but it isn't just that. I realize I will have to comply with rules and regulations wherever I go, yet these schools are devoid of originality and only perpetuate a tradition of worn-out curriculum and unimaginative faculty. I have one more appointment left before my academic options run out. I sit in the drawing room with my mother, trying to map out a strategy, determined even to compromise on my insistence for novelty and independence.

"Mom, I really wish these interviews had come off better. I fear I'm not repaying your trust very well," I tell her with genuine regret. "I only hope Dad doesn't think I'm doing this on purpose. My difficulties re-entering the system have nothing to do with the sort of mind-frame I cultivated in London, when I could defy you both with total impunity."

A streak of gray passes across my mother's eyes.

"Total impunity?" She muses. "Do you seriously believe your father didn't have the means to bring you home if he had wanted to?"

I'm unsettled by her assurance. Something inside the edifice of my confidence begins to crumble.

"Listen to me carefully," she says, rising from her seat and choosing an armchair closer to mine.

"I don't wish to take away any of your accomplishments in London. You showed initiative and abnegation, and I'm satisfied that you comported yourself honorably – as far as I can tell, of course; your sister Isabelle was unusually quiet about that two-hour conversation after your return...but I don't want you to think your father waited helplessly for your next phone call. He had other options he chose not to exercise."

"I know he's resourceful, mom," I answer her, "and I don't mean to be argumentative, but for once in my life I was out of his reach. He didn't have a clue as to where I was staying."

My mother stares at the embers in the fireplace.

"You don't know the half of it," she says gently. "I promised your father you would not be made aware of certain facts, but I see that it is necessary to enlighten you. He thought it important that you believed yourself completely independent in London. He felt that if you were left alone with that certainty and succeeded in disentangling yourself from this situation, you would gain confidence and maturity. And though it cost me sleepless nights and untold worry, I went along with his assessment. It was a risk, but well worth the effort. You could have used this total 'impunity' – as you call it – to darker designs. You might have turned into a juvenile delinquent, or much worse, but you didn't. Instead you grew up quickly and made the necessary adjustments yourself."

"But mom," I ask again, somewhat mystified, "you keep alluding to my feeling of impunity as if it were some sort of delusion, while in fact I was free to go anywhere I wanted and there was nothing he could have done about it."

"You proceed from a false assumption," my mother replies. "I agreed with this plan on one condition: that we could intervene quickly if things got out of hand. You don't think for a moment that I would willingly place my sixteen-year-old son in jeopardy, do you?"

"Go on," I answer, both intrigued and crestfallen, "I want to know."

"All right," she says softly, steadying herself in her armchair. "The day you called from London, your father cancelled his appointments and left for Paris. He went straight to *La Piscine*, the headquarters of SDECE, the French intelligence services, and saw Colonel Mercier. How he gained access into that fortress and secured a private meeting is beyond me."

"Who's the Colonel?" I ask with growing unease, as the curtain slowly rises on shadowy backgrounds and events.

"Mercier is head of special operations for counter-intelligence," she informs me. "Apparently he worked with your father during the war when they were both in the R.A.F. I say 'apparently' because as usual your dad didn't elaborate. I met the Colonel once at a reception a few years ago. He had by then risen to a position of importance in the intelligence community, and I thought it odd how he remained so deferential to your father."

That afternoon, I finally learned how the shadows and fog of London held in their mist presences I never suspected. Colonel Mercier ordered a tap on my parents' phone and all my calls were traced. Once he had ascertained my whereabouts, he contacted his alter ego at MI5, the domestic branch of British intelligence, and requested his assistance. The Englishman was only too happy to oblige. Six months before, the underage daughter of the Queen's equerry had eloped with an older man to the south of France. Under Mercier's orders, the intervention section of the SDECE tracked them down to a romantic villa in Provence, stormed the place, retrieving the girl and placing her on a military transport back to England. Singing the praises of the French, the grateful father discreetly drove to an R.A.F. base and collected his heavily sedated daughter. The whole operation was of course completely illegal, but no one complained since, officially, it never happened.

Soon after my arrival in London, MI5 contacted the Metropolitan Police who easily located the hostel. That same day Colonel Mercier called my dad in Paris.

"What would you like us to do?" he asked. "If you wish, we can have Eric picked up and detained within the hour. He's in England illegally since you did not approve of this trip, and his travel documents can be instantly rescinded."

But my dad thought otherwise. Now that he knew exactly where I was, and that I could be apprehended at a moment's notice, he gave me the opportunity to redeem myself. Once more, I'm amazed at his restraint and insight, and grateful that he chose not to reveal any of this the night I came home with a less than humble disposition.

That evening, I wait sitting on the front steps. And when my father comes home, I greet him more effusively than the day he picked me up from the airport. He sees the look in my eyes and the knowing smile on my mother's face, and hugs me back, grinning at her approvingly.

"Napoleon was right," he observes with a studied sigh, "state secrets should never be entrusted to a beautiful woman."

In private matters, as in war, my father still favors stealth over ostentation. Like the shadow of a hawk upon its prey, real power defines itself by remaining unseen.

My last interview is scheduled for Monday afternoon, and my parents do their best not to intensify the tension that is already palpable. Sobered by my mother's recent revelations, I'm determined to give this an all-out effort. The Louis XIII Institute is located in the Marais district of Paris, near the architecturally exquisite Place des Vosges. I know of its academic reputation—everyone does. Last year alone, ninety-eight per cent of its students passed the baccalauréat, that dreaded national exam, while most private schools in the capital were well-content to advertise an eighty per cent rate of success. Each year in June, nearly half the candidates fail this one-week ordeal, the nightmare of every eighteen-year-old in France. So it is with some trepidation that I sit today in the admissions office. So much is riding on this interview that I'm unable to devise some obfuscating strategy, and pretend to be someone I'm not. When the door to the inner sanctum opens, I walk in without artifice, determined to be me for once in my life.

The room is impressive, the way I imagine a cabinet minister's office, but even before the secretary closes the door, the man behind the desk rises and promptly steps forward to greet me.

"I'm Mr. Marchand, dean of admissions and professor of physics, and who the devil are you?"

He knows full well who I am, my file rests on his desk. But his voice is warm and his handshake firm without insistence. He is at least six feet tall, in his late forties, with the vitality and mannered charm of a country squire. I introduce myself and take the seat he obligingly offers. He studies me for a moment.

"May I offer you something to drink, Eric?" he enquires as naturally as if I were a guest in his house.

His amiability intrigues me. I'm used to school administrators whose authority rests on theatrics, but he appears confident enough to come down to a teenager's level. Most of all, the interest in his eyes seems genuine.

"May I trouble you for a cup of tea?" I reply, still unaccustomed to such hospitality.

"A wise choice on this cold and dreary afternoon," he remarks, nonchalantly leaning into the intercom.

"A cup of Darjeeling for Mr. du Plessis. I'll have a vodka tonic. Please hold my calls for half an hour. Thank you, Rachel."

And so our meeting begins. I'm impressed with the tone Mr. Marchand immediately sets for the interview: it is both relaxed and professional. I have never experienced such courtesy and sophistication in a school setting before. The man's intelligence and wit sparkle through his eyes. He is direct without condescension and wastes no time getting to the heart of the matter.

"You're obviously aware of the situation. I have carefully reviewed your academic record and it is, well, to put it mildly, an interesting document," he begins in a slightly sarcastic and formal tone.

"There are different ways to explain the dismal results you've accumulated thus far. Either you are learning disabled, or you've been using your grades to express some measure of discontent with your family, society, or a bit of both. Since I don't believe for a moment that you are mentally impaired, I'll pay you the compliment of being blunt. Some applicants impress me from the start with their brilliance and the record of their intellectual achievements. But your transcript is almost surreal in its pattern of academic failure. From where I sit, it speaks of a concerted effort to run aground at all costs."

He stands up behind his desk, finishes his drink and sits in the armchair directly across from me.

"I run a fairly successful establishment here," he continues. "It demands most of my attention and energy. I don't have time to indulge students with neurotic states, narcissistic dispositions or existential attitudes. Our goal here is not just to ensure that you pass selective, state-mandated examinations, it is that you do so with a total dedication to excellence. I have agreed to this interview solely as a favor to your father, and my decision is this: I will admit you conditionally as a late arrival, due to, shall we say, compelling circumstances. I trust you will be discreet as the Sphinx and prove yourself worthy of such departure from the rules. I see from your record that you've earned quite a reputation for insubordination and histrionics. Don't expect much of an audience from your classmates around here. The competition is cutthroat and your errors will be their gain."

He stands, signifying that the meeting is over, and shakes my hand.

"I may be making a mistake. You have three months to prove me wrong," he continues, the look in his eyes now implacable. "By February your grade point average will rise to a minimum of A minus, across all subjects, and you will take your place among us on a path to academic excellence, yes?"

He opens a door leading out of his office through a discreet corridor.

"You have everything you need to succeed," he adds, pointing to my temporal lobe, "and I trust you will make the right decision."

His voice takes on an unexpected edge just as he is about to close the door.

"Because if you don't, Mr. du Plessis, rest assured you will be out of here like shit through a goose."

When my father returns home that night, and learns of my being admitted to the Louis XIII Institute, he doesn't say much, but his comportment clearly shows he is relieved, and that the ball is now squarely in my court. This is the first and last time he personally involves himself in my education, and with the crisis now over, he recedes once more into the background.

Despite the fact that she needed him during the last three weeks, my mother should not be construed as a demure housewife stuck in the patriarchal traditions of French society. In addition to the typical obstacles cluttering a woman's path in the 1940's, she found herself hindered early in life by her physical appearance. Her mother came from an ancient Christian community lost in the sands of Northern Syria, and passed on to her daughter stunning blue eyes set in the smooth features of a Chaldean beauty. This Middle Eastern ancestry was diluted in the Celtic blood of her father, imparting upon her an exotic charm that seldom failed to attract attention. An enviable predicament for any woman, but a curse when you decide, as she did, to defy tradition and study medicine in 1942.

From the far reaches of its sprawling colonies, France conferred a significant amount of foreign blood upon its population. Though the bourgeoisie and aristocracy did their utmost to conceal such ethnicity, affecting instead impeccable pedigrees of Nordic lineage, my mother took pride in her Arabian heritage. Both my sisters benefited from this legacy of attractiveness and intelligence – I'm the only one bemoaning the chromosomes she passed on to me. I look in the mirror and see them rising with a vengeance, slowly transforming me into a caricature of Colonel Kadafi.

My mother was born in Hanoï in 1921. North and South Vietnam were then known as French Indochina, while France consolidated a colonial empire stretching from the shores of Tahiti to the Khmer temples of Cambodia. The thought of exporting the democratic ideals of Danton's republic to the jungles of Madagascar or the cannibals of Guyana, was deemed a noble endeavor. Besides, even when greed didn't add zeal to the enterprise, the French would have colonized half the planet for no other reason than the British who were actively conquering the other. England and France had fought their last battle at Waterloo, but their rivalry continued unabated. For another one hundred and fifty years, they vied for influence and prestige, settling outposts of their formidable cultures from the frozen plains of Labrador to the backstreets of Casablanca.

The French upper-class joined in this imperialistic effort by providing diplomats, admirals and judges on a Gallic mission to rescue savages from their ignorance. Economic opportunities were also unique, and if many failed to find fortune in the colonies, others flourished and pursued overseas a life of privilege not seen since before the Revolution. My maternal grandfather accepted a lucrative offer to leave his practice in Paris and become dean of the school of medicine the French had established in Vietnam in 1902. He and my grandmother lived in a sumptuous mansion in Hanoï, surrounded by ten acres of meticulously kept gardens and ponds, with a staff of a half-dozen natives looking after their every need. Celebrated like a little Annamese princess, my mother grew up spoiled and sheltered, speaking Vietnamese and sleeping in a four-poster bed shrouded in reams of mosquito netting. I saved a black and white photograph of her, taken in 1926, as she leaves for school hand in hand with Dinh Van, her manservant. In an odd reversal of cultural identity, the ageless Vietnamese butler forsook his traditional silken robes and proudly dressed in Western garb. He insisted on an incongruous three-piece suit that once belonged to my grandfather, with lapels as stiff as the expression on his face.

Life in the exclusive enclave of colonial administrators was not devoid of interest. Far from the scrutiny and constraints of Parisian society, French officials indulged in escapades with underage girls, while their proper wives slipped away on Saturday night into the stupor of opium dens. Other pastimes were more in a league with Indiana Jones. My mother's uncle, a farcical engineer who had traded a monotonous career in textiles for the green forests of Indochina, was an avid race car driver. The most prestigious event of that time was the yearly Hanoi-Bangkok rally, which ran through rain forests, crumbling bridges and jungle trails, pitting drivers against mudslides, monsoon and highway robbers. In 1925, the record time was held by the British naval attaché who completed the hazardous journey in a blazing two and a half days.

After twelve to fourteen hours of horrendous roads, drivers stopped for desperately needed sleep in roadside bungalows, getting back behind the wheel as quickly as they could. My great-uncle surmised that the cars used in the competition were all fairly identical in their capacity to survive the grueling journey. If the weather held, then the deciding factor had to be the ability to race on through with as little sleep as possible. All competitors eventually stopped to rest, sheltered from torrential rains and the attacks of enraged baboons leaping upon passing cars, their teeth ripping the canvas roofs like razor blades through virgin silk.

My mother's uncle was endowed with an unusual ability: he could sleep at will, almost instantly, regardless of need. He consulted his brother on the medical implications of his plan, and satisfied that it was safe, proceeded to sleep almost uninterruptedly for eighteen hours before the start of the race. He was not the most capable driver of the lot, but that year, stopping only for refueling and bare necessities, he completed the arduous trek in thirty-two hours, without any rest. Wresting the title from a baffled British diplomat, the wiry engineer established a record that held until 1933, the year the road between Hanoi and Bangkok was finally paved.

Grandfather didn't approve of such revelries. He believed that his behavior, and that of the ruling class in Indochina, was scrutinized each day. To him, high moral standards commanded respect in a more meaningful way than the fear of the French Navy. He advocated an industrious and irreproachable way of life, while the indiscretions of the colonists and their disregard for the law humiliated the natives who endured colonial rule with smoldering anger.

Unimpressed by the vacuity of their rulers, a bastion of young Vietnamese intellectuals became receptive to the revolutionary rhetoric disseminated by Chinese and Soviet agitators. In any impregnable fortress, the greatest danger always comes from within, and bright students received scholarships from the French government to study political science in Paris. There, in the cafés of the Quartier Latin, rubbing shoulders with Jean-Paul Sartre and leftist activists, they became convinced Marxists, acquiring at the Sorbonne, and at taxpayers' expense, the tools needed to transform political discourse into action. Back in Vietnam, they quietly began to sap the foundations of French Indochina. When the war ended in 1945, France tried to maintain control over the peninsula, but it was too late and the sidewalks of Saigon were thinning down to the dirt. In less than eight years, the French were forced to withdraw, and the hundred-year dream of *Indochine*—an odd mixture of noble idealism and insufferable arrogance – came to a precipitous end.

My grandfather didn't wait until then. Sensing the political charade unraveling, he resigned his position in 1932, leaving behind his ethereal mansion and joining his wife and daughter on an ocean liner back to France. At the age of eleven, my mother came to live in Paris, a glamorous place which from the shores of Vietnam had loomed with magical excitement. Her father resumed his practice on the fashionable Avenue Victor Hugo, a five-minute walk from the Champs-Élysées, and she grew up shying from social circles and immersing herself in her studies. When she graduated with honors at the age of twenty, she was expected to join the ranks of privileged young women navigating the salons of Parisian society. But war broke out, the Germans occupied Paris, and the restrictions proved inauspicious to romantic prospects. This hiatus in the social structure facilitated my mother's decision. Following in her father's footsteps, she entered the University of Paris medical school, one of only four women in a class of a hundred students.

Films of Paris in the early 1940's, courtesy of the German propaganda office, show the City of Lights in a rather sorry state. With little or no illumination, food rationing, deserted avenues and empty parks, Paris appears grey and abandoned, its monuments closed, the Louvre amputated of its collections, and the once resplendent menagerie of the Vincennes zoo succumbing to malnutrition and neglect. Schools and universities were striving though, the only places with youthful enthusiasm and intellectual defiance. At least books in libraries were left untouched by the war. Paris was occupied by the Wehrmacht and its civilized officers, but even they shrank from the incarnation of pure evil: the SS and the Gestapo who terrorized the French capital with less subtlety than hordes of plundering Vikings a thousand years before.

German uniforms were everywhere, wolves in armor roaming streets made for musketeers and lovers. Most students sought refuge in their studies, welcoming them as a shelter from the daily reminder of occupation and defeat. Food became an obsession in a city known for its celebration of gastronomy. Shortages and rationing compelled the most uncompromising gourmets to settle for unappetizing substitutes. In the course of two years, obesity was almost eradicated from Paris, while three-fourth of smokers quit due to the disappearance of tobacco. Rationing coupons restricted the consumption of meat and fish to a once-a-month luxury. Carnivorous cravings and expediency slowly cracked the veneer of polite society, and neighborhood cats and pigeons began to vanish, reincarnated later as rabbit and quail in the windows of butcher shops.

But survival tactics could not always hide the toll the German occupation took on the population.

"I thought myself fairly resilient," my mother remarked, as she recalled her medical school days. "The reality of war remained somehow muffled and distant when you were a student living in Paris. But its ugliness and cruelty also intruded on your daily life, when you least expected it."

And my mother's magnificent eyes welled up with tears as she remembered.

"By 1943, there were practically no Jews left in French universities, and their absence from the medical faculty affected the quality of instruction in several clinical departments. As I left the hospital one day in December, I came upon a small gathering on a sidewalk of the Boulevard Saint-Michel. An adolescent boy was being detained by a squad of SS in uniform. Apparently, they were not satisfied with his identification, and suspecting that he was Jewish, they forced him at gunpoint to drop his trousers and underwear. I stopped. We all knew what it meant. This despicable act was their favorite way to identify Jewish males, since no one else in France was circumcised."

"There he stood, half-naked on this December afternoon, shivering and shamed. But in his humiliation the boy rose like a beacon of righteousness in the midst of his tormentors. With his curls tousled by the chilling breeze, he kept staring at the crowd, a silent indictment in his eyes."

My mother's voice faltered and she looked away in the distance.

"*A Light to the Gentiles, and the Glory of Thy People Israel...*" she whispered, quoting the Gospel as if lost in thought.

"Is it true that many Parisians collaborated with the Gestapo?" I asked, trying to dispel her sadness.

"Some did, but I can't speak for all," she replied. "Anti-Semitism is rampant among the French, and war has a way of magnifying people's good qualities, as well as their inner demons. But not everyone was so abject," she added. "I witnessed a fair number of spontaneous acts of courage and kindness, among the students in particular."

"Please tell me," I asked, eager to preserve her testimony.

"I believe it was February 1944," she began. "The Germans' hold on Paris had become more tenuous due to the number of occupying troops sent to the Eastern front. The tide was turning against the Nazis, but the Gestapo continued the charade and redoubled its effort to harass the population. Racial laws were still strictly enforced, and resisting them proved as dangerous as ever. The SS became convinced that more Jews remained hidden in the Quartier Latin, so the Paris Kommandantur issued a new order and plastered it on every street corner. Within one week, all remaining Jews in the district were to display the yellow star with the word *Juif* plainly visible on their outer garments. There would be no exceptions, and failure to comply would result in immediate arrest and deportation."

"And was the order followed to the letter?" I enquired.

"As a matter of fact, it was," she answered, "but not in the way the Gestapo had anticipated. One week later, at 7:30 in the morning, the SS appeared near every strategic intersection in the student district, to see how their directive was being obeyed. And the answer came, loud and clear: pouring into the streets on their way to class, nearly all students wore a yellow star. Even ordinary folks proudly displayed the infamous patch on their clothes."

"I was so proud of my compatriots that day," she added. "I stood there with other students, and we wore our yellow stars for an entire week, until the Gestapo gave up and cancelled patrols in the district."

But for my mother, hardships and difficulties did not always originate from the occupation of Paris. As if the war were not enough to make the students' lives miserable, the presence of female students in the medical school attracted the censure of traditionalists. She routinely found herself the target of hazing incidents, some more comical than others. The day she arrived at the university hospital to begin her clerkship in urology, she was met by the department head at the top of an imposing flight of marble stairs.

"Good morning, mademoiselle," intoned the distinguished surgeon. "You must be the third-year student we expected today."

"Good morning Doctor," replied my mother, "I'm indeed the one, and ready to begin."

"Well, young lady, you need not trouble yourself any further. Here's the report card for this clerkship. I gave you an A. Just take it to the registrar's office on your way out."

"I'm afraid I don't understand," my mother answered, who with ingenuous enthusiasm had looked forward to this moment.

"Then, I will explain," retorted the professor, now aloof and condescending. "There is a misguided fringe in this school, entertaining the notion that women can be trained as physicians. I will not argue the point, but suffice it to say that as long as I am chief of urology in this hospital, no female student will be permitted to examine a single one of my patients."

She stared at him with incredulous dismay.

"You go on now. If it must be, I suppose you can amuse yourself by trying to become a gynecologist or a pediatrician. But while I am here, you and your kind will not set foot on this ward. Good day, mademoiselle."

"How did you put up with this sort of attitude?" I once asked her, amazed that she continued her studies undaunted.

"I did the clinical work at a dispensary in the suburbs, and learned to catheterize men at the VA hospital," she replied with a chuckle. "In the eighteenth century, the great naturalist Lamarck defined intelligence as the ability to adapt to new situations; so I decided to ignore a few incurable idiots on the faculty. And we also practiced an early form of feminist rebellion," she added. "The other three women and I graduated in the top ten per cent of our class."

In time, the last remnants of sexist resistance in the medical profession were overcome and the next generations, without fanfare, sit-ins or bitterness, gave my mother and her friends the retribution they deserved: by 1990, half of all general practitioners in France were women. The best thing about dinosaurs is that they become extinct.

It is now the end of February, and midterm grades are being sent out. Remarkably, my parents have refrained from asking about academic performance or results since my admission to the Louis XIII Institute back in November. But I have worked harder than I can remember, and not just to satisfy my parents or placate the scrutinizing gaze of professors. I did this for myself, out of a sense of self-esteem I didn't know I possessed. There's something else, too. The faculty is like nothing I have experienced before. They're distinguished and witty, yet not above continuing their afternoon lectures in neighborhood cafés, where the merits of national health care or the futility of Nietzsche are argued around glasses of dark beer and a mountain of fries. In the academic environment of the sixties, dominated by unimaginative curriculum and stilted pedagogy, these educators bring about an unexpected transformation: they make former rebels passionate about learning.

I know that academically I have done rather well, but the jury is still out on several major exams. The dean's office has not once called my father, and I take this as an encouraging sign. Strolling into class, Professor Marchand casually hands me my midterm grades without betraying any emotion. I grasp the piece of paper: I have an A in every course. I look at him and a broad smile appears on his face.

"I like it when someone proves me wrong," he quips, "because it means I'm learning something." And just before leaving the room, he lays a thin volume on the edge of my desk. It's a cookbook printed in England, *Twenty-One Ways To Roast A Perfect Goose*.

I savor the irony.

Later that week, I receive two letters from England. The first is from Michelle, inquiring about my reinsertion at home. The affectionate letter speaks of her concern for my well-being, but it is also bereft of romantic notions. I anticipated a correspondence in keeping with the motherly tone she adopted before I left, but no one likes to be proved right when the heart bears the brunt of one's perspicacity. My answer to her is insipid, hastily jotted down on a prepaid postcard, courteous to a fault. And yet the memory of her lips intrudes on my irritation and continues to haunt me.

The second letter is from Emily. My English is improving, but I still need a dictionary to translate a few words. Her handwriting is impeccable, almost like a schoolgirl applying herself on ruled paper. I will later discover that American girls do exactly the same, perpetuating a tradition of clearly readable prose, when most continental young women insist on illegible scrawl. Emily's letter is sweet and unaffected. Spring break is just a month away and she's contemplating a three-day weekend in Paris, wondering if I would be her guide and see my way clear to spending the entire time with her. I'm ecstatic and intrigued by such straightforwardness. I would love to call her in London, but I fear my inadequate English will make me sound like a fool. I write her that very night, trying not to show how thrilled I am.

I also wonder. After several false starts, blunders and unrealized hopes, am I getting any closer to discovering what sex is all about?

I confide in my parents, not really asking for advice, but welcoming suggestions and bits of wisdom. Throughout my adolescence, I've never talked to my father about sex. Not that he would have taken offense or declined to answer, it's just that I didn't feel comfortable. My mother became my preferred source of knowledge on the subject. Her medical education helped a great deal, but so did her sense of humor, which in these matters is sometimes all a teenager really needs. This was France in the early sixties. Sex education didn't exist in schools and in most families the subject was never brought up. Neither contraception nor abortion was available, and parents felt that information along these lines amounted to tacit encouragement. My parents disagreed, and believed the problem was not whether children obtained information, but rather how accurate the information was. In these matters, my mother's wisdom and progressive views were first illustrated to me at the age of thirteen.

I was home from boarding school for spring break. As I stepped into the house one afternoon, I met my sister at the top of the stairs.

"Before I forget, Mom wants to see you," she said.

"Is it something bad?" I asked, with the trepidation of a teenager with a guilty conscience.

"I don't really know. She just said she needed to talk to you the moment you got home," she replied. "Mom didn't sound angry or anything...but she looked kind of serious."

I went upstairs with growing unease. Women know how to herald trouble in the very way they initiate conversation. My mother had a look in her eyes and a certain inflection in her voice whenever she wished to communicate something unpleasant, a disposition I would later recognize in the ingenuous way most women begin with "we need to talk."

I found my mom in the library.

"Please close the door,' she said, her soothing tone exacerbating my anxiety. I sat on a sofa opposite her, quickly reviewing in my head the untold mischief of which I might be guilty. But because of mounting panic, or a temporary state of blamelessness, I couldn't think of any.

"The maid found these under your mattress when changing the sheets this morning. Would you care to explain?" she asked in a detached tone.

And to my horror I saw in her hands the girly magazines I kept hidden under my bed. In 1963 I didn't even smoke, so the extent of my lawlessness was limited to petty larceny and publications appealing to the prurient interests of a thirteen-year-old. There is hardly anything more embarrassing to a teenager than his parents' accidental intrusions on his sexual fantasies. My face turned crimson as I searched for an explanation. But my mom was merciful. She only let me squirm for a brief moment before rising from her seat and sitting closer to me. She opened the magazine, which by now looked distressingly cheap and sordid, casually flipping through the pages while I cringed with embarrassment. Back then, real pornography wasn't available to an adolescent on a modest allowance. The black and white photographs only depicted naked women in suggestive poses, typical of the tawdry publications of the time.

"It's perfectly normal for someone your age to become interested in sex and naked women," she began. "What I object to is the inherent trashiness of this sort of magazine. Just look at this," she went on, "it's utterly devoid of artistic merit. These women are distasteful prostitutes well past their prime."

She brought the pages closer to her face.

"And some of them, judging from the clinical nature of their poses, even show evidence of venereal disease and physical abuse," she added with a look of consternation.

I wished I could have disappeared under the floorboards.

"This is not the way you should discover the beauty of a woman's intimacy. These pictures are demeaning and salacious. And don't think I haven't noticed your reading my old textbooks of gynecology and obstetrics gathering dust on the top shelf of this library," she went on with distressing accuracy. "These volumes are not intended to be erotic in any way. The plates they contain are illustrations of diseases and pathological states, hardly a celebration of life and desire."

She walked to her desk, retrieved a hundred-franc note and placed it in my hand.

"You're thirteen. If you must go through the typical adolescent stage of voyeurism and fantasy, then so be it. But I would prefer that you not acquire this sort of worthless publication." She said matter-of-factly. "Take this money. Each month, if you wish, you may purchase a copy of *Playboy* magazine. Their tasteful depiction of nudity can almost pass for art, and if you're going to indulge in imaginary conquests, I'd rather it be Raquel Welch than some faded streetwalker with a habit."

And with that, she dismissed me and never again brought up the subject. I think I became the only kid in the neighborhood who didn't have to hide when buying *Playboy* magazine from the newsstand in St. Lazare train station.

To a thirteen-year-old, sex is either reduced to a selfish urge, or aggrandized as a sort of sensual Holy Grail. But relegated to the gutter, or placed on a pedestal, women still remain for teenage boys a fascinating mixture of desire and apprehension. When she talked to me or my sisters about sex, my mother was unique in her ability to demystify, while inculcating in her children a deep-seated sense of awe and wonder.

By spring break I achieve an academic milestone I haven't reached since the fifth grade. I'm at the top of my class, and not only do I enjoy this status, I will no longer settle for anything less. The Louis XIII Institute is pedagogically years ahead of other colleges. Away from the constraints of traditional French lycées, I find a perfect niche in this unusual haven. Nestled within a private park in the heart of the Marais district, the school itself is a regal anachronism when compared to the depressing classrooms of state-run lycées. And to add a touch of scandal to its originality, the institute is housed within the walls of a nineteenth-century whorehouse, once tolerated in this irreproachable neighborhood. And today, while struggling with a tedious biochemistry exam, I can see my classmates on the ceiling, fifteen feet above my head, reflected in mirrors installed a hundred years ago for the edification of lecherous customers.

Winter term is drawing to a close, with both faculty and students in dire need of a break. I am weary of battle. Emily will arrive in a week, and I look forward to the holidays. The saffron rays of an early spring insinuate themselves into my room, filtering through the curtains, glancing off the walls and settling on my face like the warmth of a woman's breath. The textbook slips from my hands as I surrender to the sweet lassitude of a tranquil afternoon.

Seven

EMILY'S ARRIVAL IN Paris is my first romantic rendezvous without witnesses or chaperon. The weather forecast calls for sunshine and unseasonably warm temperatures, as if everything conspired to make this event subtle as a postcard. I should be ecstatic, strolling down the Champs-Elysées at seventeen with trees in full bloom against a radiant sky, but this bucolic setting fills me with apprehension. How should I comport myself, and what must I do to win Emily's favor? Am I the sole purpose of her visit, or did she plan this outing long before we met in London? I'm probably getting paranoid and needlessly worried, suffering the appointed lot of all anguished teenagers.

I decide to confer with my sister Isabelle and gain some strategic advantage from a woman's point of view. As usual, her advice is inescapably logical.

"First of all, don't let her see you sweat," she warns with maternal solicitude. "You must project a debonair and confident image of yourself."

"How can I?" I reply. "I'm a complete wreck. Why not simply tell her how awkward I really feel? I read somewhere that women are sensitive to the plight of underdogs."

"To a point," she replies. "But remember this: teenage boys are attracted by physical appearance, while girls are drawn to power and confidence."

"And another thing," she goes on mercilessly, "don't pretend to be experienced, or she'll figure you out for a fraud instantly. The last time you tried that approach it was with Vivian, and you narrowly missed getting laid." She concludes with a chuckle.

"But you're not making any sense," I protest. "On the one hand you want me to be honest, and on the other she's not supposed to know that I don't have a clue."

"All in good time," she answers, getting ready to leave and consign me to despair. "It's as Blaise Pascal once said: 'The heart has its reasons that reason itself does not understand.' You intellectualize too much. Relax and banish expectations from your mind. Be spontaneous and remember to look out for her first. Be attentive to her needs, the rest will follow naturally."

"Thanks for nothing. What if she finds me dorky and changes her mind the moment she sees me?" I whine, fishing for some encouragement, as my sister lazily stretches against the doorframe. "I wouldn't worry about that," she replies. "Emily had plenty of opportunities to find out when you were in London, and apparently that wasn't enough to dissuade her from coming over." Isabelle does a swift about-face and disappears down the corridor, whistling *God save the Queen*.

I'm not any more confident than before talking to her, though I should be grateful to have a sister who can quote from a seventeenth-century French mystic. Good advice to be sure, pragmatic and sensible: the last thing a worried teenager needs.

The little I know about the way girls think, I owe to my sister, though the insight I gain often leaves me more disconcerted than enlightened. I recall a few years back, when she was infatuated with Cédric, an insipid senior from the local lycée, whose charm seemed solely to rest upon his brand new Jaguar E. He also was two years older than my sister, who had not yet reached the age of consent, and this had raised my parents' objections. Had I been Cédric and seen the look in my father's eyes, I would have steered clear of our driveway.

There were two phones in the house, both connected to a single line. In France in the sixties, calls were billed according to length. We were rationed to short conversations not exceeding ten minutes, with our parents turning merciless enforcers, placing a kitchen timer next to the phone when my sisters retreated to the library, even hanging up occasionally on long-winded suitors. Pleas for leniency and extensions were inexorably met with the same response from my father:

"It isn't a question of money, but of proper breeding. If this young man wishes to expound on his feelings for you, he should have the courtesy of telling you in person."

And my mother would back him up, adding for good measure:

"He can always write, can't he? Nothing like a long letter to measure the depths of a man's worth, and the true nature of his intentions."

In the parking lot of the girls' lycée, where Cédric and his friends held court after classes, the young Lothario had noticed the stars in my sister's eyes and said he might call on Saturday afternoon. So right after lunch on that fateful day, Isabelle kept watch like a hawk, perched on a stool next to the phone, glaring at anyone who might even think of using it. This was long before the days of caller ID and call waiting, and our family became hostage to my sister's hopes as she remained there like a statue, biting her nails, checking the clock, ready to pounce on the receiver at the first hint of a ring. We stoically endured this ordeal for nearly three hours, my father wisely choosing to drive to a nearby café for a business call, rather than confronting an exasperated teenager on the brink of a meltdown.

The phone finally rang. My sister jumped from her stool and retreated to the center of the drawing room, as if the long-awaited ring had turned into a strident death-knell. Frantically, she gestured for me to answer the phone. I picked up the receiver. It was Cédric, asking to speak to her with the mannered voice of a movie star. Getting a clue from the look on my face, Isabelle mimed her reply: she wasn't home and could he please leave a message. I stood there flabbergasted, but proceeded to do as she wished. I wrote down his message and placed the receiver back on the old Bakelite rotary phone.

"What's going on?" I asked, completely dumfounded. "You had us all walking on eggshells for three hours, precisely to make sure you wouldn't miss this guy. And when he finally calls, you're not home! What on earth is wrong with you?"

My mother kept observing us with a quiet smile. She didn't seem surprised, and looking away from her book, she even cast a knowing glance in my sister's direction.

"What did he sound like?" Isabelle demanded to know. "I mean, was he eager in any way? Did he appear disappointed? What were the exact words he used? Did he say when he might call back?"

But I refused to provide the details she needed, still outraged that she didn't answer herself.

"You really hoped he would call. Wasn't it what you wanted the most?" I went on, bewildered by such a flagrant departure from common sense.

"Of course it was," she replied.

"Then why didn't you grab the phone and tell him how long you'd waited, and how thrilled you were?"

Isabelle let out an indulgent sigh and shook her head.

"Because that's precisely the point," she said. "Cédric, or any other boy, must never know how much I care, and least of all the time I spent by this phone waiting for the call."

"But what's wrong with being honest, simply sharing your true feelings for him?" I insisted, mystified by her answer.

"Because, dear brother, the moment he learns how much I like him, he will exploit it, use it as leverage, walk all over me and lose what little respect he may have. Instead, keeping him guessing, and preferably agonizing over my true feelings, is the only way I can survive unscathed in this world."

My mother resumed her reading with an approving smirk, and even the maid, chasing dust bunnies under the sagging bellies of antique armchairs, nodded approvingly.

And thus my first insight into the psychology of women left me confused and worried. With such diabolical means at their disposal, what chances could I possibly have trying to gain their attention? More than ever, girls appeared unpredictable, fascinating and decidedly dangerous.

On the night before Emily's arrival I measure the true extent of my predicament. On my sister's advice, I decide to shave.

"Always do that a day early," she suggests. "This way you'll have a bit of a five o'clock shadow the next day, and Emily will like that."

"But why would she?" I retort. "Mom said I should look neat and smell nice."

"Mom means well," Isabelle replies, "but she's been corrupted by motherhood. The fact is, most girls like the bad boy look. It's the forbidden fruit aspect, the hint of danger, the attraction of the abyss... trust me. What aftershave are you going to wear?"

"I wasn't planning on using any," I answer, increasingly disoriented.

"Borrow some of dad's," she says. "He wears *Monsieur,* from Givenchy. It's an expensive classic from the fifties, discreet, suave and irresistible. Use it sparingly."

My sister sees the look of panic in my eyes.

"I didn't mean to worry you. From now on, I'll just quit giving advice. You'd still win her heart even if you wore overalls and a tee shirt," she adds comfortingly.

She takes a few steps toward the door but turns around, unable to resist one last recommendation.

"Whatever you do, don't talk about yourself. Be a good listener and you'll do just fine," she concludes with a sweet smile of encouragement.

I appreciate her help, but as the evening wears on, I find myself increasingly apprehensive. I do have one legitimate concern, though, and it has to do with finances. I had carefully saved my allowance over the last three weeks, even jumping over turnstiles in the subway to avoid paying the fare, but I'm still well below what is necessary to treat Emily to a couple of decent restaurants in Paris. This is 1967, so there are no credit cards, and I'm too young for a checking account. The last thing I need to worry about is my ability to pay for food or entertainment. I had already broached the subject with my mom, but failed to alert her as to the seriousness of the situation. I need a loan. This calls for a man-to-man talk and my father happens to be in his study.

An imposing blueprint covers his drafting table. With a fountain-pen and India ink, he is adding a bit of décor to one of his architectural drawings.

"Well, well...if it isn't Romeo," he chides from the large table swung at a thirty-degree angle. "I was wondering when you'd show up."

"I just came by to say hello," I reply defensively. "Why is everyone in this family under the impression that I need advice?"

"Oh, I wouldn't presume to give you any," my father replies good-heartedly. "I just thought your visit may have been prompted by, shall we say, pecuniary considerations?"

I open my mouth in protest, but he silences my objections with a wave of his hand.

"It's all right, son, I've been there," he says reassuringly, resting his pen and ruler upon a side table. "In fact, I once went to your grandfather with a similar request when I was sixteen. I needed money to buy perfume for the daughter of Wilson Schneider, whose attention I craved. I fared so poorly I left his study without a cent. So let's see if we can do a little better with you," he adds, taking a banknote out of his wallet.

I look at it in disbelief. It's five hundred francs, which in 1967 represented four times my weekly allowance. I'm ecstatic, but also wary about accepting it.

"What's wrong?" my father asks, sensing my hesitation.

"Dad, I don't think I can accept," I mumble reluctantly. "It would take me too long to pay you back, if ever."

"I appreciate your prudence," he replies, "but I'm not offering you a loan. This is a gift."

I jump with gratitude and rush around the drafting table to thank him.

"Is there anything else I can do for you?" he asks, patting me on the shoulder. "You seem a bit frazzled."

"Oh, it's nothing really," I reply unconvincingly," but tonight I don't have any confidence in myself. In fact, I'm a bit scared, like a general on the eve of a decisive battle."

"And well you should," he answers with a wink, "considering the power of the enemy. Throughout history, women have proved the undoing of fearless leaders and conquerors."

"But what can I do to stop worrying until I meet her at the airport tomorrow?" I ask, hoping for a bit of fatherly advice.

"If I knew the answer to that," he whispers, "the international conspiracy of women would consign me to a dungeon and throw away the key. Just keep in mind the words of Turenne, Louis XIV's most dreaded general, whose name sent shivers through ranks of British soldiers. On the morning of the battle of Arnheim, with the French outnumbered three to one, he was being fitted with his armor while eating breakfast in his tent. As his valet helped him with a gauntlet, Turenne noticed that his hand was trembling. He looked at this uncharacteristic manifestation with some surprise and remarked: 'Why, this carcass of mine is shaking. It would shake even more if it only knew where I'm taking it today!'"

A persistent knock on my bedroom door awakens me well ahead of the two alarm clocks I positioned around my bed the night before. My mother finally opens up and comes into the room.

"Wake up, sleepy head, you've got a telegram," she announces, resting it on my pillow before drawing the curtains aside and opening the windows. My heart sinks. It's probably Emily telling me she cannot come. My fingers tear through the blue envelope of the French postal service, revealing words on strips of white paper glued upon the form. My spirits are instantly revived. It is indeed from Emily, but it's only a change of plans.

Will use limo from airport to Paris. STOP. Meet me Hotel George V at 2pm. STOP. Emily.

This is good news, for the prospect of trying to find her in the airport was not particularly appealing. In fact, I was seriously worried that I might miss her altogether in the crowd. I also get more time to prepare and spend the better part of the morning staring in the mirror, rearranging my hair every ten minutes. My dad finally puts an end to my preening.

"I don't have to be in Paris until 1:30. I could drop you off and spare you rush hour in the subway," he suggests.

"That would be great," I reply, bolstered by the prospect of my dad accompanying me.

"And where is this English princess staying?" he asks.

"The Hotel George V, near the Champs-Elysées," I answer with feigned nonchalance.

"Well, Your Grace, that's what I call visiting the continent in style," my father quips admiringly before closing the door.

There are only a few four-star hotels in Paris worthy to be called palaces: the Ritz, the Crillion, the Plaza-Athénée and the Hotel George V. These magnificent establishments, sailing as flagships of decadent luxury, stand above other princely accommodations in the French capital. At first I am surprised by Emily's unexpected means, until I remember that her father probably enjoys complimentary accommodations at some of the finest hotels in Europe, reciprocating with the hospitality of the Devere Cavendish. This adds another touch of excitement to my day, since the closest I have ever come to the George V is a quick look at the entrance lobby while strolling along the regal avenues of Paris' eighth district.

My father drives me into the heart of the capital and drops me off in the courtyard of Emily's hotel a little after a quarter to two. The inside is astounding and truly deserves its reputation as one of the most distinguished palaces in the world. Its vast foyer exudes luxurious warmth, basking in the glow of crystal chandeliers and seventeenth-century tapestries. The George V scintillates with opulent comfort, yet its refinement comes with discretion and taste. It takes a moment for the casual observer to notice the genuine Louis XV furniture or the Dutch masters on the walls. As for the legendary service, it is exquisitely subtle. You don't actually notice the staff until you need something. Anyone penetrating deeper into the hotel is watched. Hesitation or inappropriateness seems to make staff members in red livery materialize out of nowhere. The tourist who comes in just to gawk, the intruder who doesn't belong, or the opportunistic thief looking for quick work, finds himself discreetly escorted out with muscular courtesy.

I decide to walk in boldly, as if I owned the place. My Christian Dior blazer and Grenson designer shoes, expensive presents from my aunt last Christmas, meet with the approval of the reception desk. For good measure I even borrowed my dad's signet ring with his coat of arms engraved in 18-carat gold. It's a bit pretentious, but in a place like this, where guests are constantly scrutinized, you cannot leave anything to chance. As I make my way through the lobby, trying to appear as natural as possible, a voice whispers my name directly behind me. I turn around and come face to face with Emily. We both burst out laughing and stand there for a moment, just looking at each other. I haven't seen her in almost six months and don't quite know how to greet her. The French kiss an acquaintance on the cheek as a mark of friendship, but they don't readily hug someone. Such physical closeness between strangers, with bodies touching even for a brief moment, would be considered inappropriate. Emily forestalls my hesitation by breaching both Anglo-Saxon and Gallic protocols. She puts her arms around me, greeting me with a warm hug and then, as if to cast my shyness to the wind, kisses me squarely on the mouth. We find a comfortable sofa in the foyer and sink into its velvety comfort.

"Sorry for the sudden change in plans this morning, but my dad had already booked me on the limousine out of Orly. I thought I would spare you the madness of the airport. Gosh, it's good to see you! You look...older, somehow, in a nice sort of way," she adds with exuberance. "How about a drink and then you'll tell me everything that happened in the last six months?"

I love her enthusiasm and straightforwardness, something I'm not accustomed to with French girls. In the sixties, her Gallic counterparts favored aloofness and distance over the new and liberated British spontaneity, a candor no longer paying heed to the formalism of continental dating.

The moment of surprise over, I realize what is different about her. She's cut her hair. Her magnificent red mane is gone. But the new look, cut short to the top of her shoulders, is breezily alluring. She wears corduroy jeans and a V-neck sweater, radiating the same carefree charm that caught my attention in London. The apprehension and worries of the last two days evaporate, and I'm captivated by the sparkle she radiates. We talk for over an hour in the foyer and she compliments me on my English, noticing how it has improved. But she gives me too much credit, and encouraged by my progress, Emily talks as if I were completely fluent. It's not that I really mind. I love the sound of her voice and could sit here under her spell for hours. Even if I fare better than last year, I still miss about a half of what she says and try to cover the gaps with smiles and nods of interest. Besides, by letting her do most of the talking, I stick to my sister's advice and may even pass for an excellent listener.

Emily has already checked in and is eager to immerse herself in the life of Paris, beckoning just outside the bay windows of the hotel. She's come to France once before, traveling with her parents for a weekend when she was seven.

"I was miserable," she recalls. "It rained incessantly and I stayed cooped up in a hotel eating chocolate éclairs in front of an incomprehensible TV set, while my parents visited the Louvre and went out to the opera. So it's up to you, Mr. Frenchman," she coos in my ear, "to show me if this place lives up to its reputation. The little I saw from the limousine looked fabulous."

We leave the silken womb of the lobby and find ourselves on the avenue, blinking at the sun. I didn't prepare an itinerary and just decide to improvise, turning right on the Champs-Elysées and treating Emily to the spectacular sight of one of the world's most beautiful avenues. While we walk, she tells me of her life during the last six months and the unexpected difficulties of her second semester at Oxford. I'm delighted she possesses none of the reserve British girls are supposed to display, according to the stereotypes of my generation. She's spontaneous and lively, with a contagious giggle. I am enjoying my assignment as tour guide, pointing to sights around us while she marvels at the splendor of it all. The great cities of the world are those where you can walk unhindered for miles, and be greeted on every street corner by the legacy of centuries past. I couldn't hope for a more romantic and breathtaking backdrop for our first day together. Crossing halfway down the sprawling thoroughfare of Avenue Montaigne, I grab Emily's hand to keep her from venturing into a sea of oncoming cars. Drivers will not stop for jaywalkers in Paris.

On the cobblestones of the French capital, British civility is abruptly replaced by the rude comments of drivers passing within inches of terrified tourists.

Far from being shocked, Emily finds the whole incident hilarious, as if nothing could dim her natural ebullience. It's only when we reach the vicinity of the Petit Palais that I realize she's left her hand in mine. We walk for nearly an hour and turn left into the Rue Royale to enjoy a well-deserved rest at Ladurée, the finest Salon de Thé in Paris. Its succulent pastries, laid out in window displays like precious jewelry, have tempted passers-by since 1860.

"Can we see Notre-Dame cathedral?" Emily inquires, voluptuously enjoying every bit of her second *nougatine fourrée au caramel*. The delicate icing has broken off into thin, translucent fragments that dissolve instantly on her lips, leaving a sensuous sheen upon her smile.

"Of course we can," I reply, subjugated by her charm. "But if you don't mind, we'll take a taxi, just to avoid the crowds along the Seine."

There is an affinity between us not built upon familiarity or the gradual lessening of guardedness over time. We share neither foundation nor vested interest on which to build a relationship. I know precious little of her family and she asks nothing about mine. Together we have no past, and no immediate plans beyond the next twenty-four hours. This absence of structure or expectations encourages a closeness that would have taken weeks to establish, and we both welcome this newfound emancipation, the sweet intimacy of strangers.

Resting her feet in the back of the cab, cushioned by the legendary suspension of the *DS Citroën*, Emily leans over me and gently brushes her lips on my cheek. The chasteness of the kiss, mingled with the sugary fragrance of her breath, slips into me like guiltless thirst.

French girls favor being cast in the role of fortresses to be conquered with a siege, according to genteel and romantic rules of combat. In this artificial construct, they only communicate the vaguest of clues as to any eventual success, while the bashful suitors are supposed to remain virtuous incarnations of Percival. I don't know if

Emily is representative of other English girls, but she is worlds away from the societal hypocrisy I've been taught to accept. When the taxi reaches our destination in the Ile de la Cité, we step out hand in hand towards Notre Dame with the inculpable zest of teenagers in love.

As we round the corner of the Hotel-Dieu, the oldest hospital in Europe, the cathedral suddenly comes into view, its towers gilded by the afternoon sun. The majestic façade, chiseled with statues, bas-relief and the exquisite lace of its rose window, stops Emily in her tracks.

"This is incredible!" she exclaims after a moment of stupefaction. "And to think I didn't even bring my camera. Can we go inside?"

"I'd be delighted to show you," I answer with a touch of Gallic pride. "I think you'll be impressed."

The entrance to Notre Dame lures you in like a fantastical cave. Once your eyes make the transition between daylight and half-darkness, you are seized by the palpable atmosphere that reigns within. The tourist aspect of the place fades away to reveal the true solemnity of flagstones gleaming in the shadows, polished by centuries of kneeling supplicants. Emily and I proceed under the arches to the side chapels. Ensconced on both sides of the nave, they offer a more discreet and yet arresting display of the cathedral's inner treasures. The walls are lined from floor to ceiling with thousands of thanksgiving plaques, the rising emanation of answered prayers and gratitude. You can attend services in Notre Dame and be dazzled by its splendor, even shaken by the thundering voice of its Gargantuan organ. But you can also slip in through a side-door at 5:00 a.m. and hear mass with a handful of early risers in a tiny chapel, far removed from the ostentation of public worship. And there, transported to another time, you are overcome and humbled by eight hundred years of spirituality, standing guard over the sanctuary like a host of invisible souls. As you leave, the rising sun pierces the darkness like fragile arrows sailing through the stained glass.

We stop in front of an ancient baptismal font and Emily grips my hand. Seized by the ethereal beauty of the alcove, she drops a handful of coins in an alms box and lights a thin candle. We stand there together as a hundred points of flickering light dance in the shadows, bathing Emily's face with an unearthly glow.

Twilight greets us as we leave the cathedral. Emily quickly recovers her naturally impish disposition, but I sense that the sharing of this moment has brought us closer together. We leave the Ile de la Cité and cross over the river into the heart of the *Quartier Latin*. French universities have nothing even resembling the campuses of American colleges. Instead they consist of disparate buildings and facilities scattered in an urban setting, often without much of a common bond. The University of Paris' campus is the city itself, especially the "Latin Quarter" sprawling through much of the sixth district of the French capital, alive with hundreds of shops, cafés and restaurants. I take her through winding streets and mysterious alleyways dating back to the 15th century, narrow passages forcing visitors through gauntlets of tourist traps. She seems to bask in this atmosphere, where whiffs of Ethiopian cuisine blend with the aromatic scents of Vietnamese food and Greek gyros. We walk along the rue Saint-André des Arts and head back to the river in search of quieter settings. I'm thinking of inviting Emily to dinner in a classy traditional restaurant with a view, when she catches sight of a *bateau-mouche*, one of the glassed-in, flat bottom boats cruising along the Seine.

"Would you mind very much if we got on one of those?" she asks with childlike excitement. "I've always dreamed of doing that!"

I think of Paris river boats as such a tourist attraction that it never occurred to me to mention them. And so we board the longest *bateau-mouche* of the fleet, a luxurious barge-like ship offering a two-hour night cruise on the Seine. And despite its surreal commercialism, I must admit the experience is quite enjoyable. The ship boasts a reputable restaurant on the upper deck, and I propose that we dine onboard while gliding lazily on the river.

We're practically alone tonight, huddled around an immaculate dinner table, enjoying the unseasonably warm breeze.

"I'm afraid this is as crass as booking a carriage ride through Trafalgar Square," I whisper in her ear, embarrassed by the postcard atmosphere of this place.

"I think it's absolutely charming. It's so sweet of you to do this," she muses, the lights from the river bank reflecting in her eyes as the ship reaches its cruising speed. "This is the most gorgeous place I've ever seen."

We slice through dusk and sunset on top of this nearly silent ship, while the heart of Paris comes to life in a fleeting parade of illuminated splendor. Strange how you tend to forget how dazzlingly beautiful a place is when you've lived there all your life. The dinner over, I take a bottle of Sauternes and two glasses and invite Emily to join me astern. The rear deck is completely deserted, affording us a shadowy shelter. She stands up against the railing, her face faintly lit by the lights of the city, before its reflections disappear into the somber waters of the Seine. I stand behind her with my hands around her waist, while the rustling leaves of passing trees whisper in the night. Neither of us feels the need to speak as Paris unravels its seduction from both sides of the river.

I feel completely at peace, floating with her along the Seine without a care in the world. Emboldened by the glow of the Sauternes, and the inner conviction that she's calling out to me, I let my hands venture under Emily's sweater, gently laying them flat against her stomach, feeling her blood coursing under my fingers. She leans her head back and moves closer against me. Her skin is inviting, soft as silk, and my hands slowly continue upward until they reach her breasts. Both of us stop breathing at the same time, my lips turning dry as I discover she isn't wearing a bra. Even as they lingered over her lissome figure all afternoon, my eyes never noticed a thing.

There is something delirious in the touch of her cool and naked breasts under my hands, as the lights of Paris slowly recede behind us. I let my teeth nibble the back of her neck while my hands take a downward path, below her navel, settling in the outer rim of the belt she wears low on her hips. Emily's hands reach around me and lock behind my back, drawing me closer into her, teasing my desire.

The sudden growl of the ship's engines startles us both. The *bateau-mouche* is docking along the darkened pier we left two hours ago. Emily playfully takes my hand and pulls me along, forcing us both to leap onto the river bank before the ship completely stops.

The steward on the platform shakes his head with a grin, as we run up the embankment giggling like kids.

Paris offers a nocturnal landscape so unique as to remain indelible in the heart. And those who surrender to its timeless charm discover that it hides and protects them when they wish to disappear within its realm. From resplendent landmarks we slip into the mantle of enigmatic alleyways and discreet parks, walking around the Ile Saint-Louis, with Notre Dame silhouetted behind us against a dark purple sky. Our bodies take turns hindering our steps, so we stop in the shadows, holding each other, our hands and lips teasing us to despair. Prolonging the inevitable inflames us both, and the cadence and restraint we instill in this surrender ordains our breaths like a maddening metronome. Lust is a cry of frustration, but desire consumes itself in willing subjection. It is a beast running through a forest at night, the undulating sheen of sable fur over a patch of sand and heather, with neither reason nor the threat of a thousand guns to deter it from its course.

I had planned to end the evening at the terrace of Berthillon, the finest sherbet and ice in all of France, but the hunger of our eyes and mouths won't be satiated even by such sumptuous fare. I hail a taxi and we find our way back to Emily's hotel, past the majestic gates of the Louvre and onto the Champs-Elysées, its coruscating life beckoning from both sides of the avenue like a parting river of neon and lights.

The George V greets us with the soothing comfort of a luxury liner. Emily's key is brought out to her before we even reach the front desk. I slow us down as she heads for the elevators.

"I need to make a quick phone call. Would you mind waiting for a moment?" I ask her.

She turns to me with a slight frown of inquisitiveness.

"I've got to call my parents and tell them I'll be late," I whisper, blushing with embarrassment.

"That's very sweet of you," she replies. "Go right ahead. We must have walked for hours and I need a bath anyway."

She steps closer to me.

"Just don't be too long. I'm in room 237," she adds before dashing inside the elevator with a fluted laugh. The bell-boy in livery is still looking at me with a knowing smile when the doors shut and she disappears from view.

A few years before, when my parents and I had our serious sex talk, my mother made a simple but non-negotiable request:

"If and when the day should come that you spend the night away from home, you need not secure our permission. The only thing I ask is that you spare us a sleepless night of worry and let us know. We insist upon it."

And so tonight, still marveling at the liberality of my parents' views, I remember my promise and make that call. I'm somewhat apprehensive, though, as if the final test comes here and now, under the gilded chandeliers of this palace. I find a courtesy phone and dial the number. It's a bit late and it seems to go on ringing forever. My mother finally answers.

"Hi, mom! Sorry to call this late. I hope I didn't wake you," I blurt out rather nervously.

"It's quite all right, we were watching a late-night movie. Have you run out of money and can't afford a ride home?" she asks half-mockingly.

"No, mom, not exactly. I just called to say that I wouldn't be coming home tonight."

There is a brief pause at the other end. A silence that feels interminable to me.

"I understand," my mother finally replies. "Well, have a wond.... I mean...I just -"

She pauses again, and then resumes with a slight strain in her voice: "Thanks for remembering to call. Be safe, and we'll see you sometime tomorrow."

I place the receiver into its cradle and walk back precipitously toward the elevator, my heart now racing. And as it whisks me away to the floor above, I feel that a part of me has been left behind forever.

The second floor of the hotel is just as extravagant as the lobby. Regal carpets line the palatial hallways, gently lit by soft fluorescent lights concealed in the moldings. The fragrance of fresh flowers permeates the air as I proceed along the corridor, my own silhouette following me, reflected by a succession of Venetian mirrors. The hotel detective, impeccably dressed in a classic three-piece suit, suddenly materializes beside me.

"Good evening, sir. I believe the room you're looking for is located at the far end to your left. Is there anything else I can do for you?" he asks obsequiously, as if expecting me all night.

I thank him and continue down the hall, a bit startled. I look back once but he vanishes as seamlessly as he appeared. I turn the brass door handle and let myself in. The room is stunning, a medium-size suite with a study attached. The main lights are turned off, and the bedroom bathes in the glow of a massive floor lamp. The drapes are drawn over the French windows and the place seems to shimmer like a soft, inviting retreat. I hear the water being shut off in the bathroom and remove my shoes and socks to rest my feet in the plush carpet. Echoes of Chopin stream from an invisible source. I'm admiring the artwork on the wall when Emily opens the bathroom door. She is wrapped in a white towel with water still dappling her face. Her apparition is both expected and subtle, and I just stand there transfixed by the sweetness of her expression.

"I seem to remember that you prefer baths, so I have drawn you one," she says with a smile. "Come on in. I hope I didn't make the water too hot."

There is a delicious disproportion between her casualness and the fact that I've never disrobed in front of a girl before. The air tingles and yet all of this feels strangely natural.

"Take your time. I'll dry my hair and fix us something to drink," she adds, blowing me a kiss and scampering out of the bathroom.

The hot suds are wonderfully soothing, but I find myself unable to linger in this bath for long. I get out and literally burst into the bedroom. Emily is sitting on the bed, fixing her hair, and as she rises to greet me, I realize she is naked. She stops halfway across the room, silhouetted against the suffused glow of the lamp, and looks at me. I'm in awe of her sylphlike gracefulness. Her skin is very pale, almost silvery-white against the crimson tones of the room. Her hips are fuller than I thought, with finely delineated thighs. I've never seen anyone more beautiful in my life. She walks on over almost hesitantly, water shimmering on her shoulders. The tips of her breasts are so fair they almost disappear into the paleness of her skin. She draws nearer and kisses me. Gently at first, teasing the inside of my mouth, and then by degrees more forcefully, taking possession of my lips as her hands remove my bathrobe, letting it drop to the floor. Emily's kiss is like the embrace of her bare skin, tender, agile and aggressive. I stand there against her, savoring her breath, taking it deep within me, when she takes me by the hand, leading me toward the bed. She pulls back the thick comforter, sending it tumbling onto the floor with surprising ease.

We leap upon the bed, flinging ourselves into the delicate touch of satin sheets with an odd mixture of reserve and abandon. There is a sensuality that speaks only through the eyes, the dizzying sensation of losing oneself in a woman's gaze, suspending for a moment the embrace of her flesh just to look upon her. Emily's eyes no longer reflect their soft bluish hues. Her pupils widen in the shadows and take on a wild, almost ferocious expression. I begin to feast on her body, starting with her silken shoulders, slowly working my way to her breasts. But she takes hold of my head and firmly places my mouth upon her stomach, gradually pushing me down between her hips, luring me further below.

I discover pleasures I never knew, as she lies back upon the bed with her hands like talons in my hair. This is a delectable kiss, more intimate than the touch of her mouth, a sensuous path of unknown appetites and ravenous thirst. She tastes of coriander and musk and I immerse myself into her, as if she were a pool of sweet water in the scorched earth. Little by little, Emily's desire radiates into me, measured out by the tightening grip of her fists upon my hair, the sweet effervescence of her pleasure intruding into my mouth with exquisite impudence.

When I finally raise myself up and over her, glistening with her fragrant sweat, my longing has turned into primal hunger. She slides down closer to me as I take hold of her hips, lifting her off the bed. And I do not know if it is I who penetrate her first, or she who impales herself upon me, but like the hollow of a wave ensnaring a swimmer, her thighs merge us into one, searing my flesh and branding me within her. I struggle to recover my breath. Every part of me dissolves into pleasure, the world being suddenly reduced to the dimensions of this bed.

Words gradually distort into syllables. This is a fire I stoke and yet cannot control, its intensity gaining upon me like an incendiary wave. And as we thrash upon the bed, the mattress cover comes undone and pulls away, revealing the grating surface of the bedding, a sudden contrast of coarse fabric against our skin. From my lips comes a growl I can't repress, just as Emily begins to moan. Her voice is a halting, almost plaintive counterpoint to mine, a modulated and sensuous song of life. It rises and falls in pitch and intensity, reaches an apex and sustains itself in utter abandon, her fingernails clutching my back, lacerating my flesh. My own surrender comes with no such grace, more like the brutality of lightning as it thrusts upon a field.

An hour later, Emily sleeps beside me as we both lie across the ravaged bed. I savor this moment, as if it were unique, trying to prolong its intensity. And I remain there for a while, not daring to move, attentive to the way passion gradually abates and dissolves into contented weariness. Emily's resplendent curves nestle against me like a perfect fit, as the room radiates with warmth and silence, shielding us from the world. But she stirs in her sleep, suddenly grasping my hand and keeping it against her cheek.

I extricate myself from her tender grasp and silently slide off the bed, moved by an insistent thirst. There is champagne left in a crystal glass and though it has lost its chill, it is wonderfully refreshing. I sit naked on the floor, my head against the side of the bed in the glow of the floor lamp, a slow torpor invading me as I struggle to make this moment last. I hear Emily's gentle breathing as she sleeps upon the bed. But I am wearier than I think, and in an effort to take another sip I lose my grip on the glass. It tumbles softly upon the luscious carpet and I watch, mesmerized, as the bubbles disintegrate into the rug. Illuminated by the golden rays of the lamp, the champagne rises into the thick Persian hemp, sparkling through the ancient threads with the ebullience and brevity of love itself.

Emily returned to England a day later. Although both of us were moved to tears when the time came to say goodbye, we remained without illusion as to the future. We shared a memorable weekend in Paris, but our time lay outside of established norms, of relationships, of events past or yet to come. We corresponded for a few months but never saw each other again.

And yet, to this day, Emily's hazy eyes have remained as vivid as her smile in my memory

❧≪

Two months later, my mother catches me daydreaming in the library.

"How would you like to earn some extra money and further your education a bit?" she casually asks. This is the first week of summer break and I really don't feel like doing anything. Besides, my mother's query sounds too chirpy to be entirely innocuous.

"What would it entail?" I reply cautiously, already searching for a reason to decline.

"The hospital needs a part-timer for the next three weeks. The pay isn't too bad, and as a pre-med you would gain a day-to-day exposure to the realities of hospital medicine," she explains.

"Thanks, mom, but no thanks," I reply lazily. "It all sounds too reasonable to be any fun, and I'm not going to empty bedpans for little more than minimum wage. I need a break."

My mother changes strategy.

"Are you still planning to go to Italy in July?" she asks innocently. "You could probably use a little extra cash in your budget. Lunch alfresco in Capri isn't exactly cheap," she adds, driving a wedge into my resolve. "It's entirely up to you, of course, but as an incentive I'm prepared to match everything you'll make."

The look in my eye tells her she's already won.

"OK, then," she muses on her way out. "I'll call Dr. Voynet in administration and you can start on Monday."

Our community hospital serves as a mid-level care facility for the suburban population of Saint-Germain. It boasts an esteemed maternity ward and a competent medical staff, though critical trauma is referred to larger medical centers in Paris. Officially, I've been hired as *brancardier,* or stretcher-bearer, though patients are brought in on wheeled contraptions I only have to push. When my father found out about my summer job at the dinner table, he couldn't resist reminding me that Hitler was once given the same duties in the First World War. I quickly discover why the pay is actually better than minimum wage: I'm expected to work three nights a week, a detail my mother curiously omitted when she described the job.

Still, this is not a demanding task and it does provide a close-up look at the daily routine of a hospital. It is a mixture of bustling daytime activities and the quiet eeriness of darkened corridors at night, both a revealing introduction to the assorted miseries of human life. I spend most of my time in the emergency department, tucked away in a side-room until called for. My lowly position makes me transparent to staff and patients, but I'm saddled with a surly supervisor, Mr. Lenormand, who runs the stretcher department like a taxicab service. Humorless and unfriendly, he disapproved of me from the start. My getting this job is a decision handed down to him from on high, without his being consulted. This is demeaning to his pride and authority, as if his profession were trivialized by the fact that I can fulfill my obligations without prior training.

"Just a snobby college student," he retorts when asked about me. "One of the doctors' kids pretending to work for the summer. He'll quit before the end of the week." Gaunt and wiry, he is unsuspectingly strong, picking up patients twice his size. When on break, he spends his time sitting at a table across from the holding room, chewing on celery stalks and totally absorbed in a thick yellow book, *The Dangers of Sex-Education in Schools.* Some of the ER doctors know my mother and at times allow me to remain in the treatment area. Life is fairly dull in an emergency room, hours of inactive boredom punctuated by surges of instant, tightly focused activity. I sit back out of everybody's way, watching physicians and nurses work with precipitous calm, as the clock on the wall ticks away, orchestrating the shuffling of their shoes upon the green linoleum floor.

One of the younger doctors has taken me under his wing. A fourth-year surgical resident from the prestigious Cochin hospital in

Paris, Dr. N'Doumbé is originally from Cameroon. According to my mom, some of the senior physicians are a bit ruffled at the sight of this tall, good-humored African, the first black surgeon ever to practice in this hospital.

"Yes, I know," he remarks with a smile of resignation. "Older physicians on the staff would be more comfortable if I were relegated to the traditional role of orderly. At least, once in a while, they could indulge in the sort of condescending kindness that passes for liberality."

He is kind and patient, and sectarian comments once made behind his back were quickly stifled by the expertise of his surgical skills. I like the way he sometimes orders me to prep and mask and sit next to him as he cleans and sutures a patient's wound. I'm grateful for the privilege.

"It's quite all right," he is fond of saying. "I'm trying to influence you, so that after medical school you might choose surgery as a specialty. And besides," he adds with a chuckle, deepening his sonorous baritone, "who could have predicted that the nephew of a white colonialist would one day be taught by Dr. N'Doumbé, the son of a plantation worker?"

The premature unit is located on the fifth floor of the maternity ward, directly above the delivery rooms. Lately, at the end of my evening shift, I've been finding excuses to visit the ward. My interest is neither clinical nor humanitarian, but rather motivated by the presence of nursing aides whose youthfulness brightens the dreariness of the place. One of them smiled at my white coat the first time we met, but when told of my professional insignificance, she proceeded to ignore me.

It is almost midnight when I step out of the service elevator and make my way through the restricted area. With its heat lamps, cumbersome incubators and the glow of ultraviolet lights, the premature unit has the odd appearance of a greenhouse, an isolated laboratory growing fragile and exotic flowers. Tonight the ward is quieter than usual. All the way at the back of the room, three girls are hovering over an incubator. My arrival briefly startles them before they return their attention to the problem confronting them.

"Are you sure he's dead," one of the nursing aides asks, visibly troubled.

"I believe so," answers the other. "He's been unresponsive for over an hour and I can't get a pulse or a breath sound."

I draw nearer. The small, motionless body of a premature baby lies on his back upon a thin yellow mat. Through one of the openings in the incubator, the aide passes the bell of a stethoscope, pressing it against the baby's chest. Most of the staff has gone home. The attending nurse is out of her depth, but stubbornly refuses to buzz the ER or consult the pediatrician on call.

"The baby was doing very poorly all day," she tries to explain, "and when she left, Dr. Langlois said she'd be surprised if he lasted the night. I think he was dead before I came on duty."

There is something surreal about all this. I get closer to the glass, and the three girls are now desperate enough to look upon me as if I could be of help. I don't know how I dare do this, but I put on a pair of gloves and a mask and remove the top of the incubator to reach inside. I gently prod the little body but to no avail. Then I take a deep breath and slowly turn him over on his stomach. The skin on his back is marbled with yellow and purple streaks. Death has already sunk its teeth into his tender flesh.

I draw back and take myself out of the picture. As if suddenly set free of their apathy, the girls go into a flurry of phone calls, filling out forms and ledgers without apparent emotion. I'm struck by the casualness of it all, the pitiful reality of this lifeless form and the glaring incompetence of the staff.

The night nurse finally gets off the phone.

"Dr. Bertrand says to just take the body to the morgue," she directs the other two with regained assurance. "The pathologist will want to do a post-mortem tomorrow. One of you will have to take him there, because that place gives me the creeps at night."

The girls look at each other as if they're about to draw lots. I'm not sure why, but I step forward and volunteer.

"My shift is over, but I've already wheeled three bodies to pathology this week. I know the way and I don't mind."

They seem relieved and place in my arms the dead baby, swaddled in thin white cloth like a mummy. I can't wait to take him out of this place, so I leave without looking at them, sadness and contempt in my heart.

I take the service elevator to the basement of the hospital and follow the utility tunnel to the morgue, a destination of cold antiseptic darkness behind shining metal doors. Pipes and conduits hang alongside the walls, dripping with humidity like the sweat of the earth. Amber lights pass over my head at regular intervals. There isn't a sound except the hiss of scalding steam coursing through the insulated pipes. And as my steps echo in the tunnel, I feel an odd sensation that I am not alone. I walk on with the little corpse nestled against my chest, its lingering warmth permeating the cloth as if it were passing into me.

Eight

TWO YEARS HAVE passed, a whirlwind of activity punctuated by brief intervals of lassitude and stillness. Except for family vacations and an occasional diversion, that time was largely devoted to academic pursuits. The career goals I had set for myself, and the compelling drive to excel at the Louis XIII Institute, convinced me to study with an intensity and application I had never known. I was hardly alone in this headlong pursuit of success. My classmates, like fellow runners scratching at my heels, provided relentless motivation as I gradually turned into something of a nerd. I reached the top of my class with a near-perfect GPA and didn't intend to budge from this vantage point.

Even my own family found this metamorphosis difficult to accept. It was radical enough for my mother to arrange a few Sunday afternoon talks between me and an old friend of hers: the renowned Dr. Sliosberg, at the time chief of behavioral medicine at the hospital. She became concerned about the compulsive nature of my academic life, as if the steadfastness of my efforts concealed some sort of burgeoning personality disorder. The eminent scholar was a decent man with a wicked sense of humor and a predilection for Asian women. He alleviated my mother's concerns by pronouncing me mentally fit, with a healthy dose of obsessive-compulsive behavior.

It should not be construed that my devotion to academic pursuits had pushed my life into the shadows of asceticism. I remember Christiane who was a year ahead of me. Because of our differences in age and rank, we were not competing against each other, at least not academically. We shared a fascination for fencing and it provided us with a different sort of battleground. Both of us favored the epee, the weapon of choice for blending swordsmanship and athletic abilities. We would meet at the university club late in the evening when the place was deserted. Fencing is one of the few forms of combat in which a woman can defeat a male opponent regardless of his strength or size. In a dexterous hand, the sword becomes an uncompromising equalizer. We started out in regulation uniforms, the electronic arbitration system keeping count of the hits. But soon, masks and jackets became incidental as we traveled back in time when duels occurred daily on the streets of Paris, steel and skill leaving blood on the cobblestones.

It was obvious from the start that neither of us would let the other win, either out of deference or courtesy. Our bouts were fierce, as we both took this competition quite personally. In time, we got rid of the electric timers and disconnected the wires tethering us to the arbitration system, preferring to continue outside the perimeter and in complete disregard of the rules. We were well-matched, but she enjoyed a slight advantage, winning about fifty-five per cent of our duels.

One night we lingered past closing hours and were left on our own, with instructions to switch off the lights and lock the doors on our way out. I recall Christiane finally removing her mask an hour later, shaking off the sweat glistening in her hair under the glaring mercury lights. We called it a draw and left the smooth parquetry of the court, both worn out but exhilarated. She didn't proceed to the women's dressing room but followed me instead into the men's quarters. I sat on the narrow bench between rows of steel cabinets as she took off her shoes and socks. I looked at her and didn't move, uncertain of her intentions. Silently she unfastened the padded vest protecting her against the blunted tip of our blades, and then casually removed it with a graceful and seamless gesture. The uniform had artfully concealed the voluptuousness of her breasts, and I just sat there as she took off the rest of her clothes. She had narrow hips, with endless thighs chiseled to lustrous perfection. Christiane proceeded to the showers, ripping down the plastic curtain standing in her way.

We ended up in the stalls, water hammering our skin like torrential rain, her hands and body mauling me across the uneven tiles of the floor. It proved brutish and intoxicating, as if it were an extension of our fencing bouts. We didn't become friends, but enjoyed a few more encounters before returning to the obsession of academic pursuits. I can't recall ever kissing her.

The approaching reality of summer, with its inexorable schedule of exams, gripped the senior class in a frenzy, hurtling us into one last rush to succeed, like tired horses catching a scent of the stables in the distance. I graduated with honors, a year ahead of schedule, but not as valedictorian. I finished third, my own disappointment unable to dim my parents' pride, and at the end of June I registered at the School of Medicine. Congratulated by family and friends, I rode a sweet wave through the rest of the summer, feeling invincible, as if I could do no wrong. My father rewarded me with a vacation of my own choosing. In some traditional quarters, a journey through the capitals of Europe was still seen as the proper conclusion to a young man's education. But to my dad's surprise, I opted for quite a different destination and went on a two-week discovery of the Soviet Union.

In the 1960s, Russia still loomed in the popular imagination as a great unknown. For most of us, Moscow and Leningrad conjured up all the clichés of cold war novels and Bond movies. I don't really know why I made that particular choice, and though I ended up missing the nightlife of London and the charm of Venice, I also experienced for the first time a most radical sense of alienation. We took off from Orly airport in a rudimentary Aeroflot jet, herded by Soviet stewardesses as attractive as Rosa Klebb. The cabin pressure had only been set to military standards, and it drove corkscrews into the passengers' ears once we started our descent towards Moscow. We spent the next fourteen days sightseeing in small groups, whispering everywhere, tiptoeing across a landscape as cheerless as if it had been painted from faded photographs, trying our best to ingurgitate the most dismal food. Our sense of constant foreboding turned into paranoia when we learned of the Red army's invasion of Czechoslovakia, just as we reached Leningrad. I still recall the malodorous commodes of the

Metropole Hotel, clogged by indigestible Russian newspapers. Cut up in squares, the morning edition of Pravda was distributed to every guest because of a shortage of toilet paper.

The people in the street were kind and hospitable, going out of their way to help, apparently resigned to this regimented despair. It was as if I had stepped through a time portal, transported to a bleak reconstruction of Europe during the great depression. There wasn't much to do outside the activities orchestrated by the state tourist authority, so I decided one afternoon to set out on my own and pay a visit to the local zoo. I have a predilection for botanical gardens and zoos, because I'm convinced that the preservation of wildlife within an urban setting becomes a symbolic microcosm of society. The Paris zoo is a study in Cartesian planning and Gallic inefficiency, while the London botanical gardens stand as a celebration of civility and neurotic restraint. The Moscow zoo, with its pink rock castle entrance on Gruzinskaya Street, was a faithful mirror of the unimaginative environment from which it sprang. Deserted and dreary, the place seemed to shroud its visitors in inescapable doom. I was greeted by a once magnificent polar bear, slouched in a cage and stripped of lethal imperiousness. It had wedged its massive nose between the iron bars, a stream of breath filtering into the open air, as if it could distill itself out of this prison.

A week later, when I finally landed back in Paris, even the ill-mannered frown of the French police felt like a ray of sunshine.

※

The first semester of medical school proves a rude awakening to those who don't know the meaning of hard work. I discover a level of studying and a vastness of material to absorb I never imagined. The six-year program blends premed with the four-year curriculum of an American medical education, and a viciously selective exam awaits at the end of the first year, with a failing rate exceeding sixty per cent. Grades and test preparation become an overriding obsession, with social life coming to a standstill and every parcel of energy dedicated to the pursuit of academic success. By All Saints' Day the bustling life of Paris has become an impediment to preparing for exams, so my great-uncle invites me to spend the upcoming vacation in isolated study at his estate in Savoie. There, in the chilling silence of late autumn, the Alps become the ultimate refuge.

My room looks out onto the orchards covering the hills like a tapestry of pear-trees laid out in espaliers. Now bereft of their gold and green foliage, they stand in the distance like thousands of dark Menorahs, their tufted ears sinking in the morning haze. A quiet peace reigns over this place where I was born and later returned for summer vacation. I still treasure memories of carefree evenings in hammocks, lazily stretched across the sprawling verandas, and the taste of bergamot ice cream as the sun set behind the walls of the park. I never realized back then how it would all shape my preferences for particular colors and hues.

The vast wrap-around porches were painted in resplendent white enamel, and on sunny afternoons I would watch the sunlight disintegrate upon the wood with such brilliance as to make me wince. I just sat on the lawn, feasting my eyes upon the immaculate porch and the way it stood against the crisp yellow leaves of the silver birch. At the age of five, I noticed subtle changes when sunlight played upon the house. Around seven o'clock, the limpid clarity of the wood began to fade in the gathering dusk. Purple shadows and a sort of grayish sheen came creeping in under the veranda, stretching tentacles against the alabaster purity of the columns. This slow transformation worried me, for I was never sure if my favorite spot would recover from such a change. And I recall running back to the porch the next day after breakfast, and the smile coming to me as I rubbed my hand against the restored luminescence of the wood, bursting back to life in the morning sun.

The past slowly ordains our predilection for tastes, scents and colors. It took me years to appreciate why much later, thousands of miles from this place, I became drawn to a particular spot on the lawn of the University of Virginia. There I would sit with a smile on my face, inexplicably charmed at the sight of the Rotunda, its gleaming white colonnades against the purest sky, leaves billowing in dazzling shades of yellow.

And tonight, as I struggle to absorb reams of anatomical drawings, memories return to the stillness of this room and populate empty hallways with the sound of running feet, bringing back echoes of children's voices outside my window. Though I spent much of my childhood in this privileged enclave, shielded from the rest of the world, it is also here that I first became acquainted with death.

My great-aunt had a heart condition which she concealed from everyone save her chambermaid who had been sworn to secrecy. She secured her silence by explaining that this diagnosis, with its regimen of medications and restrictions of all sorts, was simply incompatible with her lifestyle. She went on offering her friends and acquaintances a façade of dignified maturity, indulging her cigarettes, foie gras and nightlife unreservedly. Death came swiftly one July morning, arresting her heart and drowning her in the pool. In those days funeral parlors didn't exist in France, since the very thought of entrusting to strangers the care of the dead would have seemed indelicate. As was the custom, my great-aunt was laid out in state in one of the drawing-rooms on the first floor. She wore a regal dress and lay there, almost shrunken amid the flowers cradling her in multicolored rows. I remember the mixture of dread and awe that came upon me and my sisters as we were ushered into the room. In the oppressive thickness of the air, I stood in front of a catafalque looking like a scene from *Sleeping Beauty*, disturbed that I felt no sorrow. How do you behave as a boy in a roomful of distraught adults when you do not share in their grief? I liked my great-aunt, but all I could do was repress the thought that her death might shorten our summer vacation. Kneeling on the prie-dieu, I looked surreptitiously at my sisters for guidance: they both seemed genuinely affected, and I thought of myself as a cold-hearted, unfeeling monster. I loved my great-uncle, and feared him too. So as an attempt to atone for my selfishness, I spent the next two days shedding the most abundant and insincere public tears I had ever cried.

The funeral was but a prelude to a gradual discovery of the fragility of life. The estate had originally been acquired for leisure and vacation, but my great-uncle found it impossible to remain idle during the summer months he traditionally spent in France. The orchard surrounding the mansion rapidly multiplied and prospered into a veritable sea of apple and pear trees covering the adjacent hills. What had begun as a hobby, a remedy against wasteful inactivity, turned into the most prosperous agricultural venture in the region. Buildings sprang to accommodate the sprawling enterprise, along with houses for hired farmhands dotting the landscape like a company town. Cavernous hangars were built to store a harvest sold as far as Italy. As a child, I loved the scent emanating from the warehouse in August: intoxicating fragrances of Anjou pears and Fuji apples hanging like a mist in the warm summer air. Half the production was processed as apple juice, which my sister and I drank liberally from the press, our tennis shoes stuck to the sugar glistening on the cider house floor.

There was one building I particularly liked: a tall, six-storied structure without walls where crates lay like rows of dominoes, three hundred feet deep and twenty feet high. I was strictly prohibited from entering this area and yet regularly broke the rule, wandering off after dinner to the aromatic stillness of the storerooms. An industrial crane reached into each level and maneuvered blocks of a hundred crates at a time like a monstrous praying mantis building a nest.

A couple of tall ladders extended from the ground to the third floor of the open building. The temptation proved so irresistible that I climbed up there, and perched in a niche among the stacked up crates, enjoying my sister's favorite caramels. After a while I got up and walked to the ledge that looked out onto the alley. I thought it quite entertaining to push one of the ladders off and send it flying against the wall of the next building. Had my great-uncle caught me in the act, I would have qualified for a memorable spanking, my eleven years of age notwithstanding.

But I was alone.

The intended mischief was not in itself particularly nefarious, but it rested on a disastrous ignorance of physics. The energy needed to push the ladder away required more strength than I thought. Unaware of the danger, I stepped up to the ledge and began shoving the ladder. It started to move like an oscillating pendulum, bouncing back each time with a little more force, gaining enough momentum to escape my reach. After one last effort the ladder flexed, arched and fell away. But the swaying motion carried me too far from the ledge and I lost my balance, slipping off an invisible tightrope onto the concrete sixty feet below.

How many people have died in this manner? From bored construction workers to reckless teenagers, it was a fairly inept way to exit this life prematurely. I remember fragments of time whistling by as my body vacillated, arms thrashing through the air. But the breath of Providence emerged from the night like a sudden breeze blowing on a wisp. I regained my balance and fell back to the safety of the ledge. Scurrying down the other ladder, I ran to my room and lay in the dark, waiting for my legs to stop shaking.

To this day my great-uncle's magnificent house remains in my memory a blend of origins and finality, the place where I nearly joined my ancestors in the family crypt at the age of thirteen. As I entered my teenage years, I became fascinated with cars, motorbikes and the enjoyment of pure speed. My actual experience was limited to the excitement of a ten-speed bike, and that summer a formidable object gripped my imagination: a bright red Moped sometimes used by the kitchen staff. It may not have been a Harley, but it was a forbidden fruit well within my grasp, shining with all the tempting power of its polished chrome. Easy to start and operate, it reached the awesome speed of 35 mph.

And there it stood all day, idle and unappreciated in a corner of the garage, like a race horse shimmering in a stall. I approached my parents, careful not to display the sort of enthusiasm which always seems to elicit negative responses from adults. I casually remarked that I had already operated a Moped in Paris, in the alleys of a park with older kids. But my mother's verdict fell like a cleaver on a block: it was illegal to ride a motorized bike until I reached the age of fourteen. End of story. I knew that just as well as she did, so I decided to go behind her back and lay siege to my great-uncle's patience, pleading my case for an exception to be made. The law could not to be circumvented, but, I argued, traffic regulations only applied to public thoroughfares. As long as the Moped was operated on the private roadways of the estate, it was as lawful as it was safe. Perhaps my great-uncle's legal background appreciated the case I was trying to build. He looked at me and said:

"If you exercise caution and agree not to leave the park, I see no reason why you shouldn't enjoy yourself."

No one else knew of this stratagem, and my dad had returned to Paris the night before. So I spent the next three mornings building an exemplary record of responsible riding, that is until my mother discovered what I had been up to. We were at the pool. She turned to me with a look of irritation in her eyes, but the searing July sun, the magnolias rustling about us and a delectable Tahitian punch wore down her resolve and she reluctantly agreed. I had won. I was free.

For an entire week, I diligently abided by my great-uncle's injunction and remained on the long sandy alleys of the estate. But soon they became too familiar and repetitive and I found myself at the massive iron gate, peering enviously at the asphalt unraveling into the distance. The lure of the open road proved irresistible to my fragile sense of discipline. I longed to discover the surrounding county and found a willing accomplice in my forbidden explorations: Floriant, the son of a tenant farmer. He was almost fifteen and owned a sleek Mobylette. We began to spend the afternoon together, riding through the countryside. For a kid used to a ten-speed bike, 35 mph felt like sheer exhilaration. But I knew nothing of traffic laws and began throwing caution to the wind. Racing against Floriant on narrow country roads became an addictive pastime, while my family imagined me safely puttering along through the orchards.

It was a sunny afternoon as we ventured beyond the hydroelectric plant. With my friend close behind me, I leaned into the endless curve of a deserted road, unaware that it led directly to a T-Shaped intersection. I couldn't see over the thick hedges bordering the road and I sped on, hypnotized by the dizzying proximity of the asphalt. A yield sign flashed into view, but too late. From my left, a car sliced through the intersection like a shadow closing fast upon me. It was a Citroën Traction Avant. The massive sedan had for a generation reigned as the vehicle of choice for both Parisian gangsters and the French police. Over the noise of the engine I heard Floriant yelling something, but as I turned to look at him, the car sprang forth like a viper out of its lair.

Today it seems odd how my brain recalls only in slow motion such a rapid succession of events. The Citroën met me in the intersection at 60 mph. I wasn't even upright on the Moped, still leaning out of the curve, so I should have been run over and killed instantly. But somewhere beyond Eden and Sheol, where beginnings and ends are grasped in a single glance, it had been decided otherwise. The massive front end of the sedan swatted the bike with such violence that it bent the frame to a forty-five degree angle, throwing me like a rag doll ten feet into the air. The Traction Avant possessed a narrow, elongated windshield more suited for an armored vehicle than a family car. I came down head first and impacted the glass just one inch above the metal rim. Bouncing off the hood, I was flung past the passenger's side and dragged two hundred feet before the car came to a stop.

Floriant later gave a detailed description of the accident, but my own recollection consists of still frames stripped of any notion of time. I remember lying face down on the asphalt, slowly moving on all four in search of my glasses. For some reason, finding them became the only thing that mattered to me as I kept picking up my hands, trying to escape the scalding surface of the pavement. I never found my glasses because my hair kept falling into my eyes, obstructing everything. I stopped and tried once more to brush it aside, but could not. Then the sky went dark. Only later did I realize that I had a crew cut and couldn't possibly be hindered by hair falling in my eyes. In fact, I was hemorrhaging from two gashes on my head, the blood pouring down my face and blinding me.

Floriant sat next to me, looking very pale. I saw his lips move as if he were talking, though I couldn't hear a sound or feel any pain. I never saw the driver; after the collision, he remained slumped at the wheel with a broken collar bone. A passing car slowed down, its driver soon speeding off to call for help. I remained lying in the road, the summer heat raining down on me, intrusive, relentless, with the song of cicadas all around, so shrill it could have petrified the air shimmering over the asphalt.

I will never know the identity of my savior, the Good Samaritan who stopped and came over to us. Breaching all protocols, he picked me up and carried me to his car. I lost consciousness as he laid me down across the back seat. At some point I came around, wondering where I was, intrigued by the blood splattered over the seat, smearing the fabric and slowly dripping onto the floor mats. The driver stormed through the gates of the small hospital in Albertville, and as nurses and orderlies rushed me inside on a stretcher, he got back into his car and drove off without a word. For weeks my family tried to find him. Later I became fascinated by my mysterious rescuer, attributing to him fantastical powers to explain his selfless discretion. I concluded he was either a spy or an outlaw on the run who couldn't risk being identified.

Alerted by Floriant's family, my mother and great-uncle had left the house precipitously and hurried toward town. The community hospital lay at the foot of a mountain range. My mother knew it well. Ironically, I had been born there, on the second floor, thirteen years earlier. The surgeon on call was a temporary replacement, a retired colonel doing a weekend favor for his nephew. He stopped the hemorrhage and left thirty-seven stitches in my head, but when my mother burst inside the recovery room, she wasn't too reassured by what she saw. On a Sunday in August, the X-ray department was closed. The radiologist had the only key, and that afternoon, chancing that no one would need his services, he had gone fishing. There were no cell phones back then, so his wife and kids proceeded to track him down through all his favorite spots along the river. No one could tell with complete assurance whether I had suffered a skull fracture, and my mother grew restless by the minute, debating the merits of a transfer to the university hospital in Grenoble, only an hour away. The radiologist finally came in discreetly through a side-door, and I was wheeled off to X-rays, the bright neon lights in the corridor passing over my head and stabbing me in the eyes. There was no fracture after all, only a severe concussion, but they kept me under observation for a week. My mother camped in my room, checking vital signs day and night, worried about a subdural hematoma and neurological sequelae.

I stayed at my great uncle's for another two weeks of convalescence. The only benefit I ever reaped from the accident was an exemption from PE that lasted an entire year. I never again rode a Moped, and to this day have declined every offer to experience the pleasures of motorbikes. But bizarre dizzy spells and twitches persisted on and off for months. When I finally consulted a neurosurgeon in Paris, he examined me and burst out laughing.

"I haven't seen this sort of surgical care since the field hospitals of World War II. In fact," he added, trying his best to remain serious, "the stitching in your scalp is reminiscent of techniques used in veterinary medicine. The edges of the wound were so poorly approximated that some of your hair follicles have grown inward under the skin...Still," he concluded with an indulgent smile, "that old drunk probably saved your life."

❧

My parents have broken out a bottle of Château Haut-Brion 1955 to celebrate my midterm grades, and my father informs me that he's found a studio in the Rue de Rivoli where I can move in by Christmas. I walk around the house with a smile on my face, numbed by the glow of this fabulous Bordeaux and the sweet prospect of independence, when my eyes notice the letter waiting for me in the entranceway. The handwriting is familiar, and yet I can't immediately recognize it. Looking at the back of the envelope, the elegant and imperious scrawl reveals Michelle's name. I'm shocked, not having heard from her for over two years. Her motherly condescendence and the power differential she wished to preserve between us had eroded my interest.

Michelle's letter has been mailed from Paris, yet I recall her adamant oath never to return to France. I tear through the envelope and read. She now lives in an apartment near Montmartre and teaches English literature while finishing her dissertation. The tone of her letter is rather sweet, even a bit seductive, wondering what has become of me and extending an invitation to catch up with each other's lives. I call the number she left under her signature. Our conversation is awkward but pleasant; Michelle's voice is readily familiar, while she struggles a bit to recognize my own. We decide to meet next Saturday for dinner at her place. I feel a bit odd after hanging up. Part of me remains curious and excited, remembering her rapturous kiss, but the other is also puzzled. I'm no longer intimidated, the intervening years having closed the gap that once stood between us. I feel confident, thrilled even, with the insidious thought of possessing her at last, and not as an adoring adolescent, but this time ravishing her against a wall. This is uncharacteristic of me, a compensating mechanism to atone for my once ardent and unsuccessful worship. When Saturday evening finally comes, I have grown so casual that I don't even dress up for the occasion.

A cold drizzle clutches me as I emerge from the warm subway. Montmartre still remains an odd mixture of crass commercialism and undeniable nostalgia, a refuge to artists and prostitutes. In a jarring contrast between lust and spirituality, the basilica of the Sacred-Heart shines high above the garish neon of the red light district. Michelle's flat is located on an unassuming back street, sheltered behind oaks and a quiet courtyard. I pause for a moment after reaching the third floor, standing at her door with something like stage fright tempered by lust. I ring the bell and Michelle opens, welcoming me with a kiss on the cheek. She's still the same, with that aura of mystery about her, a smile like sweet sorrow over those perfect lips. She looks upon me with amused inquisitiveness.

"You've changed quite a bit," she finally decrees – "for the better, I mean."

"And what's so different about me?" I enquire.

"You're taller, with broader shoulders too," she replies, "but it's not so much that. Your eyes are not the same."

"Is something the matter with them?" I ask, intrigued by this cryptic pronouncement.

"They've seen the wolf," she adds with a grin, "Something in the way you're looking at me. I should have known you wouldn't remain ingenuous – a pity."

The apartment is luminous but rather Spartan, with low Japanese tables, floor lamps and large black and white photographs framed on the bare walls. Michelle adopts an amiable tone, and I detect none of the residual sensuousness which in arrogance I expected from a woman whose intimacy I once shared. We talk freely as night settles upon the square, the glittering life of Montmartre mirrored in the window panes. At her request, I recount what has passed in the last two years. I gloss over personal relationships, the scarcity of information eliciting a faint but knowing smile from her. I linger on my family and the first year in medical school. Silhouetted against the pale background of the opposite wall, Michelle loses some of the mythical presence my youthfulness once imparted to her, as if my mind is now furiously updating all the memories I had kept.

For the first time she tells me of her past, delving in matters of a personal nature with disarming honesty.

"I never told you anything in London," she says almost contritely. "You were too young, and frankly I chose to maintain between us a certain distance to discourage your sweet infatuation. I had arrived in England under conditions more inglorious than your own. You hadn't a clue back then, but I too was running away, though for quite a different reason. I lived in Le Havre, a port city whose boredom and ugliness are only matched by the mediocrity of its middle-class aspirations. I was engaged to a good-looking and very decent man, the crusading district attorney, fifteen years older than me. A marriage of convenience arranged by my parents, and tolerated by me with the obedience of a sow resigned to the butcher's knife. The wedding was to be a magnificent affair in the church of Saint-Joseph, decked out for the occasion with all the trappings of a padded snare."

Michelle pauses, as if she can see it all too clearly, but when she continues, her voice is steady and devoid of self-pity.

"I don't quite know how I found the strength, or the madness, to do this. But as I sat in the sacristy, waiting for the bridesmaids to come in, I suddenly came to a decision. I got up, scribbled a few lines on the back of a seating card, and disappeared through a side-door. I fled in my wedding gown, flagging a taxi and running up the stairs to my apartment. Though I hadn't planned for any of this, I was stunned how controlled and unemotional I remained. Taking the suitcase my mother had packed for our honeymoon, I changed and went straight to the harbor, catching the afternoon ferry for Folkestone. I left behind a humiliated man, two hundred guests in the pews and a family so devastated we're still not speaking."

I'm stunned by this account, my mental image of Michelle going through a complete metamorphosis, taking on an alluring veneer I never anticipated.

"It remains one of the better-known scandals in the history of Le Havre," she goes on, "a city stifled by etiquette and traditionalism. The letter I sent a few days later cleared up any misunderstanding, and gave my ex-fiancé the evidence he needed to secure the commiseration of all."

"What do you mean by *evidence?*" I ask, mesmerized by this unraveling tale.

Michelle looks at me with a quizzical grin, like an older sister about to expose the Tooth Fairy.

"The same sort of evidence I withheld the night I refused to make love with you," she answers softly, her words now as prudent as if the air between us had become brittle. Michelle's gaze is fixed upon me, her almond-shaped eyes free of hesitation. And in the silence, things begin to coalesce like ice cubes melting to the bottom of a glass.

I keep searching for a hint of a smile in her face but cannot find any. I'm on my own. My eyes go from the window to the sofa and back to her. They scan the room, lingering on a jewelry box gleaming of lacquer and precious wood, before settling on the portraits against the walls. I recognize Gertrude Stein, Frida Khalo and Marlene Dietrich.

"Yes, I've always been drawn to the beauty of women," Michelle adds almost casually, tipping the ashes from her gold-tipped Sobranie, an expensive habit she acquired in London.

And with brutal simplicity, it all comes crashing down in my head. I can't tell if I'm just overwhelmed by the truth or embarrassed by my lack of perceptiveness, as the veil is finally drawn aside. None of this alters the attraction I have always felt for her. Indeed, in a manner I don't quite comprehend, the revelation of her Sapphic affinities exacerbates my desire. But I feel cheated, as if my teenage infatuation has suddenly run aground.

Michelle senses the rush of conflicting emotions assailing me and comes to sit by my side.

"What could I possibly have said, back then, to a kid with stars in his eyes, lost and hungry on the streets of London? Forgive me for not telling you the truth, but I don't think it would have helped. And if it makes any difference," she adds with a smile, "I didn't force myself to please you that night. I'm not bisexual, but I did enjoy what passed between us. You were still undefiled and your androgynous teenage skin tasted sweet. I thought you should know."

She cradles my chin in her hand, the way she used to, and gives me a taste of her lips, a reminder of the sensuousness she once inundated in my veins. Michelle sits there, desirable and forbidden all at once, unsettling as the eyes of a young nun glimpsed under her veil. When we part later that night, there is neither judgment nor regret between us. We make plans to meet again, but I know it will never happen. I walk absentmindedly through the streets of Montmartre trying to find the metro. Mixed emotions buzz around my head, awakening memories now re-enacted with a different feel and context. My recollections of London are passing through a sieve, never to feel quite the same again. I reach the Place Pigalle and the vulgar neon of its porn shops. The subway entrance, with its art deco iron gate, beckons me like an escape hatch cut into the pavement.

"How about it, handsome?"

The young hooker's voice startles me out of my reverie. She comes from the shadows of the stairs and stands in front of me, dreadfully thin, her silver make-up and glitter more suitable for a children's party. I quicken my pace and vanish into the enameled corridors of the Metro.

❧ ❧

Clinical rounds are the most interesting part of my schedule. The curriculum for the first two semesters is limited to basic sciences and anatomy. However, with a view to initiate us to the actual practice of medicine, we are required to log in ten hours a week as observers in the various wards of the teaching hospital. Our white coats make us look like physicians and help conceal our ignorance. Shadowed by residents who take us under their wings, we're encouraged to ask questions, sitting in on physical examinations or observing surgical procedures from the glassed-in deck of the OR. But in the relentless bustle of this medical hive, with hundreds of patients ambling about and threatening to overwhelm the resources of the hospital, we are drawn in deeper than expected. Nurses and doctors use us for just about any menial job that comes along. Some days, we matter even less than the maintenance crew, wheeling patients to X-rays, cleaning human waste from the floor, alternately cajoled and berated by everyone on the staff. But there are unexpected compensations, like an invitation to listen to the sound of mitral stenosis, or spending half an hour perched on a stool, watching a breech presentation in the delivery room. At times our desire to participate more fully in our environment is granted beyond our wishes, as happened two weeks ago while I sneaked into the surgeons' lounge in search of an Orangina.

"Du Plessis, I need you in here!" a resident calls from one of the examining rooms, before pulling me aside in the corridor. "I've just been called upstairs for a surgical consult. Every nurse and LPN on this ward is busy, and someone needs to stay with a patient for about twenty minutes until I get back." She sees the look of panic on my face. "Listen, you don't need to do a thing. I've already examined her and she's in no imminent danger. Just stand in there as a warm body."

"But I don't know anything. How could I possibly be of assistance?" I reply, trying to distance myself from this sudden intrusion into reality.

"Look at me," the resident continues calmly. She could simply bark an order and get me to do her bidding, but instead takes the time to explain without condescension. "You have two assets you're not aware of," she says, "the white coat you're wearing and the fact that the patient doesn't know you. Now take a look." And she silently pulls the curtain aside.

The room is bathed in subdued bluish tones. On the examining table a young woman lies with her eyes closed. She moans incessantly, her face glistening with sweat, arms quivering as if she were laughing.

"I can't help you. Please don't leave me alone with her," I beg the resident.

"Get a hold of yourself," she replies. "Your presence alone can help, and you've heard of the placebo effect of a white coat. A simple act of kindness in this place can work wonders, so get in there, sit by the table and hold her hand."

"But what if she's dying or something," I retort, reaching for any excuse to get out of this situation. "What if she's suffering from...a *surgical abdomen?*" I blurt out, using a term I heard in the emergency room. Again, the resident's patience overrides her mounting exasperation at being lectured by a first-year student.

"*A surgical abdomen*, eh? That wouldn't necessarily be an erroneous diagnosis," she answers, "but this patient doesn't fit the profile, at least not at this stage. We're waiting on her lab work, but I have a hunch this case is more psychosomatic than surgical."

"How can you be sure?" I ask, "I mean, she looks like she's really in pain."

"Let me explain something," the resident replies. She switches to a more professional and detached demeanor, but the kindness in her eyes doesn't waver. "Her medical history is unrevealing. Vitals are normal. There is no sign of inflammation, trauma or internal bleeding. Patients presenting with a surgical abdomen often experience deep visceral pain. They'll lie still, trying not to move their peritoneum, taking shallow breaths from the lungs, not speaking very much. Now take a look at her: she's nearly hysterical. Observe how she breathes from her abdomen, thrashing about and shouting. I could be wrong, of course, but thus far nothing in this case is suggestive of a surgical emergency. Now get in there and keep her company until I return."

And as I cautiously step into the cubicle, she turns around and whispers "Of course, if her abdomen were suddenly to rupture and splatter internal organs all over the walls, you might want to buzz the head nurse."

I sit next to the woman writhing in pain and introduce myself. She opens her eyes and acknowledges my presence by sitting up. I put on a soothing voice and enjoin her to remain calm until the surgeon has returned. Then I ask her name, but she just falls back on the examining table and continues to moan in anguish. I take her hand, and she instantly grabs mine with all the strength of despair. Above us, a fan slowly churns the antiseptic warmth of the room, the amplitude of her cries remaining steady as I sit on my stool, useless and embarrassed. But if there is little I can do to alleviate her pain, she in turn is teaching me something. I thought of myself as a compassionate and patient individual, interested in medicine because of a deep-seated desire to serve others. Yet in the span of fifteen minutes, as the patient's cries do not abate, I sense a surge of exasperation taking over me. To my dismay, I don't react to her visible torment with patience and kindness but try instead to stifle a thought forming in my head. It's a firm and angry "Will you shut the hell up?" silently directed at her sobbing despair. Dr. Schweitzer I'm not. When the resident finally returns, I feel unworthy of the opportunity she gave me and horrified by my selfishness. I evade her scrutinizing gaze and hurry out of the room, but she catches up with me, gently placing her hand on my arm.

"Don't be too hard on yourself," she says with a tired smile. "You did just fine. Compassion comes from the heart, but true empathy takes time. It is something learned, usually at the expense of our pride."

Today my fellow students and I casually stroll through the revolving doors of the hospital. We're wearing bow ties, white coats impeccably pressed and stethoscopes casually slung around our neck. We feel invincible, cool enough to impress at least some of the newer nurses, but we are stopped in our tracks before reaching the elevators. Professor Chardin, the dreaded chief of medicine, has intercepted our cavalcade and gathers us to attention in the middle of the hall.

"Good morning, gentlemen. You certainly look fine and dandy on this beautiful day, though I can't recall seeing any of you last night for the clinical roundtable on pain management...no doubt you had something better to do?"

He pauses as we squirm uncomfortably. We all went out with visiting Irish nurses, thinking our absence would scarcely be noted.

"And another thing," he goes on. "I don't approve of medical students carrying stethoscopes around their necks, like some sort of reptilian appendage, and none of my residents ever do. If you're wearing them in the hope of being mistaken for physicians, I'll set your minds at rest right away: there's no danger of that, though you do succeed in looking ridiculous."

By now, nurses and attending physicians have gathered around us, delighting in our public upbraiding. Even a few patients are listening in.

"I expect academic excellence and professionalism from all students," Dr. Chardin continues, his voice rising above the background noise of the hall. "The ostentatious display of a stethoscope is as pretentious as it is impractical. Should you have to run to the ER, it will probably fall on the floor, and when you lean over a bed, it might sling off your neck and hit one of our patients...an interesting lawsuit indeed."

The old clinician pauses long enough to enjoy the look of discomfiture in our faces.

"Gentlemen," he goes on with slow, sarcastic admonition, "stethoscopes belong in the pockets of your coat. A physician's presence on a ward is made manifest by the experience and confidence he projects. His authority should rest on knowledge and dignified bearing. Real doctors have no need for props. Leave that to Hollywood and nursing aides."

And then he leaves, making his way to the elevators with a gaggle of grinning residents. Crestfallen after this cold shower, we bury the incriminating instrument deep in our pockets when Dr. Chardin abruptly turns around and fires one more volley in our direction.

"One last word. I like your bow ties. They're elegant, quite professional and less likely to colonize bacteria. Who knows? There might still be hope for some of you."

⊱⊰

I get home exhausted from a wrenching day and the tedious commute, hoping to immerse myself in the bluish fragrance of a bubble bath, but my mom ambushes me before I even make it out of the foyer.

"I know you're busy," she reminds me for the third time this month, "but you haven't visited your great-grandmother for quite a while. She's one of the most undemanding persons I know, but yesterday even she remarked on your absence. I think she misses you terribly."

I like my great-grandmother. She's ninety-two and lives in a splendid apartment in Neuilly, on the west side of Paris, guarded by two scheming Portuguese maids. Large bay windows allow the sun to flood her terraced refuge, a rain forest of rubber plants haunted by Hemingway cats. Today she's resting in the winter garden, snuggled in an old fur coat, with the mythical skyline of Paris in the distance. She's in relatively good health, with a prodigious memory and an agile mind. Seizing my arm with the tenacious strength of the elderly, she makes me sit beside her, looking me over with the intensity of a hawk. Born in 1877, she has lived through the glory and horror of modern European history.

"How's medical school?" she asks, while the chambermaid lights one of her Turkish cigarettes.

"It keeps me busy, but my grades are good," I answer, resisting the temptation to say anything about her persistent use of tobacco. My great-grandmother still smokes five cigarettes a day, but her physician has given up advising against it. She just loves to remind him how she's attended the funeral of his three predecessors.

The oldest daughter of an Alsatian squire, she was the heiress to every lake, meadow and forest around the city of Colmar. But in spite of her privileged upbringing, she was graced with an uncommon human touch, enjoying scandalous popularity because of her unseemly feminist views. Alice-Hortense Lacour de Jurru, her unforgettable maiden name, married well and moved to Paris at the age of nineteen. Her provincial origins were met with cold aloofness in Parisian society. And perhaps because of this undeserved snobbery, she exhibited the exquisite politeness and generosity found in the true nobility of the heart, especially to those in her service. And today, her meddling chambermaids still watch faithfully over her like two acrimonious griffins.

"I'm amazed how you've remained devoted to other people's trials and misfortunes," I tell her admiringly.

"Thank you for the compliment, but I'm not nearly as exemplary as you think," she replies. "I learned not to linger on vicissitudes. The example of my own mother was inspiration enough for a lifetime."

"I don't know a thing about her," I remark. "She must have been exceptional."

"She was the meanest and most malevolent person I've ever had the displeasure to know," my great-grandmother retorts, without apparent anger or bitterness. "In coldest fact, I resolved at the age of seven to become the exact opposite of everything she represented."

I'm astonished by this revelation, and perversely intrigued by such a character now relegated to a forgotten past.

"Can you tell me about her?" I press my great-grandmother, now the sole repository of information that will perish with her.

"Perhaps I'll pass along a few details," she says as I ensconce myself in a plush armchair.

"Let's see," she begins pensively, "that would make her your great-great-grandmother. She was born in 1848, just as Louis-Philippe, the last French king, was unceremoniously stripped of his crown by hordes of irate Parisians. Her unpleasantness and irascible disposition were legendary, and remained unchecked largely because of her immense wealth. She took her constitutional down the Champs-Elysées every evening at precisely six o'clock, in the company of her steward and chambermaids. Tall and corpulent, she would march down the sidewalks of the avenue oblivious to the rest of the world. Among her many eccentricities, she couldn't abide the sight of anyone directly in front of her. Sheltered under a parasol and flanked by her entourage, she was an imposing sight arrogantly sailing the footpath, forcing unwary sightseers off the sidewalk by waving an ivory walking stick."

"After the Great War broke out, she became incensed when my brother enlisted for the front, even after she had bought him out of his military obligations." My great-grandmother pauses, her crystalline voice belying her age.

"I loved my brother, a tender soul named Charles-André, but he was no match for her. You can imagine how badly he needed to escape to volunteer for trench warfare. Yet her determination proved unstoppable. A year later, upon learning that his unit was enjoying a week of rest and recreation from the front, she made up her mind to visit him. But her connections at the *Ministère de la Guerre* were categorical: this was impossible. No civilians were allowed to travel within a hundred miles of the war zone. She was undeterred. Alone in the back seat of her resplendent Packard twin-six, she set out from Paris in the company of her chauffeur, with two French flags flying on each side of the majestic hood of her car. They drove east towards the German border, before reaching the first military checkpoint a hundred miles from Paris."

"She had the most unflappable aplomb," my great-grandmother adds, lighting another cigarette. "As a young girl, I lived in fear of her indiscriminate visits to my boarding school. She condescendingly looked at the officer and declared: 'I am Mrs. Lacour, young man, and that information alone should suffice. You have your orders, so let us through.' Unprepared for such a grand apparition and intimidated by this woman's assurance, the young lieutenant opened the barrier and waved her on, unaware of any such order but petrified at the thought of committing a major gaffe. She used the same stratagem at each successive outpost, gaining in arrogance as she went. The military police let her through, convinced she would never have gotten this far without official approval. She roared into the courtyard of the Epinal military camp like Marshal Joffre on a surprise inspection. My brother was aghast as she alighted from the sumptuous car, assisted by an overwhelmed corporal. She had prepared well for the journey. Her chauffeur distributed three cases of Dom Perignon champagne to the men, while the commanding officer was greeted with a magnum of aged cognac. She stayed for dinner in the mess hall, feted by everyone, and drove off that night between two rows of saluting honor guards. Charles-André was mortified and crushed once more under his mother's indomitable will."

"I guess my brother knew he would never be free of her," my great-grandmother adds softly. "He died two months later, slaughtered with the rest of his unit during the battle of the Somme. They said the ground was drenched in so much blood that the grass didn't grow back, leaving meadows looking like a cratered moon."

I do not wish to distress her further with such searing memories and bring our conversation to a close, but she turns around, setting her quiet gaze upon me.

"Don't be sad," she says. "It was probably for the best. Even I was not to enjoy any personal freedom until my mother passed away."

"How did she die?" I ask, curiosity getting the better of my resolution.

"Oh, her death was in keeping with her life," she replies with an appeased smile I didn't anticipate. "She died as extravagantly as she had lived, in her mansion in Nice, on the Riviera. To subjugate the city council, she had paid for the renovation of the hospital and the entire cost of the museum of fine arts, sinking half her fortune into these projects. She detested my sisters who became convinced she meant to deprive them of their inheritance by squandering her fortune in charitable donations. She became a recluse, her behavior growing more bizarre, and cut off all contacts with friends and family. Sleeping during the day to live only at night in the midst of her prodigious art collection, my mother became interested in spirituality and religion, with a particular fascination for Judaism."

"In September of 1921, she was taken seriously ill and diagnosed with some form of fulminating gastro-enteritis. But even disease and bacteria seemed to be wary of her. She took a week to die, lying in pomp and ceremony on a monumental four-poster in the center of her bedroom suite. Her paranoia had intensified in later years and she had lost all confidence in banks. At her request, the bulk of her remaining fortune was transferred into treasury bonds, payable to the bearer, and hidden inside her mansion."

"My sisters' sagacity and occasional indiscretions from the staff finally revealed where she had concealed the money. The tall windows of her panoramic bedroom, looking out onto the scintillating waters of the Mediterranean, were framed with heavy velvet drapes. She had directed her seamstress to hide the treasury bonds inside the thick bottom folds of the curtains. In time, all of us became aware of the secret and my older sisters spent sleepless nights worrying about the fate of their inheritance."

"Were they really scared she might give it all to charity?" I ask, transfixed by the image of this miserly old despot, inciting invidious greed in her children while lying in bed, cocooned in paper like a dying moth.

"Oh, no," my great-grandmother replies with a chuckle, "she had a habit of keeping scented candles about the room, their fragrance soothing her rheumatism. My sisters would lose sleep, imagining the house on fire, and their money going up in smoke. But now she lay there in agony, slowly slipping into a coma. I was away in Sardinia when it happened, but my three sisters and their husbands were all dutifully in attendance. The last two days, no one dared leave her room for more than five minutes. She finally went into kidney failure and the attending physician informed the family that her death was imminent. The moment she lost consciousness, my older sister Gentiane got up and spoke.

'I'm not aware of the provisions in Mother's will,' she said, 'but I do know this: what's left of her wealth is in her art collection and those treasury bonds. The paintings are all catalogued and accounted for, so we'll have to wait for the attorneys concerning their final disposition. However, the Department of Taxation is unaware of the bonds' existence, and I for one do not intend to be deprived of my fair share. So for the sake of our children, I suggest we drop all pretenses and get to business.' And taking a pair of silver shears from her purse, she walked to one of the curtains and started ripping the seams."

"That's incredible!" I exclaim, "What did the others do?"

"Well, Anémone, bless her heart, stood by the bed in disbelief, holding on to her mother's hand," my great-grandmother goes on. "But as the tearing of fabric intensified, she too joined in the fray. Mother began to breathe with difficulty, her râles and gasps rising above the sound of clicking scissors and rent velvet. Outraged by the children's disgraceful behavior, her physician tried to convince them to wait until she had passed away, but no one listened. Mother died without anyone even looking at her."

"I don't mean to be callous about this," my great-grandmother remarks. "Everyone's conduct on that day was appallingly uncivilized. Yet it must be acknowledged that the ties of filial love between my sisters and their mother had been severed long before, if indeed they had ever existed at all. Much of the art collection was auctioned off, except for the Degas still hanging in my living room. But of all the heirlooms and memories salvaged from my mother's estate, your great-uncle probably owns the most valuable one," she concludes.

"And what is that?" I beg to know, my curiosity piqued by the lilt in her voice.

"It's her death certificate," she replies. "And in spite of her later spiritual aspirations, it isn't exactly Kosher. With majestic strokes of pen and ink, the medical examiner had listed the cause of death as an indigestion of fried pig's feet."

Nine

I MOVE OUT OF my parents' house over Christmas break. It is a rite of passage, defining my independence and giving me almost unlimited privacy. Of course, it's all a matter of perspective: my father pays the rent and gives me an allowance, but he soothes my wounded pride by observing that a medical student can't accommodate a part-time job in his schedule. The place is small but endowed with the glow of recently acquired autonomy: two rooms on the sixth floor of a brownstone, recessed behind the marble colonnades of an historic Parisian avenue. Despite its exiguity, the studio is the envy of my classmates because of its prestigious location. The Rue de Rivoli runs alongside the Louvre, with glittering arcades on both sides of the street, home to some of the most exclusive stores in Paris. It is the sort of *pied-à-terre* that attracts attention, and I'm counting on its allure to improve my social life. I can't resist the vanity of acquiring a set of business cards with the address engraved on impressive cardstock. Of course every movie set has a back lot, where reality meets the pavement: the elevator stops on the fourth floor, forcing me to climb a narrow flight of stairs to an unheated corridor.

"This is actually a bonus," my mother remarked when she helped me move in. "It motivates you to be charming, so the ladies won't notice that you occupy the servant quarters of this palace."

Independence notwithstanding, my mother also hopes I will get homesick and spend an occasional weekend at her house.

"I'm trying to do what I should and kick you all out of the nest," she says with a sweet smile, hugging me the way she always has since I was a boy, "but it's not easy. I keep bumping into the memories of my children in every room of the house." A haze passes across her eyes, a rare weakness in that magisterial charm.

In the first two months I spend alone in this apartment, I find that all my time is devoted to studying. The place is as quiet as a vault, and the discretion afforded by the thick ancestral walls helps foster my academic diligence, rather than the wild decadence I had fantasized. An invitation in March finally breaks the monotony of this abstentious existence. It is from one of my fellow travelers to the Soviet Union, and he's throwing a party to reunite all the unfortunate members of last year's "Russian campaign," with prodigious amounts of caviar and vodka. The invitation also gives directions to his home on the Avenue de Madrid in Neuilly, an address that reduces the pretensions of my own lodgings to social embarrassment.

A week later, I discover a catered reception sprawling over the top floor of a resplendent villa. Glistening through the terraced gardens, its illuminations add unusual warmth to the end of winter. It is a pleasant evening, but I feel out of place; most of the guests are older than I, established professionals and affable entrepreneurs with whom I have little in common. Studying medicine in my dungeon has robbed me of the social veneer necessary to navigate these waters. But my host is attentive and notices my awkwardness. He guides me to the upstairs library and introduces me to a younger guest, before thoughtfully abandoning us in this quiet setting. And it is there, between rare first editions and a monumental collection of erotica, that I discover Adrienne.

She possesses a discreet charm, clear eyes and a natural presence that speaks of unassuming intelligence. We talk undisturbed for an hour, but nothing of substance passes between us. I give her one of my pretentious business cards and she reciprocates with an invitation to a party at her father's house in Normandy. As I walk back along the Avenue de Madrid, I feel puzzled. She elicits in me a measure of interest, yet it remains untenanted by infatuation or lust, as if I were merely playing a part in a script.

Adrienne had dropped out of school, preferring to take a year off and evaluate her options. She is the daughter of the Count of

Chalindry, a gentleman farmer of considerable means, and hails from a family whose connections extend beyond the borders of France. In the sixties, the daughters of wealthy aristocrats had no need to study for a career, but a graduate education was considered advantageous in social circles, offering proper suitors the validation of one's intellect. A significant number of debutantes obtained law degrees without the slightest intention to practice, and it almost became a fashionable ritual, precisely because it was frivolous.

She's bright, but devoid of ambition. In granting her request for a sabbatical year, her father insisted she would agree to some sort of volunteer occupation to maintain contact with the right sort of people, giving her a taste of what she was missing. Pulling a few strings, he found her a position as social secretary with the Ambassadors Club, the exclusive retreat at Orly airport where diplomats and celebrities enjoy privacy in the company of their peers.

The following Friday, Adrienne calls me for a favor.

"You know I was planning to drive you to my father's place for the party this weekend," she coos into the phone. "The problem is, I have to replace someone this evening and I'd rather not return to Paris to get my car. Could you pass by my mother's house? She'll give you the keys and you can pick me up at the airport tomorrow."

I agree instantly, my motivation less than honorable: Adrienne owns a gorgeous Alfa-Romeo coupe. I don't have a car of my own and the thought of having this high-powered beauty all to myself is irresistible. I leave from Paris the next morning, opening the sunroof, wearing shades and a white scarf as if I were the Red Baron in flight. My experience with cars is limited; the Alfa-Romeo's manual transmission is new to me, and for some odd reason I can't shift into fourth. I end up coasting in the right lane with an engine revving higher than it should, cruising at 55mph and unable to unleash the Italian horses huddled under the hood. Several drivers shake their heads as they pass me. I decide to close the sunroof, keeping a nervous eye on the temperature gauge and feeling ridiculous in this castrated sports car.

Adrienne will never know how long it took me to get to the airport. She waits in the drop-off area and greets me with a cheerful smile. I place her traveling bag in the trunk and surrender the wheel. She's an accomplished driver and swiftly negotiates the congested interstate leading out to the coast of Normandy. Why have I agreed to this road trip? She's fun and attractive, with sensual lips and bangs cut in a perfectly straight line above her eyebrows. I guess I'm flattered to escort her for a weekend out of town. I gaze at Adrienne as she effusively describes her professional obligations from the night before. She looks as wholesome as a Coppertone commercial, her thighs melting into the chestnut leather of the seat.

It takes three hours to reach her family home. Adrienne had said nothing about the place and I'm in for a shock. Overlooking the craggy coast, her father's castle rises in the splendor of the noonday sun. Almost Scottish in its austerity, it looks more like a fortress than a palace. There are few medieval strongholds left in private hands. The coast of Northern France was once dotted with them, but gunpowder and cannonballs in the sixteenth century brought an end to ramparts and battlements, replacing them with the luminous architecture of the Renaissance. We drive across the drawbridge, through the gates and into a narrow courtyard. Once inside, the castle looks much smaller, the thickness of the granite walls taking in most of its size. Bolting from the car, Adrienne leads me to a flight of stairs, and a rotund middle-aged man greeting the flow of arriving guests.

"Eric, may I present my father, the Count of Chalindry? Father, this is Eric," she intones in an almost theatrical delivery I didn't expect.

The Count darts his gaze into my eyes while offering his fingertips to hold. He looks like a country priest, with a deeply furrowed face and a proud mouth. Since he's rather short in stature, I remain politely in the stairs two steps below, allowing him the advantage of looking me in the eye. Our mutual distaste is instantaneous. I suppose it is the fate of any young man showing up in the company of his daughter. Adrienne leaves us alone for a moment, and for her sake I engage in a bit of polite conversation. He knows of my grandfather and his work, but doesn't elaborate upon the nature of this acquaintance. I feel a bit marginalized in the decorum of this ancestral courtyard, when the Count casually asks which year I happen to be at the medical school.

"I'm a third-year student at Lariboisière Hospital," I blurt out almost defensively.

I'm not quite sure what possessed me to deceive him like this. Perhaps his overbearing demeanor, a feeling of insignificance within these walls and a childish need to impress my host, but I instantly wish I could take back my hasty words.

"I'm pleased to hear that, young man, and look forward to chatting with you over dinner," he replies with a hint of interest, before releasing me into his daughter's care. I'm angry at myself and embarrassed by this ridiculous subterfuge, as I pick up my bag from the car under the disapproving eye of the butler. Adrienne remains in the courtyard a while longer to greet her guests, and I choose to say nothing about my conversation with her father. A maid guides me up the tower steps through an interminable corridor leading to the eastern wing.

"You will be very comfortable here, sir." she explains. "The Count wants all his guests well-rested before tomorrow's festivities. And here we are."

I expected a private bedroom and discover instead a sort of small dormitory with a half-dozen beds lined up against the walls. The maid sees the look of puzzlement on my face and volunteers an explanation.

"The men will sleep here and in the adjacent rooms, while the young ladies are lodged in the west wing of the castle," she says cheerfully. I thank her and storm back to the courtyard in search of Adrienne.

"What's the meaning of this?" I ask abruptly, though I can see in her eyes she's embarrassed enough as it is.

"Dad is very old-fashioned," she says. "He would never permit unmarried couples to sleep together under his roof." And then she gently takes hold of my arm, resting her head on my shoulder.

"It's only for two nights," she sulks, "we'll be together the rest of the time."

But I'm unwilling to accommodate her.

"I'm sorry, Adrienne, but it won't do. The sleeping arrangements are intolerable and I've no intention of being treated like a teenager at camp," I reply testily, well-aware that my anger is fueled by that dismal performance earlier on with her father. But I'm her guest, and should simply bow to my host's antiquated views and avoid distressing her like this; yet something in me perversely instigates against indulgence. And it is then that I realize she cares for me more than she has let on. To my surprise, she looks up with plaintive, almost submissive eyes and whispers, "I understand. Maybe later on tonight, once my father has retired, you and I can discreetly leave and find a room in the village?" I'm subjugated by her offer as she takes my hand, resolutely guiding me to the entrance hall.

The dinner is an elaborate affair. We all sit around an ancestral table, chandeliers mirrored in the veneer of weathered oak and ironwood. The staff has placed everyone according to pre-arranged name cards. To my surprise, Adrienne sits across the table half a dozen chairs to my right, while I'm seated directly to the left of the Count. I don't know to what I owe this mark of distinction, but I would rather spend the evening in his daughter's immediate company. Yet the dinner is enjoyable, with animated conversation in the glow of exquisite wines. I try to engage the guest to my left, but our host seems most eager to converse exclusively with me.

"My daughter is a fragile, easily dominated young woman," he begins in a condescending tone, "and I think it essential that she be properly looked after."

So this is it. He has arranged to be seated next to me so he can deliver a fatherly lecture.

"I hope you're comfortable here at the castle, and I regret that I cannot accommodate each of Adrienne's guests in private quarters," he goes on. "You know how fickle women are. At first, she talked of a half-dozen guests, and only yesterday were we informed to expect more than twenty. Of course, I had to segregate everyone by gender, and place folding beds in several of the suites."

The Count pauses a moment to answer a query from a servant, and then turns his attention back to me.

"We live in troubled times indeed. Our values undermined daily by unprincipled ideas, the worst of which being undoubtedly this deplorable sexual permissiveness. Well, I am pleased about one thing, my boy," he declares peremptorily, seeing to the proper level of my wine glass. "Within these walls, where family values and decency have prevailed for five hundred years, we will not give modern France even the semblance of impropriety. The reputation of every young woman entrusted to my protection tonight will be beyond reproach. As is, by the way, my daughter's," he adds, his face now uncomfortably close to mine.

I'm at a loss for words, politely nodding at my host's remarks, my eyes trying to find Adrienne through the blur of candle-lit faces across the table. I begin to squirm uncomfortably in my seat, unaware that the worst of the evening is yet to come.

"Since you are my daughter's escort for this weekend, I feel sure you understand my interest in you," the Count goes on, unwilling to release my attention. "I am particularly impressed with your studies. To be a third-year student at your age is quite an achievement. You appear not much older than twenty."

I brush aside the remark with shamefaced modesty, but behind the compliment his line of inquiry has grown more pressing.

"You must be one of those precocious students, graduating from college a few years early, and your parents are no doubt very proud of you," he adds with an insistence that makes my toes cringe inside my shoes. "Of course, I do know of your ancestors, noble souls who served France with distinction. And perhaps you're unaware that the histories of our families briefly merged at some point in the past, in 1641 to be exact. According to my archives, a Baron of Chalindry was killed by a Captain du Plessis in the moat of the Louvre."

"You don't say," I manage to utter, holding my glass a bit tighter in my hand.

"It must have been quite a duel," he goes on persistently. "Even the court chroniclers remarked on it at the time. Your ancestor's sword was driven so savagely through the eye of the Baron that the blade came out six inches in the back of his skull. It proved impossible to dislodge, so the du Plessis in question, one of the King's muske-teers, left the field abandoning his weapon in the dead man's head."

The Count calmly finishes his wine before concluding with a sarcastic tone.

"Of course, this may have been less the feat it appeared to be, since the Baron of Chalindry had limped for years...a wound he sus-tained at the siege of La Rochelle. But all of this is ancient history," my host concludes with a comforting slap on my back, "and I am de-lighted to have you as a guest tonight. By the way, how is Professor Schlésinger carrying on these days?"

"Professor who?" I stammer, caught off-guard and completely ignorant of the name.

"Why, Charles Schlésinger, of course, the head of dermatology at Lariboisière. As a third-year student, you must have been the tar-get of his legendary wit more than once," he adds, a look of surprise in his eye. "Don't tell me he finally retired?"

I don't know what to say and try desperately to extricate myself from this quicksand.

"How is it, sir, that you seem familiar with the faculty at the University hospital?" I enquire, trying to evade his questions.

"Charles is an old acquaintance of mine, though we haven't seen much of each other lately," the Count answers. "But that's beside the point. What I'd really like to discuss with you are the new treatment protocols for atrial fibrillation. Since you're going through your car-diology clerkship at the moment, I'd appreciate your insight on the matter."

I feel collared like a foal in the jaws of a wolf trap. The Count knows exactly what he's doing, and his exposure of my deceit is all the more embarrassing that other guests have left their own conversa-tions to listen in on ours.

"Will you excuse me for a moment?" I reply unconvincingly, getting to my feet and wiping the sweat off my brow. "I fear I may have indulged your excellent Armagnac a bit too liberally."

"Let me help you to the restroom," he replies with feigned so-licitude, "You do seem a little pale all of a sudden."

But the Count has no intention of releasing his grip so easily. He escorts me out of the dining room, and just as I'm about to break free he overtakes me in the deserted corridor.

"I may look like an uncouth farmer to you, young man, but I also happen to be an M.D., University of Paris, class of 1935," he begins. "I retired last Christmas after thirty-two years as the only cardiologist in the county. You may think your little games rather funny, Mr. third-year medical student, but you don't impress me at all. Not in the slightest bit."

I try to mount a feeble defense, but he pounces on me.

"If you're going to pretend to be someone you're not, I suggest you research your role a little better. If there's something more deplorable than a liar, it is assuredly a mediocre one...." And he briefly turns away to acknowledge the greetings of a passing guest.

"Do enjoy my hospitality this evening," he goes on, "but rest assured that I will inform Adrienne of my disapproval." And just as he is about to rejoin his guests, he can't resist one last jab.

"History has an interesting way of settling old scores in the most unpredictable manner," he concludes with a contemptuous sneer. "The last meeting between a Chalindry and a du Plessis proved disastrous to one of my ancestors. But tonight, my lad, it does seem that I have you at a disadvantage."

The Count swiftly turns around and disappears into the bluish reflection of the tapestries lining the corridor. Troubled and disoriented, I mechanically follow an animated group of guests leaving the dining hall. Shortly thereafter I find Adrienne in the billiards room, wearing a resplendent smile.

"I'm so glad you and dad talked during dinner," she says exuberantly. "He never speaks with any of my friends, so you must have made quite an impression on him."

I will not inform her of what passed between the Count and me. I'm embarrassed enough as it is, but mostly angry at myself. I have every reason not to feel ashamed of my academic achievements, and yet I chose to lie and present myself in a less than flattering light. I usually don't care about aristocratic traditions, or the vestigial sense of duty that passes for good character, but I must admit that I feel humiliated tonight, and in need to obtain satisfaction from my distinguished host.

Adrienne is unaware of my particular disposition. The party is now well under way in the west wing, with a local band providing the entertainment. Out of a door dissimulated in the oak paneling, her father appears and bids her good night. He also shakes my hand as if nothing had transpired between us, before retiring to his apartment for the night. Once he's gone, she takes advantage of the ebullience of the festivities to lead me to the courtyard and discreetly drive out into the countryside. I'm flattered by her eagerness to leave so precipitously, disobeying her father and neglecting her guests just to spend time with me. And yet, despite her charms and the enticing intimacy of the night, my heart is not in this. I know my presence here tonight was motivated by the anticipation of lust, but an unclean thirst for revenge now renews my interest in Adrienne.

There's a village just a few miles from the castle where she hopes to secure a room, but the charming country inn, with its thatched roof and red beams protruding from terracotta walls, is closed until the beginning of June. We meander through the darkened streets when Adrienne comes to a sudden decision. She drives off a mile out of town, and leaving the main road through an open gate, takes us both into the surrounding meadows. The car seems to glide silently over the spring grass, until we come to a stop by the side of a barn. The night air is invigorating and not inordinately cold. She opens the sunroof, revealing a sky matted in luminescent clouds. Our desire condenses in the air, and the fields all around are surprisingly warm, as if they were breathing along with us. Wisps of slow-moving fog rise from the ground, settling like gauze upon the bare trees. Slowly, Adrienne sheds her clothes, with a hesitation I attribute as much to modesty as to the coolness of the air. We make love in the car, oddly whispering to each other, as if to harmonize our lust with the stillness enshrouding us.

It's only later, as we rest our heads contentedly upon the cool touch of the leather seats, that I get the feeling we're not alone. And indeed, slowly taking form around us, something emerges from the fog, silently encircling the car. Adrienne smothers a cry and buries her head against my chest, but as I discern the identity of the intruders, I can't repress my laughter.

"Look. Just take a look," I encourage her playfully, "Let me introduce you to our guests."

A half-dozen horses stare at us, hoping for something to eat, before turning around and disappearing back into the fog.

We return to the castle an hour before sunrise. The contrast between Adrienne's desire for me to stay and my pressing wish to leave this place is telling. And while she sweetly articulates her wounded disappointment, I keep averting my eyes, as if she might read in them the absence of any feelings. Upon realizing that she cannot dissuade me, Adrienne lends me her car, offering to pick it up at my place on Monday. I drive off in a huff, part of me wanting to spend another night, and the other wondering what she will think after her father mentions our conversation. I feel weary and abject, as if I've robbed her of her intimacy.

And yet, gradually, as the hum of the engine soothes my exasperation and the rising sun illuminates the interstate, a sordid sense of satisfaction begins to settle in my thoughts. Yes, Adrienne's father may have had the better of me, but when he finds out about last night, rage will consume him like a torrent of bile, the sweet illusions of his daughter's virtue turning into spikes in his heart. "Revenge is an expensive luxury," Richelieu once said—"Even statesmen cannot afford it." But this morning, against my own principles, I allow the poisonous satisfaction of vengeance to wash away an evening's humiliation. I tell myself that in possessing his daughter, I've also taught that overbearing aristocrat a lesson. But I reach Paris unaware that the Count of Chalindry is not quite done with me, and that Richelieu's remark on the folly of revenge will prove accurate once again.

It all begins a week later. I wake up in the middle of the night in a sweat. The heat circulates like a desert breeze throughout the small apartment, and yet I feel shivery and uncomfortable. When I finally answer the urge to visit the bathroom, I'm appalled by the discovery of other symptoms. It burns when I urinate and a ghastly discharge is dripping out of me into the commode. The clinical picture is fairly straightforward, but I choose total denial. After all, I'm a lowly first-year student who doesn't know anything, and shouldn't presume to diagnose an actual illness.

At nine a.m., I walk through the doors of the student health department. It is housed in a decrepit building wedged against the massive towers of the Conciergerie, the austere medieval structure that served as Robespierre's revolutionary tribunal. Today, it is occupied by the Parisian headquarters of the French police, and the neighborhood makes you feel as if you were summoned to an interrogation, rather than seeking the help of modern medicine. By the time I get to the reception desk, I'm walking like a duck, trying valiantly to resist the urge to pee. For the past two hours, I've felt as if I were passing razor blades.

The clinic is staffed with interesting characters. To discourage malingering or frivolous excuses, it is comprised of retired military physicians, practicing part-time at the clinic and trying to dissipate the boredom of their retirement. Most of them were officers from the medical corps who saw combat in Indochina and Algeria; and with years of clinical experience stretching from Hanoi to the Sahara, they're a formidable challenge to medical students complaining of imaginary ailments.

Colonel Deniau is a soft-spoken, retired flight surgeon, bearing a striking resemblance to David Niven. As is the custom in France, I'm asked to shed all my clothes and stand in front of him, shivering on the green tile floor. None of these American hospital gowns I was to discover years later, as a typical Anglo-Saxon effort to preserve a patient's privacy. The French approach to physical examination cares less about modesty than it does about pragmatism. The air force doctor is kind enough not to prolong my ordeal.

"We'll collect a smear from the discharge, a urine specimen, and a blood sample for the lab. I trust you already know you're infected with venereal disease," he says matter-of-factly, as I stand there thoroughly humiliated, trying to put my clothes back on with a semblance of dignity.

"Why the hell don't you use prophylactics?" he asks with a voice completely devoid of moralizing.

"I hate condoms," I reply sheepishly. "They're unromantic and smell as if a car had burned its tires around your bed."

"That may well be," he answers with an acquiescing grin, "but when this episode is over, I'll bet you a bottle of Scotch that your personal aesthetics will yield to common sense."

The lab tag bears a red, ominous request for a "B.W." That's short for "Bordet-Wassermann," the standard serology for syphilis. I look at him with panic.

"Relax, my boy." He answers soothingly. "I think that's quite unlikely, but we can't take any chances. Come back at five this evening and we'll know a bit more."

I stay in the Quartier Latin for the rest of the day, huddling around small tables in cafés, trying to sit still next to the crowds of students descending the avenue like a chatting river. By three o'clock, I'm convinced I've contracted the most dreaded venereal disease on the continent. And I remain slumped in my chair, haunted by visions of Nietzsche screaming in restraints in a psychiatric hospital, lost to the labyrinthine madness of tertiary syphilis.

I must look a sight when I return to the clinic, because the old military doctor rises from behind his desk, greeting me with a reassuring smile.

"The good news first," he intones in a jovial manner. "Your blood test is negative." I heave a sigh of relief and drop in an armchair.

"That being said," he goes on more seriously, showing me the paper in his hand, "This isn't a lab report, it's a roll call at the zoo."

I stare at him with eyes of renewed despair.

"You've got gonorrhea *and* trichomoniasis. We'll have to hit the enemy with the firepower of a B-52," he declares, shaking his head. "I'm going to give you an intramuscular injection of two million units of penicillin G in each buttock. And then, you will scrupulously ingest all this metronidazole over the next ten days. I'll see you in two weeks, and we'll repeat the lab work. I'm afraid your intestinal flora will join your urinary tract in celebrating this event." He concludes half-jokingly, as the nurse brings in the hypodermic.

I return to my apartment with the enthusiasm of an army retreating from Russia in winter. I ache in more places than I did when I started out this morning. My doctor's parting advice is to take advantage of this situation and study the illness from a patient's perspective. A practical suggestion no doubt, but my heart is not in it. I know that within two weeks I will likely be freed of this ordeal and resume my life as if nothing ever happened. But I'm mortified and angry. I may not have had romantic illusions about Adrienne, but even her sensuous memory has now dissolved in the sordid reality of a lab report. I'm also furious to have been taken in by her demure and chaste appearance, a well-rehearsed act that defeated even her father's clinical eye. I call that night and give her the news over the phone, slamming the receiver so hard a part of it cracks in my hand. A few days later, a kind soul will tell me how popular a hostess she had become with the distinguished clientele of the Ambassadors club, bedding celebrities in the plush comfort of the overnight suite. For weeks, I will ignore Adrienne's attempts to contact me, slowly allowing my disgust to run its course. In time, bitterness becomes indifference, but, as Marivaux observed, the sort of indifference that can still turn into hatred if you torment it.

Even after receiving a clean bill of health, I still feel something gnawing at my pride. That night, Adrienne's father taught me a lesson in proper manners and integrity; and I sought to repay the sting of his correction by possessing his daughter. I'll never know whether the price I paid for this unprincipled revenge ever came to his attention, but in the end it doesn't really matter. In this private duel of ours, the Count of Chalindry had dealt the final blow and avenged his ancestor at last.

৵৵

"Pediatrics, ladies and gentlemen, is a challenging specialty, a passion I hope some of you will embrace." The voice of the silver-haired clinician resonates against the marble walls. Narrow and steep, the small amphitheater seems to suspend us over our professor and his examination table. The windowless room is two hundred years old, with stiff portraits in gilded frames creating an atmosphere of elegant claustrophobia. The introductory lectures are usually fascinating and the seasoned pediatrician holding forth in our midst is well-liked for his perceptiveness and wit.

"The examination of the pharynx in a three-year-old patient can easily degenerate into hostility and confrontation. But your ability to perform this simple task without incurring the wrath of his mother will be a factor in the making of your reputation," he declares with a glint in his eyes.

"And indeed, the success of your practice will rest not so much on your clinical acumen – though that must be beyond reproach – as it will on your ability to secure a mother's trust. So here's your quandary: to examine the throat of a screaming child without appearing brutal or coercive. Well, here's a little technique borrowed from veterinary medicine, which," he adds with feigned compunction, "is likely to be the nature of your practice with most toddlers."

By now the affable and good-natured physician has captured the attention of every student in the room.

"While the mother restrains the arms of the young patient, quickly place the palm of your hand over his eyes, pinching his nose to make him open his mouth and breathe. Then, with your other hand, gently depress his cheeks between the maxillaries. The child cannot close his mouth without biting himself, giving you time to insert a tongue depressor and visualize the larynx."

In between the laughter and the flow of more serious queries from fellow students, I take myself out of the room, back in time to my own childhood...

My sisters were both in Catholic schools in Paris, but not finding anything suitable for a boy, my mother had reluctantly placed me in a private school in Switzerland. I was seven years old, and the place had a reputation for progressive pedagogy and innovative curriculum.

"The school had been highly recommended by personal friends, and, pressed for time, I had not been my diligent self in checking further on the establishment." My mother recalls to this day with a retrospective shudder. "I knew something was amiss when the taxi brought us to the school gates from Geneva airport. There were Bentleys in the driveway, with idle chauffeurs chatting among themselves as if this were the first day of racing at the Paris Hippodrome. I had never bothered to enquire about the tuition, and I remember the choking sensation I experienced while writing out a check in the bursar's office."

Unknown to my mother, the establishment was run by an elderly German couple, two retired psychologists with unusual child-rearing theories. The place was magnificent, with manicured lawns, British nannies and a gigantic playroom looking like the toy section of a department store. But the nutritional approach to the education of youngsters was unconventional – to say the least. The headmaster and his wife had determined that refined sugar was one of the deadliest poisons threatening our health, second only to the dangers of unrestricted hydration. So we were each assigned a small plastic goblet bearing our names, with strict instructions to limit ourselves to one serving of water during meals, and a complete interdiction to drink fluids in between. The idiocy of this philosophy might have been tolerable had it not been for the particular diet we were fed each day. Faithful to her Bavarian origins, the headmaster's wife insisted on baked potatoes, lentil soup, cured ham, cheese and wheat bread in every season. She also had a predilection for the medicinal virtues of rhubarb, and served this stringy, acidic plant in unsweetened pies for dessert. Rhubarb without sugar is something of a slow, gagging torture to a child, and those who objected to the unpalatable nature of the dish were made to pick wild berries during interminable walks through the woods, just to satisfy their perverted craving for sweets. Mashed in with the rhubarb, the berries only intensified its acidity, and we ended up silently swallowing the concoction under the contented supervision of the staff.

I had promised my mom I would behave, but it proved impossible not to rebel against the kitchen police.

We were constantly thirsty, and during our required daily walks I noticed a farm nestled among the meadows bordering the woods. With three accomplices, I evaded the scrutiny of our counselors and vanished through the trees. Dodging the barbed wire we proceeded gingerly through the fields, crawling in the new grass, in search of anything that could slake our relentless thirst. And we finally discovered our own private oasis: a long wooden trough with clear water splashing ebulliently over the fossilized wood. It was a pure mountain stream, cold enough to burn your teeth, and we drank with complete abandon. My friends and I returned to the secret place a number of times until we were caught imbibing the forbidden drink, under the perplexed gaze of a dozen cows.

"You're obviously unaware of the seriousness of your actions," the headmaster intoned as we stood to attention in his office. "The reasons for the restrictions limiting your intake of fluids are too complex for me to explain, but suffice it to say that they're compelling."

I made a facial expression that implied some form of dissent, and the heavyset psychologist instantly pounced on me.

"You think you're so clever, du Plessis? Well, let me enlighten you as to the obvious benefits of this regimen," he went on passionately, as if he were hawking his wares in a marketplace. "Have you noticed how few pupils here at *L'Orée du Bois* ever wet their bed? It is precisely thanks to this rule that we can spare you the humiliation of enuresis."

I thought for a while that Enuresis was an Egyptian god out to get us all during the night. But the headmaster's obsession with bedwetting and water consumption also led to more disturbing policies. There were kids in the dorms still wetting their bed, and such resiliency to progressive pedagogy was not to be tolerated. For added motivation, the refractory children were consigned to the dreaded "Chambre Jaune," a segregated bedroom painted yellow from floor to ceiling to remind its occupants of their evil deeds. I suppose the treatment was meant as some form of radical behavior modification, but it resulted only in cruel humiliation. We thought our parents knew of this peculiar approach to education, so we said nothing at the time. I still recall the look of stupefaction on my mother's face the day she found out.

In no time I became miserable in this luxurious house of horrors and began more or less consciously to resist the conformity that was expected of me. We slept in comfortable rooms with four beds in each, neatly lined against the walls. But with the white paint, glaring overhead lights and the lingering smell of antiseptic, our accommodation resembled those of an expensive clinic. One of my roommates, a corpulent, ruddy-cheeked British boy, took a definite pleasure in bullying other kids. He detested me. I was tall for my age, but skinny, and quickly discovered that in a fight, the larger boy could wrestle me to the ground and pound my head into the floor with remarkable ease. At first, I silently endured this humiliation, resigned to the loss of self-esteem that defines the relationship between a bully and his victim. But after a while, I recalled my mother's advice when I first entered boarding school.

"Remember the motto of Field Marshal de Lattre: *Ne Pas Subir* (Don't Put Up With Anything). I made it my own when I was in school, and I'm passing it on to you. Whatever the circumstances, never allow yourself to be demeaned, or your dignity to be compromised."

I feared the British boy on a daily basis and had even modified my schedule so as not to come in contact with him at all. But we were roommates, and I couldn't avoid him forever. I felt sick at the realization that my acceptance of this subordination had turned me into a coward. I could not compete with him physically, so I began to look for other ways to get even. It finally came to me as I lay in bed wide awake in the night, worried and unable to sleep. The staff didn't want us to leave the room for any reason, and a trip to the bathroom meant we had to awake a counselor to be escorted out. Despite the headmaster's dictatorial control over our bladders, a fair number of boys still found it necessary to get up at night. So he placed in each room an enameled bucket in which we could relieve ourselves without waking anyone. The bucket could hold three gallons, and it wasn't emptied every day.

Over the weekend, the idea slowly formed in my head, and became more clearly delineated as the bully's mistreatment intensified. At two in the morning, everyone slept around me, the slow rhythm of deep breathing keeping time in the room. I silently got up and walked to the bully's bed. My tormentor lay peacefully with a faint smile on his face, looking unguardedly angelic in his sleep; but weeks of humiliation at his hands had steeled my resolve. I tiptoed over to the bucket in the corner of the room, carefully removed the lid and picked up the handle. It was heavier than I thought, and standing by the boy's bed, I hoisted the enameled container, using the night stand to steady it. I stood there for a few seconds, wishing he would awake and catch a glimpse of his impending destruction, but he never stirred. With one last effort, I lifted the bucket as high as I could and poured its contents upon his head.

The amber cascade shocked him from his sleep, and I stepped back as he bolted out of bed, took a few steps and stopped, frozen in the center of the room. The handle was still in my hand and I just stood there, swinging the bucket, ready to throw it in his face if he made so much as a move to strike me. But he didn't budge, looking like a scarecrow in the rain, urine glistening through his hair, soaking his pajamas and staining the floor. And then he started to cry, a pitiful whine that built up to an agonizing scream. The lights came on, stabbing my eyes as the counselors rushed in. And my cruel oppressor, the thorn in my flesh for the past six weeks, disintegrated before me. He began yelling in syncopated waves, hiccupping with fright like desolation incarnate. The commotion woke everyone in the adjacent rooms and the British boy, wrapped in a blanket like a maniac on a disturbed ward, was carried away to the infirmary, urine dripping in his wake.

I spent the rest of that night in a private room, a counselor watching over me and the door locked. My mother was summoned in the morning, and the timing couldn't have been more inconvenient to her demanding schedule. She pleaded with the German psychologists for two or three days delay until her arrival, but to no avail. She flew the next day to Geneva to retrieve her seven year-old delinquent, now kept apart from any contact with other students. The school also composed a formal letter, explaining the reasons for my being expelled. The description of the incident, and the clinical evaluation of its perpetrator, still reads like the indictment of a dangerous felon.

❧≈❦

I've never liked funerals. My mother theorizes that most people detest them as well because they feel as if they were witnessing their own burial. After all, given the ties of family and social class, the mourners on that day will likely be the same. I sit in a pew in the Eglise de Saint-Germain-Des-Prés in Paris. It's a romantic church, with Gothic steeples in full view of the cafés where Sartre and Camus once officiated in the secular proximity of the Sorbonne. Only the Boulevard Saint-Germain now separates the cradle of French existentialism from this stronghold of faith and tradition.

The nave is filled to capacity. Two hundred people have come to attend the funeral of my great-uncle Lucien, on my father's side. This is probably the first time in fifty years that he's in church. The crowd behind me attests to the notoriety of the departed, but what I know of him was not included in this morning's obituary in *Le Figaro*. I liked my great-uncle, his sulfurous past hidden from us when we were kids and only gradually revealed as we grew older. An iconoclast in impeccably tailored suits, he's probably grinning right now at the hypocrisy of these proceedings.

I never knew my paternal great-grandfather, an ancestral du Plessis. A violent man with a cruel disposition, he lived in contemptuous comfort on the French Riviera. While my grandfather escaped his sadism through boarding schools and military academies, his younger brother bore the brunt of the man's malevolence. Lucien was educated by private tutors and kept away from the company of other boys. He grew up alone and frightened under the watchful eyes of the house staff.

"Every Wednesday," my dad once told me, "he would be summoned for a beating."

"But what did he do to deserve it?" I asked with consternation, wondering how the dignified gentleman I had come to know and like could have been treated like this as a child.

"Nothing at all, really," my dad replied. "I learned from my own father that it was an established ritual. Your great-grandfather had Lucien brought in and stripped of his shirt in the oak-paneled gymnasium on the second floor. He would use a French army leather belt and thrash his son until the skin broke. The reason was always the same: "You're being punished for all the misdeeds you committed this week. And if by chance you're not guilty of any, I'm certain that today's lashes will remind you to stay out of trouble."

This went on until Lucien turned seventeen, and then the abuse ceased as inexplicably as it had begun. The next year he was admitted to a private college near Monaco and life went on as if nothing had ever happened. But if Lucien's back was toughened by the mistreatment he suffered, his resolve to get even patiently solidified like a stalagmite of the mind, nurturing his resentment from within.

In the winter of 1921, his parents left for their annual cruise on the Aegean Sea, while Lucien was a junior in college. In their absence, he was left with a power of attorney to supervise the staff and see to the day-to-day maintenance of the estate. A week later, he came home unannounced and dismissed the personnel with a generous severance pay. His parents' princely villa was renowned for its superb furnishings, priceless antiques and tapestries handed down from generations. He called on Cannes' most prominent art dealers and sold everything for a considerable sum. Then he quit school, took off to Monte Carlo, setting up residence at the prestigious Hotel de Paris overlooking the bay. In thirty days he squandered the money on women and gambling at the most affluent casino in Europe. After losing it all, he left for Marseilles and boarded a cargo ship for the French colonies of West Africa.

His parents returned in late January, incensed at not being met by their chauffeur near the harbor. A plebeian taxicab drove them to a homecoming they had never anticipated. The villa was cold and deserted. Broken window panes had allowed seagulls to nest in the entrance hall. All three floors were empty, bereft of their splendor, with only the magnificent parquetry still gleaming in the bleak winter light. Lucien's father ran screaming through every room until he reached the top floor. And there, in the middle of the barren library, an ornate night table awaited him. The only survivor of the cataclysm that had stripped the entire house to the walls, it stood completely alone, a leather belt resting on its lacquered top.

Lucien's dreams of exotic adventures and fame soon collided with the reality of Guinea's unforgiving weather and arid lands. But the young man who hadn't worked a day in his life found in the thankless challenge of tropical survival the education he needed. After seven years of arduous toil, he became the owner of the largest plantation in the mountains of Fouta Djallon, turning cassavas and sugar cane into sizeable profits. Once both his parents had died, he sold everything to a Portuguese competitor and returned to France. Lucien had earned enough money to live on the interest of his investments alone, but he needed to indulge a particular fancy. He dreamed of building a zoological garden in Provence, where children could come and admire the fauna of Africa. My great-uncle bought two hundred acres in southern France, commandeering landscape architects and masons to lay the foundations of his private zoo. Bypassing the established channels that provided exotic animals to the European market, he personally selected the first shipment of giraffes, gazelles, elephants and lions. Placed in the care of a local shipping line, they boarded a cargo ship from Conakry, on a journey through the Straits of Gibraltar and on to Marseilles.

But the pride and joy of his menagerie was never to set hoof or claw on French soil. As the ship passed the island of Gorée, off the coast of Senegal, it was caught in a ferocious storm. Barely a third of the crew managed to escape the splintering ship. A broken mast punctured the emergency fuel tank on the upper structure, sending waves of kerosene into the cargo bay. And when lightning coursed like a silver web through the ship's rail, it ignited a river of flames flowing into the hull. The survivors in lifeboats watched in horror as the burning ship slowly sank in the night, listening to the howls and shrieks of entrapped animals. Breaking the walls in their stalls, predators and prey huddled in terror against this unearthly foe made of liquid fire. In time, the ship listed enough to allow the ocean to extinguish the flames, the burned beasts never knowing that the watery embrace of this liberator was also their death. And over the shattering winds the elephants could be heard trumpeting in the dark, like majestic mastodons descending to their grave.

Lucien took it all in stride, losing a quarter of his fortune in the depths of the Atlantic Ocean. He settled in a quiet apartment in Paris, near the Arc de Triomphe, enjoying the comfortable idleness of early retirement. My father's side of the family was infamous for its traditionalism, and my great-uncle's return caused a stir in the tranquil waters of respectability. As a teen, I had so often heard rumors of his unorthodox lifestyle that I finally asked my dad about his uncle's reputation.

"I think you should ask your mother," he replied cryptically, the way he always did when conversation touched on a more florid aspect of human behavior. But I pressed him on the subject, arguing that the truth would be preferable to innuendos, and he relented.

"Well, the example I've always found most representative is this," he began. "Lucien had a mistress, whom he kept for twenty-five years if not with the assent, at least with the full knowledge, of his wife. He also suffered from obsessive-compulsive disorder, a condition poorly understood by medical science at the time. It had plagued him since childhood, often compelling him to make bizarre decisions. He bought a lovely apartment for his mistress, near Montmartre, presenting it to her one morning completely furnished and decorated. The poor thing never knew that Lucien's extravagant generosity stemmed from something more urgent than his devotion to her. His life was so precisely ordained that he found himself unable to deal with the changes that his adulterous visits required. So he had her apartment furnished as an exact duplicate of his own. Every piece of furniture, even the carpets and lighting fixtures, were identical, down to the wall paint and the brass doorknobs in the kitchen. Only in this manner could he reconcile his unfaithfulness with the exigencies of his peculiar disorder."

The requiem mass seems to drag on interminably. From the back of the church the thundering pipe organ rattles the pews, waves of sounds washing over the assembly and threatening the stain glass windows. A deacon sways the censer around the altar, sending wisps of aromatic smoke ascending along the arches of the nave. But the lingering scent hangs in the air like a tropical haze, casting a spell of torpor and queasiness over the front rows. This unerring sense of ritual and awe, orchestrated to perfection in Catholic worship, would have pleased my great-uncle, intrigued by the splendor of a faith he did not believe.

Lucien also was an inveterate smoker, and during World War II, along with tens of thousands of strung-out Parisians, he had learned to curtail his habit until there wasn't a cigarette left on the black market. Apparently resigned to the disappearance of tobacco, alcohol and coffee, he had chosen a dignified exile in the garden where he would read for hours. Only in the winter months, when the cold forced Lucien to move back indoors to his library, did my great-aunt notice the peculiar scent. Halfway between the acrid odor of a rug burn and the perfumed aroma of Ceylonese tea, the enigmatic smell impregnated every bit of fabric around their apartment.

Craving for something to smoke, Lucien had surreptitiously begun to trim the fringes of the antique rugs in his living-room. He did it so discreetly, harvesting only a few bristles at a time, that it took a while to notice the receding threads. He would stock his pipe, lock himself in the library and smoke in silence. He would also sleep afterwards, which was unusual since he had an aversion to naps. The magnificent rugs, woven on ancient looms in Persia, were made of pure hemp, and the story circulated in his scandalized entourage that the war had turned him into a drug addict. But the physicians in the family were quick to debunk the story. Industrial hemp does not contain enough THC to affect anyone, and the incriminating rugs were over a hundred years old. But myths are more resilient than facts, and in the sixties my sisters and I preferred to believe that Lucien had perfected the most patriotic disappearing act. And we imagined him ensconced in his library, oblivious to the Hessian hordes, his magic carpet spiriting him away to some Assyrian paradise.

Ten

MOST FIRST-YEAR students have been dreading the end of the semester. Final exams were particularly challenging and the results are brutal. Out of one hundred candidates, only forty-one are admitted to the second year of the medical curriculum. Everyone's grades are posted on large bulletin boards outside the registrar's office. This habit of broadcasting failure and success proves distressing to foreign students used to sacrosanct privacy. But to the French, this unsparing policy makes perfect sense: since taxpayers finance state universities, a student's performance should be a matter of public record. In the midst of joyful faces and scowls of dejection, I catch a glimpse of Christiane, who winks at me and returns my smile. We have both survived the onslaught.

My parents invite me to spend a week in their company, with extravagant room and board. I treasure the freedom of my apartment, but leaving its dungeon-like atmosphere for the airy and spacious rooms of our family home will be a welcome change. I enjoy a wonderful weekend with my family, before my mother casually asks me for a favor.

"This is near the middle of June," she begins, "and this year, in particular, you remember what it means?"

The chirpiness in her voice must cover some portentous announcement, but I reply just as casually, "I'm afraid I've no idea."

"Why, Eléonore's visit of course," she answers with a smile, the calmness of her words hanging like a veil over a nascent storm.

I had completely forgotten – Eléonore, my mother's closest friend. They met in elementary school and have known each other for thirty-five years. After the war, Eléonore looked for an escape from the limited opportunities of a newly liberated France. The only heir to a large textile empire, she was a stunning debutante kept on a short leash by a domineering matriarch. Salvation came in the perfectly pressed uniform of a U.S. Army Captain. They met at a USO charity ball and soon began an assiduous courtship. The young officer's social rank and fortune fell short of the aspirations of Eléonore's family, and five years earlier his eagerness would have met with distant courtesy. But these were difficult times, with food rationing and the prospect of post-war reconstruction. And Eléonore had other reasons beside practicality in selecting her marital prospects. She desperately needed to run away from her mother, whose relentless dominion proved as unbearable as the German occupation. Within six months, the couple married at the American Church near the Quai d'Orsay, and by Christmas they had left on the Queen Mary for a distant land with the quaint appellation of Virginia.

My mother bore the brunt of this separation. But her friendship continued through a rich and faithful correspondence, between postwar Paris and the predictable disillusions of a loveless marriage in America. Five years later, Eléonore returned with three children and a nanny in tow. She and my mother began a tradition of a summer visit every other year. I remember meeting Eléonore when I was six years old, but I took little notice of her subsequent visits to France, until I turned fourteen. The Americans, or "Les Ricains," as my sister and I had nicknamed them, created an exotic diversion. Everything about them, from their behavior to their clothes, was unusual. They looked different too: the boys with astronaut hair cuts and the girl wearing odd-looking pants called jeans. In time, only the daughter continued to accompany her mother for the biennial trip to Paris. Her name was Jennifer, and it resonated in my Gallic ears with a sense of otherworldliness. She was two years younger than I, and starting in 1965, I was hired as her summer guide and entertainer, while our mothers spent hours together in a whirl of social engagements. I thought Jennifer looked rather dorky, always quiet and awkward behind her thick-rimmed glasses, with straight hair halfway down her back. She spoke French fluently, but given our age difference and her less-than-glamorous appearance, I hadn't the slightest interest in her. My duties as an escort were crassly motivated by greed. Unknown to Jennifer, my mother paid me a king's ransom to take her out to the movies, to lunch, to museums and department stores. I enjoyed the food, the shows, and, for a teenager on a modest allowance, a summer salary that kept me afloat until October.

But things have changed. Due to a hiatus in their summer plans, I haven't seen Eléonore and Jennifer in three years, and have no interest in playing the part of tour guide this time around. My mother turns to me with a look of despair.

"You've always come through before. They're both absolutely charming – almost family to us, so I don't understand your reluctance to help."

I'm beginning to miss the shelter and privacy of my apartment, barely three days after accepting my parents' hospitality.

"Look, mom, I know they're very nice, but I'll be twenty this fall and Jennifer just turned eighteen. Why don't you ask my sister instead? I hang around with a completely different crowd now, and we wouldn't have anything in common. And besides -"

"Besides?"

"Jennifer is very nice, but she's basically a nerdy-looking American girl, and I'd rather not be seen in her company in the Quartier Latin."

"So that's it?" My mother replies icily. "I admit I didn't realize how much time had passed since you last saw her. I just don't know what I'm going to tell Eléonore. We had both taken your help for granted."

Mom has a special talent to sap my resolve when she really wants to. She's had years of practice and does it in style, without recrimination or argument. She just looks at me. I begin to vacillate under her disappointed gaze, knowing how much she values this special time with her friend.

"How about if I were to help for just a couple of days?" I propose hesitantly, hoping my offer will be rebuffed.

"That would be splendid...for a start." My mother answers with the satisfaction of a benign taskmaster. "I expect you to pick up Jennifer Saturday night at her mother's residence in Neuilly. We'll discuss the proper wage for your services over dinner."

That weekend, as I ride the ornate hydraulic elevator to Eléonore's vast apartment, I feel a mixture of regret and guilt. I refused my mother's generous offer to compensate me; it didn't feel right to make her pay for something I should have volunteered to do in the first place. But I really don't want to be doing this, and the excitement I once felt coming over here has given way to a sense of tedious obligation. I exit on the last floor and pause, just to put a look of convincing enthusiasm on my face. "I'm doing this one last time, just for my mom," I keep telling myself as I take a deep breath and ring the bell.

For a brief moment nothing happens, and then I remember you can never hear footsteps because of the plush blue carpeting in the entranceway. The door suddenly opens and Jennifer rushes out to greet me with a hug, before taking a step back and inviting me in. The rimmed glasses are gone, revealing delicately shaped hazel eyes. Her hair is much shorter, now barely touching her shoulders. Gone are the braces too and there's nothing the least bit awkward about her. Her cheek bones have sharpened, giving her face an almost exotic symmetry, and following her through the hallway I can't help notice the sensuous curve of her hips. When we reach the drawing-room, Jennifer turns around and smiles, dewy lips over scintillating teeth.

I'm stunned. The ungainly chrysalis I met three years ago has turned into a luminous butterfly.

"I can't believe how much you've changed," Eléonore says as she rises from her armchair. She greets me with a warm, genuine welcome, punctuated by a solid kiss on both cheeks. Twenty years of corseted life in the American South hasn't altered her Latin heritage. She decides to treat us all to dinner at the Jules Verne, the outrageously expensive restaurant on the second floor of the Eiffel Tower. And there, with the glittering lights of Paris at our feet, we spend the rest of the evening catching up with three years of life on both sides of the Atlantic. Drawn by her dazzling smile and the incisiveness of her comments, I catch myself looking surreptitiously across the table at Jennifer who radiates charm and thoughtfulness. And each time she intercepts my glances, as if anticipating them.

I stay for another two hours after we return to their apartment, discussing our plans for the coming week. Jennifer thinks she's intruding on my vacation, but she need not worry. I'm eager to show her around town once again. Her mother takes a long look at me before I bid them good night.

"You're the portrait of your mother," she remarks with a nostalgic smile. "I'm so pleased to see you tonight, and only hope Jennifer won't be too much of an imposition on your schedule. Your mother mentioned how constrained it is, so I'm most appreciative for this effort."

"It's no effort," I reply too quickly, unable to disguise my eagerness, "and I'm sure some of these obligations can be rearranged."

"We're delighted to hear that," she remarks knowingly, catching the way my eyes drift over to her daughter.

It's only later, as I hurry down the avenue to catch the last Metro, that I notice the spring in my step.

My cousin's wedding, a few days later, provides a suitable opportunity to see Jennifer for an entire day. I call Eléonore, explaining that I'm already invited, and offer to take her daughter along for the unique experience of a French wedding. At least it gives me a chance to find out if there's more to our mutual affinity than fleeting infatuation. She accedes to my request, generously pretending she can't see through this convenient artifice. My mother is not too displeased either, congratulating me on my resourcefulness, with barely a hint of irony in her voice. I borrow my father's car and pick up Jennifer for the leisurely one-hour drive to a country estate near Orléans. She greets me with a confounding mixture of restraint and eagerness, wearing a pale blue dress and a summer hat. It's a rather elegant outfit, but short enough to raise a few eyebrows at a wedding. Jennifer squirms and laughs as she gets into the car, recounting how her mother pleaded for more conventional attire. As she settles a few things on the back seat, her purse slips through her fingers and falls, spilling its contents on the floor mat. I rush to help and among her keys, handkerchief and purse, I also retrieve a disk of Ortho-Novum. She looks at me, a blush of embarrassment coloring her cheeks.

"Well, *Doctor,*" she says with a smirk, "don't look so shocked. I'm sure a lot of French girls are on this sort of medication." I remain diplomatically silent. She's unaware that contraceptives have only been legalized this year in Catholic France.

"At any rate, I was prescribed these because of cramps," she adds with natural assurance.

We burst out laughing. This is the sort of ice breaker you couldn't make up if you tried. Sharing the front seat also gives me a closer look at Jennifer. Except for a hint of eyeliner, she doesn't wear any makeup, her lustrous skin and gleaming smile needing no artificial enhancement. If the first impression she elicits is one of old-fashioned deference, it is swiftly tempered by a Latin ebullience bursting through the conventionality of her upbringing. By the time we reach our destination, we have moved beyond the adolescent complicity of previous years, to a closer sense of mutual trust.

Set inside a twelfth-century Romanesque church, the wedding is a moving experience for Jennifer. The medieval stones of the altar are covered in fleurs-de-lis, a regal adornment for the natural simplicity of this ancestral place. Later in the evening, we are invited to dine outside, on small tables discreetly set throughout the cloistered gardens of the estate. And amid a hundred guests, Jennifer and I disappear into our own world, champagne and candlelight sparkling through the dusk as it stretches upon the fields. Thoroughly immersed in our conversation, we also enjoy the silence slipping in between words and laughter. An hour ago, our hands met across the table, and they haven't let go. I feel as though things are moving too fast, but the uninhibited nature of our burgeoning relationship takes on a pace of its own, with neither of us willing to slow it down.

The air is still warm when we leave the guests and go for a stroll on the surrounding meadows. A quarter of a mile away, we find an isolated patch beckoning us to rest for a while. And taking off our shoes, we lie down upon the grass, strains from a string quartet reaching us across the night.

"What will you think of me if I kiss you on our first date?" she asks, half-seriously.

All I see are the stars etched against the sky, and Jennifer slowly leaning over me. Her face is almost a blur in the shadows, but her fragrant breath becomes an irresistible path to her lips. The sounds of the night come alive all around, while darkness covers us like a blanket over the enticing grass. Jennifer's sensuality is both inviting and hesitant, her body nestling against me while her skin seems to retreat from my touch. And as I delicately reach under her dress, she abruptly stiffens, unwilling to allow such intimate contact, as if my hands had turned into thistles against her flesh. Jennifer turns over and lies beside me, her head upon my chest.

I'm furious at my own intemperance, and embarrassed that I could so grievously misread her intentions. But she assuages my concern, the trust in her eyes still unwavering.

"You must think me quite a tease," she chuckles, "and yet, I couldn't imagine a better place to make love with you."

In the shadows, I must look thoroughly disconcerted.

"This American girl isn't as worldly as you think," she whispers, "I'm still a virgin."

The thought had not even occurred to me. Ever since that dreadful night with Viviane six years ago, I have never been with someone inexperienced. Now my embarrassment is complete, and I try to apologize for my lack of insight.

"Don't feel guilty," she protests. "I wanted this to happen just as much as you did, so I made sure to send you all the wrong signals." And she places her fingers over my mouth to silence any further excuses.

"Can we take a few steps back and enjoy the magnificence of this night?" she asks softly.

And under the incandescent sky, she wraps herself around me, holding on as if she might slip through the luscious grass and fall beneath the surface of the ground.

❧ ❦

Over the next two weeks, we see each other practically every day. I've cancelled my plans to leave for Scotland with a couple of friends, so that I can devote all my time to Jennifer. We gradually avoid public places, preferring calmer retreats away from the bustling crowds, talking about anything imaginable and strengthening a natural bond between us. I have known lust and infatuation before, but this urgency upon my senses thrills and preoccupies me all at once. I value self-reliance, preferring solitude to any compromise with my independence. But here, settling within me, is this sensation that things become more meaningful when I share them with her. And this revelation is disquieting, the more so that I'm enjoying a relationship not based solely on lust.

Today, as we move away from swarms of tourists coming out of the Louvre, Jennifer sits me down on a stone bench in the peaceful gardens of the Palais-Royal.

"I want to be honest with you, and yet I'm afraid to come across as some sort of Victorian relic," she begins. "I enjoy your company immensely, and I certainly don't shy from physical contact with you."

She pauses to find the exact words she needs.

"The chemistry between us is obvious and I'm drawn to you on a scale I never imagined. However, I've always known I would only yield to someone willing to commit himself to me. But you're more experienced, and here in Paris, I must sound like a provincial little tart. I've dreaded this conversation, and now I'm not even sure what I'm trying to say," she blurts out, as frustration and anguish become visible upon her face.

"I'm glad you spoke," I answer, trying to alleviate the distress her honesty has unleashed upon her.

"It's not like I'm only waiting with an appetite consuming me from within," I explain. "This is also new to me, and oddly enough I find the sublimation of my desire a rather enriching experience."

"But I'm worried that my particular disposition will drive you to despair," she goes on with ingenuous concern.

"Don't be," I chuckle. "I'm not prone to asceticism, but I happen to enjoy our relationship as it stands. If it should ever turn into intolerable frustration, you'll be the first to know."

She slides closer to me on the uncomfortable bench, and rests her forehead on my shoulder.

"I hope it never does; but know this: your willingness to accommodate me is also a measure of my devotion to you." And she kisses me, her innocence smiling through the racing of her heart.

My sister Isabelle chooses our weekend family visit to drag me into the library. "Well, kiddo, I think it's time you and I have a little talk," she says, closing the door behind us.

"What's the story about you and Miss America? I hear you guys are inseparable. Are you nailing her?"

I stare at Isabelle with my pseudo-clinical frown, the one I've been working on at the hospital, trying to look serious when taking down a patient's history. And it works. She listens intently as I recount the events of the past four weeks. As always, I can rely on her absolute discretion. We know enough about our respective misdeeds to send either one of us to the guillotine.

"Wow! This is quite unexpected," she finally interjects with a sense of admiration. "My brother, the dog, becoming a gentleman?"

"If you mean the absence of sex, it's actually quite bearable," I answer. "At first, I thought I would just bide my time, slowly bringing her around to a more reasonable point of view, whittling away her virginity, so to speak, with charm and perseverance. But somewhere along the way, I abandoned that plan, realizing how important it was to respect her values, even if it meant denying my own."

"Are you planning to join the Jesuits when you finish medical school?" my sister asks with a mellifluous tone. "These admirable sentiments are uncharacteristic."

"I can't explain," I reply, a bit defensively. "I would have scoffed at such a situation only a month ago. And yet, strangely enough, what she requires of me at the moment is not as great a sacrifice as I anticipated. Actually, it almost works the other way around, as if I had found a measure of contentment in obliging her."

I expect my sister to burst out laughing at my sentimental answer, but when I look up, she is staring at me with misty eyes and that sweet smile my mother has passed on to her.

"Oh, my gosh, I had no idea," she says softly, standing up and giving me a hug. "You've got to promise me to tell mom before going back to Paris tomorrow."

"Tell her what?" I ask, completely without a clue.

Isabelle shakes her head the way all three women in our family always do, when imparting wisdom to the males of the clan.

"For the first time in your life," she replies, "you may be in love with someone other than yourself."

By the middle of July, Jennifer is spending all of her time with me, or as a guest at my parents' house. We have yet to share a single night anywhere, but in deference to her wishes and our respective weakness for each other, I haven't offered the use of my apartment. My mother and Eléonore watch our idyll with mutual enchantment. Mom and I have talked, but, curiously, she has refrained from discussing the matter. For the two of them, this is a sort of childhood dream come true. They met when they were six years old, and my mother still remembers how they would fantasize about their children falling in love with each other. Now, thirty-five years later, they're looking at us with all the sweet indulgence of gratified parents. But my father, usually removed from such considerations, is becoming irritated.

"Your mother has lapsed into some sort of quaint sentimentalism," he remarks to me in private, "at least as far as you and Jennifer are concerned. When I dared raise an objection the other day, it was roundly dismissed by both your sisters and your mom."

"What did you say?" I ask, intrigued that he would even volunteer a personal opinion.

"I observed that she and Léonore seemed to be floating on clouds whenever the conversation turned to the two of you, and that perhaps it was time for a bit of reasonableness to be injected into this situation," he replies, indignant that his point of view should be so readily discarded.

"What are you concerned about?" I enquire.

"Well, this is none of my business, of course, but everyone is encouraging you to board a runaway train, while simple facts are being ignored," he answers, carefully choosing his words.

"Come September you will be engulfed in your second year of medical school, and Jennifer will have returned to the United States. I don't think it's wise to make more out of this than a summer romance," he adds, before retreating behind his usual silence, as if he had said too much already.

But I appreciate his concern. In all the emotional whirlwind of the past five weeks, he's the only one speaking the voice of reason. Jennifer told me that her father, a conservative politician in Virginia, would undoubtedly take issue with the present state of affairs, if only his wife had kept him informed. But caution and common sense have been cast to the wind, and I find myself equally resilient to vigilance and circumspection. In fact, as if to ride roughshod over my dad's objections, Jennifer and I decide to leave for a ten-day European vacation. Her father would scowl at my audacity, and to reassure everyone's sense of propriety, my sister Isabelle has agreed to accompany us as unofficial chaperone. The trip is being underwritten by both our moms; we will travel as a party of three, the girls sharing rooms in hotels along the way, on a journey through Italy and Greece.

Isabelle and Jennifer have quickly become confidantes. There are times when their whispers and giggles can become exasperating, since my sister's presence gives Jennifer unlimited access to information about me. But I know I can count on her discretion about the less glorious details of my past. Her presence actually provides an added sense of balance in our interaction. Isabelle will know when to disappear if we need to be alone, while offering a cheerful and complicit presence to Jennifer. Ever the iconoclast, my sister can't resist a last bit of unsolicited advice.

"You're in an odd position of experimenting with sobriety, while possessing the key to an enviable cellar. But should you, or Juliet here, ever decide to break your vows of abstinence, just let me know and I'll move into your room while you take up residence in our quarters," she says with a wink.

The night before our departure, Jennifer's mother summons me for a private chat.

"I've known you since the day you were born," she begins wistfully, "so I'm not about to ask what your intentions are concerning my daughter. I believe such matters will in time follow their due course. There is, however, one point I would like to make."

She hesitates for a moment, and then looks at me with a mixture of imperiousness and supplication.

"I have neither the right nor the desire to interfere with my daughter's private life, so what I'm about to say is not a request, but an observation which perhaps you will take to heart. Jennifer and I are very close, and you know how devoted I am to her. She doesn't share your experience of the world, and I happen to have old-fashioned ideas about honor. Please consider restoring her to my care, in ten days, just as she was when I entrusted her to your protection."

And before I can say anything, she gives me a quick peck on the cheek and sends me on my way.

☙☙

The train leaves Paris in a torrential downpour, with lightning transfiguring the blight of the suburbs as we hurtle through the rain. But in spite of the deplorable weather, the journey to Italy is one of style and comfort. My mother surprised us with reservations on the Trans-Orient-Express, a mythical train carrying passengers with uncommon luxury between France and Greece. The sumptuous private quarters, complete with cavernous leather seats, full-size beds, private bath and a gourmet dining car, give passengers the impression of sailing on a luxury liner. From the corridor running along the entire length of our car, the panoramic windows become privileged vistas to the most enchanting scenery in Southern Europe. Later that night, as we sit in the lounge before retiring, I realize why the surroundings feel oddly familiar. The Trans-Orient-Express was once used as a setting in *From Russia With Love*. I catch myself enjoying this unexpected intrusion of fantasy into reality, as if I had to protect Jennifer from the menacing presence of Robert Shaw.

The morning awakens us to a Mediterranean landscape shimmering in the sun, leading us along the Riviera to the sparkling coast of Italy. My sister knows the area quite well, and for the next few days she proves the perfect guide through Venice, Naples and Rome. Though I've never been particularly attracted to Italy, I fall under the charm of the island of Ischia in the bay of Naples. Jennifer's excitement is contagious and I have no difficulty plunging wholeheartedly with her in this veritable feast for the eyes. My sister seems to disappear magically the moment we need to be alone, and Jennifer proves an ideal traveler, charmed by unique details she discerns beyond the more traditional tourist attractions. And neither hordes of gypsies begging in Zagreb nor the peril of Italian cab drivers can dim her sense of wonder.

We finally reach Athens and pay homage to transcendent archeology and breathtaking views, before deciding on a two-day trip to Skiathos. Back in the late 1960s, the island was unspoiled by organized tourism. A rusted ferry takes us to a small harbor nestled in tiers of alabaster homes gleaming in the sun. And it is there, on a virgin beach called Koukounaries, with the penetrating scents of figs and limes hovering in the implacable heat, that it all begins.

The wide stretch of ivory sand is deserted, as if this afternoon everything were conspiring to leave us alone. Over the waves in the distance, the aquamarine of the Adriatic extends as far as the horizon, its hues merging so seamlessly with the azure of the sky that I can't tell them apart. We find a small recess in a rocky escarpment and sit in the shade, lulled by the rhythmic breath of the surf.

"What are you thinking of?" I ask, weaving my fingers into hers.

"Us," Jennifer replies, almost imperceptibly. And the plurality of this single, solitary word instills itself into me with devastating ease.

"I'm in love with you," she says, her voice now firm and clear.

"There are moments between us so privileged when I no longer think of myself as an individual. The full measure of things, their worth and meaning, is now defined in our ability to experience them together. I'm not denying my own identity, but it is in sharing it with you that I rise above myself."

She looks straight at me, and the clearness in her eyes feels like a breeze upon my face.

"Will you come into my life, and turn my love for you into a celebration of the two of us?"

I sit there transfixed, forgetting to take another breath. No one has ever spoken to me with such disarming honesty. Jennifer's vulnerability endows her words with irresistible force and they flood into me without resistance.

"Je t'aime autant que ma propre vie," I answer. The words come out in French, and I find myself unable to continue. She puts her arms around me and I bury my head in her hair, kissing her neck, as a rasping taste of sand and salt lingers upon my tongue. I've never known such peace and contentment. Holding on to each other, we walk back along the shore, the oblique rays of the sun casting a single shadow across the sand.

≈≈

When we return to Paris, I realize how little I learned from previous relationships. I've known attachment before, but only in relation to the thrill I experienced, and the attraction dissolved the moment my own interest was no longer served. Jennifer bears no resemblance to anyone I've met. And it is not that I've gone blind or taken leave of my senses, for I can see her flaws just as clearly as she sees mine. Perhaps this acuity of mind and heart, the reckoning of our shortcomings, makes our mutual attraction more meaningful.

Jennifer's mother and mine are by now fully apprised of the situation. Though a willing accomplice in encouraging our romance, my mom finally becomes concerned and calls me in for a chat.

"You look resplendent," she begins as I sit next to her in the living room. "How are you and Jennifer getting along?"

"We're in love," I reply, "and I find my devotion to her quite addictive."

"Well, that's precisely what I wanted to talk about," she says, her voice taking on a more serious tone. "You know that Jennifer is leaving in a week, and in all probability you'll not see each other again until next year."

"I know, mom," I answer with a sigh, "that's been on my mind more than you can imagine."

"Well, then, I trust you're able to sort out the priorities and keep your head above water, aren't you?" she asks almost aggressively, as if she were afraid of my answer.

"Yes, I'm well aware of my priorities. Dad already pointed them out to me even before we left for Greece," I reply with a mild degree of exasperation.

The antique clock on the mantel strikes the hour, and its crystalline chime fills the silence suddenly settling between us.

"Have no fear," I continue, with a faint smile of encouragement. "I have years of medical school ahead of me and Jennifer lives four thousand miles from here. The voice of reason couldn't speak more clearly in my ears."

"But are you paying attention to its counsel?" she asks, as if to elicit a clearer sense of reassurance.

"Of course I am," I reply soothingly, as I get to my feet. But telling her what she wants to hear, and ending our conversation so precipitously, only deepens my mother's anxiety.

"You're older and more mature than Jennifer," she concludes as I take my leave of her. "See that you don't break her heart."

I'm not so sure that my experience or my age necessarily bestows upon me the reasonableness my mother alludes to. In some ways, I wonder if my own heart isn't more susceptible than Jennifer's. I've never been in such a relationship before, and I find the experience both exhilarating and troublesome. The closer Jennifer and I are drawn to each other, the more dependent I become. This unsettles me, though I find it difficult to live out my commitment without surrendering some autonomy. And yet, each time I yield to this compromise, I'm compensated a hundredfold by the consonance I find in weaving myself into her.

Faced with the imminence of our separation, Jennifer and I settle into an emotional cocoon excavated from the time and space still left to us. Two days before she leaves, Eléonore invites me for dinner. Knowing how much we wish to be left alone, she orders a catered meal, serving it in style in her own dining room.

And while we eat, she comes in and drops a bomb on me.

"Why don't you come and spend a couple of weeks with us in the U.S.? I was given to understand that medical school won't resume until the end of September," she asks nonchalantly, enjoying how the casualness of her offer disintegrates my countenance. A sidelong look at Jennifer reveals that she's known about this plan since morning.

"Well, it's settled then," she concludes. "When you arrive in Virginia, Jennifer will have another two weeks before returning to Duke. That should give us plenty of time to celebrate your birthday."

I'm overwhelmed, though my enthusiasm is dampened by material considerations beyond my control. But Eléonore has surmised my difficulties, waving her hand as if to consign all obstacles to oblivion.

"I've already spoken with your mother," she says reassuringly, "and we're satisfied that none of this will interfere with your studies. Jennifer's father hasn't yet been informed, but it is inconsequential. He will agree as to the merits of my plan," she adds with regal confidence.

"Mom, aren't you forgetting something?" Jennifer asks while I sit there in a daze, trying to process a torrent of emotions.

"Indeed I have," her mother replies, as if remembering a trivial detail. "I know you're broke, and I was racking my brains trying to come up with a suitable present for your birthday. Please take this and don't lose it," she says sweetly, laying an airline credit card next to my plate. "Tomorrow morning, you and Jennifer can stroll down the Champs-Elysées to the ticket counter of TWA, and book a round-trip ticket to Richmond."

The promise of seeing Jennifer within two weeks has turned my despair into furious impatience. Our parting is no longer a dreaded separation, but a prelude to a reunion across the sea. I can't remember a more perfect succession of events. Two days later I drive Jennifer and her mother to the airport, and the time comes for us to say goodbye, jostled by swarms of passing travelers. Directly to our left, beyond the cathedral ceilings and bay windows of the terminal, a white and red Boeing 707 waits on the tarmac, glimmering in the sun like a postcard. I hug Eléonore before she goes on ahead through passport control, granting us one last moment alone.

"I'll call you tomorrow, just to make sure you've arrived safely," I manage to say, staving off the emotion taking over me.

"I'm not sad; really I'm not," Jennifer protests, as the tears welling in her eyes break free upon her cheeks. She kisses me almost hesitantly at first, and then fiercely, every part of her communing with me. And for the first time, I feel the unrestrained wave of her desire passing into me.

"Once you reach the other side of this ocean, I will be yours at your own choosing," she whispers in my ear. "I want you."

And then she eludes my grasp and disappears past the security gate, stranding me here in the swarming indifference of the crowd.

આૐજ

Being away from her for the first time in two months is harder than I expected. The time has come for me to learn a lesson or two about attachment and loss, patience and commitment. I try to cheer myself thinking about my own departure in a couple of weeks, but her absence tugs at my heart no matter what I do. Back in the 60s, communication between continents wasn't easy. The Internet didn't exist, the mail was too slow and the telephone quite unaffordable. Even the simple task of calling the US from Paris took on mythical proportions. You could not dial direct and had to go through an overseas operator. She would take your request and call you back after what seemed an eternity. And when the phone finally rang, you struggled through a treacherous echo, shouting as if you could coax your words along the cable snaking its way across the ocean floor. But talking to Jennifer in the US is a cruel relief, her passionate and disincarnate voice only emphasizing her absence. I just sit by the phone in exile, like a lone astronaut crossing the terminator into night. Jennifer has a wondrous appetite for life, unhindered by social degrees or protocol. There's something unfettered in the way she gives of herself, with a smile that would conquer an army, laying to waste the vaunted sophistication of Parisian women. The pull she exerts upon my heart is as irresistible as gravity.

I'm also intrigued by the country from which she comes, as if Jennifer herself were an embodiment of her native land. I don't know much about the United States, other than its history, and the mental pictures I have derive from Hollywood productions. It's a kaleidoscope of westerns and action movies, a landscape made of creaky saloon doors, glaciers breaking off into the Alaskan sea, urban canyons and mythical skylines. And in my mind this collection of stereotypes is populated by typical Americans, like Dr. Heywood Floyd, Raquel Welch or Steve McQueen in *Bullitt*. None of them true to reality, of course, and yet all perfectly at home in this imaginary patchwork, the fantasy of every French kid born after World War II. I'm curious how the real thing measures up against the legend. In two weeks, I'll travel farther than I've ever been, and I sense that it will involve more than just reaching a distant shore. This is a personal discovery, a challenge to everything I have become. New horizons are fascinating, but in time the most rewarding aspect of a quest is the journey within.

The end of the second week sends me on my way. By now I'm as giddy as an explorer about to embark on a fantastical expedition. So why do I feel such unease weighing upon me, assailing my thoughts and stripping me of inner peace? I know what I'm doing, and understand so clearly what is at stake that I convinced my own mother of the level-headedness of my plans. I'll indulge this fantasy and be reunited with Jennifer, grounding more firmly the foundations we've already established. And then I will return, with stars in my eyes, ready to resume medical school and build the future awaiting me. A career path of quiet affluence and success, a comfortable niche in an immutable social order. The reasonableness in all this is so obvious, so compelling...and so unadventurous. A part of me is inexplicably drawn to rebellion, in my heart as in my deeds. I dreamed of being in love before, but never thought I'd make life-changing decisions just to be near someone else. I could certainly exist without Jennifer, but I'm left wondering why I would want to.

And right there, around the corridors of reckless abstractions, the first speck of folly creeps in before I can excise it from my thoughts. Slowly, insidiously at first, like an aberrant notion easily dismissed by reason, it hides and lurks around some unguarded back-door in my mind. By week's end, the unthinkable has taken rational form. As always with seditious thinking, the peril lies in indulging it long enough that it becomes acceptable.

Epilogue

MY FATHER IS DRIVING me to the airport after a cheerful goodbye to my mother, and we suddenly find ourselves struggling with an awkward silence between us. My dad is visibly preoccupied, after a commendable job of stifling his objections while Eléonore remained in Paris. But now he wishes to reiterate the arguments he once presented against my getting involved with Jennifer. I know he's doing this out of a sense of obligation, but also because he is genuinely concerned about me. As we negotiate the evening commute out of Paris, he eloquently talks of the necessity to make sensible choices in life, delineating the differences between pure fun and reckless behavior.

And I listen dutifully, touched that he should care enough to come out of his traditional reserve and intrude so liberally into his son's private life. These are noble sentiments indeed, but I can't help thinking that his entreaties are also half-hearted, as if he needed to convince himself of their merit. During the war, years before I was born, he had listened to his own adventurous stirrings and left the safe haven of his parents' home just to reach England. This he did for quite a different purpose to be sure, but apart from his determination to fight the Nazis, I still marvel at our similarities.

My father insists on accompanying me to the gate, and once we reach the concourse, he bursts out laughing, realizing that the last time we stood together in this terminal, circumstances were considerably different.

"I'll be right here in two weeks to pick you up," he says in a jovial tone. "You will remember, won't you?"

"Come on, dad, you know I will." I reply, looking at him with boundless affection.

But I see it in his eyes. He knows. He already knows I have allowed the unthinkable to infect my mind, though the time hasn't come for me to act upon it. I will return in two weeks, but part of me has already begun to untie the heartstrings keeping me here. Neither of us knows it yet, but in less than a year I will burn my bridges and cross over to the other side.

And the last I see of my father is his smile. The same smile he wore when teaching me how to scale a rock in the Alps, encouraging his son to let go of the rope, to come into his own and finally climb alone.

I step on board the plane with elated apprehension, the stewardess greeting me with clear blue eyes from another world. And taking a deep breath, I start down the center aisle without looking back.

Valentine's Day 2006 – September 2008
Radford, Virginia

CPSIA information can be obtained
at www.ICGtesting.com
Printed in the USA
LVHW030346020721
691685LV00004B/413